She was

she was also translucent. I could see a row of bottles through her head, a sensation that added nausea to all my other emotions at seeing her again. Right here in front of me was a dead woman who I had loved, alive . . . or half-alive . . . again. Edgar Allan Poe would've loved it.

"If it isn't Mr. Eshanti," she said, just loud enough for Rachel and me to hear. Her smile was as warm and inviting as it had ever been. To look at her, you'd expect her to be a model or an actress. Anything except one of the nation's top experts at destroying things.

"Cynna . . . you look . . . great."

"Oh, my heart would be all aflutter—if I still had one."

"Gideon?" Rachel said. "Who is . . . this?"

"This is Cynna Stone, Rachel."

"Cynna Stone? The bomber?"

Cynna, or the holographic simulacrum that was all that was left of her, made a pouting face. "Ooo, I hate that word. Demolitions engineer has a much nicer ring to it, don't you think?"

HELL
· · · · · · · ·
A Cyberpunk Thriller™

HELL
· · · · · · · · · ·
A Cyberpunk Thriller™

by

Chet Williamson

PRIMA PUBLISHING

ISBN: 0-7615-0069-3
Library of Congress Catalog Card Number: 94-80090
Printed in the United States of America
95 96 97 98 EE 10 9 8 7 6 5 4 3 2 1

Acknowledgments

First, thanks to John Antinori, Laura Kampo, and Dennis Johnson, the creators and writers of the CD-ROM game on which this novel is based, as well as the artists and programmers at Take 2. They made my job easy by supplying an abundance of good dialogue, a marvelously dense story, and a stunning visual realization of the world of *Hell: A Cyberpunk Thriller*.

And thanks to the good folk at Prima Publishing, in particular Roger Stewart, Ed Dille, and my editor Debbie Notkin. All publishing types should be this easy to work with!

Thanks to my agent, Jimmy Vines; T. Liam "Long Tom" McDonald for his generosity and friendship; my wife Laurie for understanding the sanctity of deadlines, and finally my son and fellow writer, Colin Williamson, for being my resident Jeremy Verdi in all things computeresque, as well as contributing a share of fine fictional ideas as well.

The worst of madmen is a saint run mad.
　　　　　　　　　　　—Alexander Pope

CHAPTER 1

The dream saved our lives. It's been driving me crazy for years, but I have to admit that tonight I was damn glad for it.

It started the way it always does. I was at my deck tracking down some outlaw techie through the bright-dark, smart-dumb trenches of cyberspace, my fingers roaming idly over the silent keys, both me and the deck turning random bits of data into logical algorithms of pursuit . . .

. . . suddenly I was *nowhere*, just in a kind of red-fire limbo I knew and remembered from dreaming of it before.

I could feel my heart thwacking away in my gut, and sweat beads popping out on my bare skin—all over, since I was naked—and I knew I was ready for the Fall, ripe as a rad-zapped apple.

Then it came. Whatever was holding me up in the middle of nothing suddenly became nothing itself, and down I went. I could hear myself scream like it was coming from somebody else's raw, burning throat, and believe me, I don't exaggerate when I use the word *burning*.

I was burning, every damned inch of me. I could feel the hairs on my body curling, crisping, turning to ash and drifting off like tiny black snowflakes. When I gathered enough balls to look down at myself, the horror I felt at my reddening and peeling flesh was nothing compared to my shock when I saw *where* I was falling to...

... straight into the gaping mouth of a monster. The bastard's face was as big across as the Capitol Dome, and a lot uglier, even after the Imperator's new gilt paint job. Now imagine the dome wide open, with fangs that could've used the tip of the Washington Monument for a toothpick, and you've got a good idea of what I was falling into.

I couldn't do a thing about it—not fly, not turn away, not even close my eyes—not a thing but fall. So I did, and even greater heat rushed up to suck me down, and I knew that I was falling into Hell, the Hell that came to earth when I was a kid, the *real* Hell, the one the demons came from, the horned and horny monsters that we share this city and the world with.

I knew I was going to be on *their* turf now, and they were going to do whatever the *hell* they wanted to with me, forever and ever. Then I went down that massive maw, and its throat seemed lined with squirming, tapered worms, curling like whelks or DNA strands, whose needle-like snouts lashed out at me as I fell past them, and every time one struck, it stripped the skin away and thrust molten fire between my flesh and my muscles until I was one seething ball of pain. I screamed even louder than before, and, mercifully, woke up wrapped in my cool bed in my cool sheets next to my cool, warm woman, and I heard myself saying those words again, that sentence that I can never finish—

Vocabulum est serus . . .

And that's all I can ever remember of it. It's Latin, sure, and it doesn't make a lick of sense. Serus? Cirrus? Ceres? The word is late? The word is cloud? The vocabulary is a Roman goddess?

I know there's more, but I can never quite get it. I even repeat those words sometimes just to see what comes next, but nothing ever does.

"Gideon?" It was Rachel's voice, low and soft, but with the hint of alarm in the darkness.

"I woke you. Did I yell?"

"No," she said. "But you said those words again. *Vocabulum est*—"

"*Serus,*" we finished together.

"*Our* words," she said. That was the really *weird* part. Rachel had the same damn dream that I did. We each had it every few months, and had both been having it for years, even before we met.

Not that it's all that unusual that people would dream about falling into Hell. What with knowing that place is real now, and with the Imperator Solen Solux's insistence on individual and collective perfection to escape perdition, Hell is something that we're face to face with every day. It's like hundreds of years ago when people thought of themselves as spiders hanging by the web over the eternal fire. Only today we've actually seen the creatures who are stoking the flames. And some, like Massimo Eddie, have even seen the fiery pit itself. No wonder his circuits are fried.

Anyway, it was a bad dream, but it saved my ass—and Rachel's too. We would have still been sleeping when the scrub team came to call.

As it was, I was in the bathroom splashing cool water on my face when I heard a *thunk*, like something heavy hitting the floor, and I started out, because I thought maybe Rachel had fallen in the darkness, in spite of the fact that this was her own apartment. Maybe I'd left my boots in the middle of the floor.

But I heard her yell, "Scrub team!" just as I heard the first shot fired. The flash from the muzzle was blindingly bright, but I could see that there were three of them, wearing ugly brown monk's hoods, their eyes hidden by wraparound gleamers to protect from flash.

I didn't see Rachel anywhere, and figured she'd dived onto the floor on the other side of the bed. I looked around desperately for something to use as a weapon, but that's the trouble with having an ascetic as a lover—no sharp-edged knick-knacks to total bastards trying to kill you. So I threw the only thing I had at the guy who had fired at Rachel— myself.

"Die for your sins, cursed of—"

Catching him in the legs and in mid-sentence, I knocked him sprawling. The other two were trying to get a clean shot at me without hitting their teammate, and with both of us scruffling on the floor, it was tough. Their hesitation gave me just enough time to grab the gun of the guy I'd downed, and bring it up at the two shooters.

Willoughby 7.

The thought came pure and sweet as a spring breeze. My fingers wrapped around the grip and trigger as though I'd been shooting this weapon my whole life. I aimed and fired with the same natural skill, somehow knowing just how it would respond, the amount of recoil, the precise counter-weight that I had to provide so that I could fire again, immediately and accurately.

I never saw a man's face get blown apart before, but it didn't bother me, nor did the fact that he was employed by the same government that I worked for. No matter what the reason, the son of a bitch had come to kill me, and Rachel too. So as his gleamers splintered and the fragments of plaz and my bullet ripped his cowled head to pieces, I already had my next man targeted.

But before I could pull the trigger, the man's head snapped to the side as I saw the flat of Rachel's hand cut into his heck like a dull axe driven hard. I didn't stop to be amazed, but shifted my gun hand the fraction of an inch while I threw my whole body to the right, firing as I fell, to evade the blast that followed as the surviving scrubber's finger pressed the trigger.

The exploding round punched a hole the size of a grape-fruit in Rachel's mattress, missing me by inches. The scrubber wasn't as lucky. Rachel had picked up her victim's weapon, and our rounds took the third man at the same time, from both sides. Either of our shots would have been lethal, but both of them meeting in the middle of the man's brain provided a result that was just plain appalling. The shower of gore went straight up, like the Fountain of the Imperator in L'Enfant Plaza.

We lay there for what seemed like a long time, me on the floor, Rachel in a half crouch, our eyes looking toward the burned-in door, expecting more attackers. But there were none so we both straightened up, and only then looked at each other in amazement.

What the hell had we done? Neither one of us had ever handled anything more deadly than a keyboard, yet the two of us, starting off unarmed, had taken out three of the Hand of God's most dangerous executioners.

The thought of what she had just done hit Rachel like a brick. She dropped her weapon on the floor, then looked with horror at the dead men whose blood and brains had just repainted her tiny apartment. She moved gingerly toward the one she had neck-chopped, and took off his gleamers as though she thought he might try to stop her. She needn't have worried. His open eyes stared glassily at the ceiling without blinking.

"He's . . . dead," she whispered.

I nodded grimly. "People tend to get that way when you break their necks." It was a dumb crack, but I needed to add some humor, however warped, just to defuse the tension, to somehow diminish the miracle we had just worked.

Rachel looked at me helplessly. "Gideon . . ." she said.

"We've got to go," I said. "The shots will bring more."

"But . . . but there's some *mistake*." She spoke slowly and distinctly, trying to convince herself. "They came . . . to the wrong place. It couldn't have been us."

I shrugged. I didn't know why the scrub, but I've been in ARC long enough to know that when you're targeted, nobody ever rescinds the order. She looked up at me in disbelief. "Do you think . . . because we're *fornicators*? Would they do it just because of *that*?"

"Rachel, who knows why they'd do it? But apparently we've done something—or they *think* we've done something—that merits the death sentence. Maybe it's a mix-up, maybe it's not. But I guarantee that if anybody from the Hand of God finds us with three dead scrubbers here, they're gonna shoot first and work out the mix-ups later. If we weren't guilty before . . ." I gestured to the dead pieces of monk meat on the floor. ". . . we are now."

"But it was self-defense!" Rachel said. "They were trying to *kill* us!"

"They were supposed to kill us. And we were supposed to die. All five of us screwed up. And the Hand of God doesn't like screwups. Now we gotta go, because whoever comes in here next won't ask questions. All right?"

She knows the way things are, and the pounding of feet somewhere down the hall was an additional incentive to make tracks. We dropped the bulky weapons, since to be seen on the street holding them would bring an instant death sentence, and opened the window. Luckily, Rachel's apartment was on the first floor, so we jumped to the ground and ran into the night.

There was no time to even grab our clothes. Rachel was wearing a long t-shirt and panties, and I had on only a pair of boxers. The first thing to do was to find some clothes, or we'd be picked up by the first Holicop to spot us.

Fortunately the area around Righteous Tower, where both Rachel and I have our apartments—or had, since we'll never be able to go back there again—is lower class residential. The Tower rises like a lighthouse out of the rat's nest of the poor, proclaiming Solene Solux's presence among those who don't give a damn whether the Hand of God or the Hand of Satan or those old dead parties, the Republicans or Democrats, rule them. They live their lives, and the only time they worship the androgynous Imperator Solux is when they need to collect their food credit.

Tonight, however, I was glad for the poor—and especially for the fact that they still used laundromats to wash their clothes. It was three o'clock in the morning, but through the back window we could see a woman letting the machines dry her clothes while she sat at a sorting table, head down, her eyes closed, the neck of the guilty bottle peeking out of a woven plastic bag by her feet.

Alcohol, certainly. It had been outlawed by the Hand, but even long before had been replaced by synalk, which gave you the buzz but spared you the hangover and liver damage. It was not, so they claimed, addictive, although the Imperator said otherwise, and what the Imperator says goes.

So synalk was banned along with alcohol, but that didn't seem to have stopped the dozing washerwoman here. Rachel is lighter on her feet than I am, so she opened the door quietly and stepped in. Fortunately, the woman had two dryers going at once, so that one could keep up that comforting humming while Rachel opened the other and took from it clothes that she though would fit both of us.

These duds left a lot to be desired in the style department. The pants were a little short, but the shirt she cadged for me fit well enough. Though people might look at us and think we were rat's-ass poor, at least we wouldn't be arrested for insufficient garment cover. An erect nipple could get you up to five years. As for a "defined genital pouch"—the harder you were, the harder your time.

Our feet were still bare, but it was summertime, and if you could avoid the broken glass and metal shards, you'd survive. Besides they weren't going to be bare long.

There was a storage facility five blocks away from the Tower that rented alcoves by the week, month, or year. I had dropped a hundred a year on the rent for a space the same size as a small gym locker. That night it finally turned out to be worth it.

"What all have you got in there, Gideon?" Rachel asked me after I had coded open the door.

"Hopefully, everything I might ever need. Money, security clearances, false ID's . . ." I wedged some of the items in my pants pockets, gave Rachel a few, which she studied in confusion, and left the rest in the zippered bag.

"Why? Why stash all this stuff?"

It was a fair question, and I had an answer for her. "Three years ago," I said, "Frank Jersey had some synalk he had gotten in a street bust. He was there, saw the deal going down, flashed his badge, and the sinners dropped the stuff and ran. All the bottles broke but one, and he showed it to me. I mentioned that I'd never even had a taste of the stuff—hell, I was only a kid when it was banned—and you know Frank."

I could feel my face cloud over. Frank Jersey is our immediate superior in ARC. "Or maybe we *did* know Frank. Anyway, he said better late than never, and opened it right in his car."

"Oh, Gideon, like a couple of teenage punks."

"If you say so, babe. Anyway, we got a little high, and when I asked him if he wasn't afraid of getting caught with the stuff, he said he was always afraid these days, that you never knew when the Hand or somebody in it would turn on you. And then he told me that any ARC agent—or anybody at all—wouldn't be dumb to keep a cache of stuff on hand, just like this, in the event that anybody ever turned up the heat. I figured he'd been around long enough to know, so I did it. Only thing I added to the mix was this."

And I showed her the handheld recorder into which I'm talking right now. My little buddy, who just listens and never talks back. And if I—or, God forbid, both of us—get any unluckier than we've already been tonight, maybe somebody will hear the story. Maybe the Hand will know they made a mistake, though it might be too late to do us any good. And maybe some changes will be made.

Or maybe, after they scour our blood, wipe our data, and dump our bodies, nobody will give a shit.

CHAPTER 2

Rachel's just reminded me that I'm so damned informal that I probably haven't even put our full names to this chip yet, and she's probably right. So I guess it's time to fill in the blanks, tell who we are and what we do, even if we don't know what we *did*.

Long and short of it is, we love each other, and we work for the Hand of God, which apparently doesn't love us. My name is Gideon Eshanti, age 32, place of birth, Washington, D.C. My colleague, friend, and lover—though that's a dirty word—is Rachel Braque, age 31, place of birth also D.C.

Rachel is Skin Type Euroid, five feet six, 130 pounds. Red hair, blue eyes, a gorgeous combination. And her face is beautiful. I'm Skin Type Afroid, six feet one, 180 pounds.

Black hair, brown eyes, and nowhere near as good looking as Rach, but you wouldn't throw bricks at me. There. Now you can identify our corpses.

We were on the Investigations Staff of ARC, or Artificial Reality Containment. Dry Ops, though you wouldn't know it from the wet work we did tonight. We were just Double-D's, decks and desks. Most of the time we sat at our decks doing research, tracking down anything that might be indicative of illegal technological work, for profit or any other reason.

I do a lot of tracking of unauthorized or suspicious component purchases, and other inferred intelligence options that might lead to the detection and arrest of anyone using artificial realities. Rachel's strength is in producing intelligence reports from human and electronic intelligence sources.

In other words, I'm the bloodhound, she's the ferret. We work great together, and find a lot of sinners, and make a lot of arrests possible.

We're not perfect, though. Sometimes we've let people slide, and been judge and jury, and nobody knows about it. I guess that's because we've got soft hearts—or maybe softer heads. But in a lot of cases no real harm is done, to society or to individuals or even to the perps themselves. And if the Hand knew about them, they would face not only judge and jury, but executioner too.

Rach worries about it. She feels that we're betraying not only the Hand of God, but God him- or herself. I decided long ago that the Hand of God and The Big Guy—and I don't mean Solux—might be on speaking terms, but I doubt it. You stay in law enforcement under the Hand for any amount of time, and you see that it's run by all too human people who use God as an excuse to do what they want.

Why didn't I get out a long time ago then? Maybe I should have. But I always wanted to work in law enforcement. My dad, rest his soul, was a cop, back in the days before the Hand. He didn't relate well to the new regime, didn't think people ought to be told what to think and who to pray to, so he took retirement soon as he could and died a couple months later. I was only fifteen. My mom said it was of a broken heart, seeing what the department had become.

But I wanted to do what he had done, and I enjoyed working with decks, so it was natural that I fell into ARC. I think they could tell that I wasn't a holy roller. My ratings for diligence and resourcefulness are always excellent, but my devotional rank is only fair. After tonight, it seems I had the right idea all along.

Not surprisingly, Rachel has pretty much the same background as I do. In fact, we went to high school together. I remember her, though I really didn't pay much attention to her then, nor she to me. I ran into her from time to time during my ARC training at the academy, but we never had any of the same classes. It was only when we were partnered four years ago that I got to know her.

For me, to know her was to love her, and vice versa. It took another three years for us to become actual lovers. When we knew how we felt about each other, marriage was out of the question if we both wanted to keep working, since the Hand frowns on partners getting married. Oh, one of us could have resigned, but the story goes that if you resign from the Hand before retirement age, it'll be tough to find another job *anywhere*. Solene Solux and her government are like spurned suitors. Leave me, and love nobody else.

So the only thing to do was to become "fornicators," as the Hand puts it. Any sexual union, romantic or not, not sanctioned through a Hand of God marriage, is illegal and punishable by imprisonment. Nobody's ever been scrubbed for it, far as I know, not even the high profile cases, like the big shot in the Department of Transgressions who was caught in a Watergate room doing the carnal carioca with a Voice of God media consultant. He got twenty years, she got fifteen, but at least they're still alive, if you can call life in the Penitence Mall living.

They were luckier than the Assistant Secretary of Piety Assurance, who had the misfortune to fall in love with someone of the same sex and get caught cohabiting. Public flogging and castration is a high price to pay for someone to get you through the night.

But I'm getting off track again. The Hand of God will do that to you. Think of one horror story, and a dozen more spring to mind. As for Rachel and me, it became pretty easy—or so we thought—to evade the Hand's eyes and become lovers. We both live in the Tower, and as far as we know the only cameras are in the stairwells and elevators. Maybe we were wrong. Still, we wouldn't get scrubbed for being lovers. Dishonored and imprisoned, yes, but not killed.

I think the seriousness of our relationship is obvious from the fact that we were, and are, willing to risk that fate. And now we're running for our lives, and dammit, we don't know why.

At least we have a place to spend what's left of the night. Dante's one of the good guys, even if he is an outlaw in the Hand's eyes. He fronts as an appliance repairman, but he's an incurable techie, dealing in tech and illicit data. Pretty innocent stuff. What he's fed us in the past about the real bad guys—including a kiddy-porn netrunner—earned him a free ride on our circuit paths.

We couldn't take either Rachel's or my car to Dante's, since they're sure to be staked out by now, and the subway was out of the question, since the Hand could follow us through our credit codes. So I stole a car.

It crashed Rachel for a minute, until she realized that since they're after us for murder, a lousy car covet-and-steal wouldn't make things worse. They can't kill you twice.

I had phony plates in my emergency bag, and the Gatesmobile was so old that my unicode popped it open right away, and we were headed to Dante's. That's his deck name, not his real one. Why incriminate a guy who's doing us a favor?

Dante lives near Union Station, and when we drove past it, I said to Rachel, "Want to hop a train, take off for parts unknown?"

"Like we could *get* on a train," she said dryly, knowing I was just dreaming.

Dante's apartment is a huge loft, one room with an alcove curtained off as a bedroom, and a closet-like bathroom with a real door. Everything else, kitchen, living area, Dante's workspace and deck, is right out in the open.

Just before five in the morning we buzzed his door, and he opened it, looking not at all sleepy. He'd been decking, and the glow of his screen was the only light in the room. Outlaws do most of their running late at night—the nets are less crowded, though it's harder to escape if you're tagged.

His eyes widened when he saw us. After all, we still were the law. "Whoa," he said. "Rachel, Gideon, hey, what's the flowchart? Cracking down on rogue techs?"

"Just the opposite," I said. "We're *getting* cracked."

He looked puzzled, but let us in, and we followed his long-haired, lanky frame into the room. We perched on a couch, and he sat at his deck at the most comfortable seat in the place, since that was where he spent eighteen hours a day. He hit a few keys, then popped off the screen.

Rach and I told him about the scrub attempt, and how we had been lucky enough to come out of it alive. His already large eyes got even larger.

"You guys scrubbed a scrub team? That's not gonna endear you to the Solux dude."

"We know that," I said. "What we want to know is what we did to piss off the Hand in the first place."

"We're ARC employees, damn it," Rachel said. "We enforce the laws, we believe in what the Hand's doing, even if they . . ." She struggled for words.

Dante finished it for her. "Step over the line sometimes? Clamp down with an iron fist on what used to be free speech and action and thought? Ah hell, it started years before the Hand . . . that goddam Clipper chip . . ." He shook himself like a wet dog and smiled. "Maybe they nailed you for being soft on guys like me. Most other ARC agents would've pulled my plug by now."

Rach shook her head firmly. "That wouldn't get us cleaned. A rebuke, maybe, but we could prove that you're a singer on more dangerous hackers, so we let you stand."

I thought back to our most recent infraction. "You know, a couple weeks ago we tagged those two kids? Your typical would-be's programming an illegal c-space. We gave them another chance, let them skip."

"They wouldn't scrub us over that," Rachel insisted.

Dante laughed. "Hey, you guys are trying to be *logical*. When's the last time Transgressions punished *only* the wicked? In case you've been blinded by Solux's holy light, this is a tyranny. Some suits in the Five Fingers get jumpy, they start purgin' anybody."

"Maybe you're right," I said. "But our first move is to find out what the Hand has—or *thinks* it has on us."

"*My* first move," Dante said, "would be to a 1087 heading for Africa. The coastal republics are kind of a high-tech free zone now. It's a little rough, but the Hand's fingers aren't that long yet."

"We're not running."

"Damn right, Rach. We've spent our lives working for this government, and I'm not going to end it by running when somebody starts shooting. I want answers, even if we have to go to Solux to get them."

"You don't want to do that," Dante said. "Look, let me surf the underground nets, see if anything's being rapped out about your case. I ain't much of a hacker, but if something leaks out, I'll hear about it. Meantime, why don't you two grab some down time. Use my bed, I got a few more hours of load left. Just, uh, don't get anything messed up, y'know?"

He gave us what was supposed to be a salubrious leer, and turned back to his deck. Rach and I took him up on his invitation, but I'm sure we disappointed him by not making a sound once we hit the mattress. Whoever said that danger puts fire into the genitals wasn't talking about us. We were scared and tired, and all we wanted to do was to hold each other until we fell asleep.

CHAPTER 3

We woke up just after nine, after only a few hours of fitful rest. Rach nestled against me, looking into my eyes. "Now what?"

"Get some other clothes and shoes," I said, then ran a furry tongue over my teeth. "And plaquers. Then. . . ."

We both thought of it at the same time, but Rach said it first. "Frank. He'd have the official e-mail on our scrub."

I nodded. Frank Jersey would have answers, and he might be willing to share them with us.

Or, I thought coldly, he might be more willing to scrub us himself. "Do you think we can trust him?" I asked Rach.

"Frank? Are you kidding? He wouldn't be a part of this. He hasn't got a political bone in his body."

That much was true. Frank had taken some pretty big risks to defend innocent people from corrupt busts, and he was the captain in charge of all the cases we handled. He knew both of us, knew how we felt about each other, and knew a lot about the techs we let slide. And he had never done a thing about it—so I thought. After last night, I don't think I'd have trusted my own mother if she worked for the Hand of God.

"We'll link him," I said. "Not from here, though. Don't want any traces. See if he'll talk to us."

"He'll talk to us. I know Frank."

Dante had crashed on the sofa, but woke up when he heard us stirring. He hauled some stale cereal and overripe fruit from his fridge and brewed up a pot of coffee. "The real thing," he said. "Colombian, loaded with caff." Caffeinated coffee's a real treat, and illegal like all stimulants. I used to have a street dealer I bought from in four ounce packets, but they caught him and cut out his tongue.

"Not a byte about you two menaces to society and to God on the nets," Dante said as he poured out the rich, dark brew. "They probably have the lid clamped tight until they decide which way they want to spin it. Can't have Hand agents being mowed down by unarmed bureaucrats now, can they? Gotta keep that terror quotient high. You got somewhere to go today?"

"We're going to pay a few visits," I said.

"Well, you ever want to crash, come on back here. Just don't bring any scrub teams with you. I tell you, though, I think you're whistlin' past the mausoleum."

"What do you mean?"

"Rachel, nobody's gonna sit down and explain a thing to you. They don't think they owe you an explanation—what they owe you is a bullet in the brain. You two are marked for logoff, and talkin' to the Man ain't gonna help. So lemme just give you a word of advice."

Rachel sat angrily, but I knew Dante was probably right. "Shoot," I said.

"When you don't know where to go or who to turn to, I know somebody with links to the underground. Not the nets, the *Front*."

Rach and I looked at each other darkly. The Citizens Freedom Front would indeed be a last resort, but I could envision us having to turn to them to stay alive.

"I don't know whether you two have got any faith left in the system, but you may want to check out what the other side has to offer."

"A week ago I'd have busted you for saying that," I said quietly.

Dante grinned. "Funny how being shot at changes a person's attitude."

"It doesn't change it *that* much!" Rachel stood up. "Don't be so sure we're ready to turn traitor!"

"Hey, Rachel," said Dante, "I have a dog and it tries to kill me, I ain't gonna feed it biscuits and pat its little head."

"Don't you compare the Hand of God to a dog!"

He looked at her dead on. "I wasn't, lady. You're the dog, and when you nuked that scrub team you bit the hand that bled you. They wanted you dead then, and they want you a whole lot deader now. The Hand is no option anymore. I'm just trying to give you another."

I put a hand on Rachel's shoulder. I could feel her trembling. "And we're grateful for it. What's the name?"

He looked at us for a long time. "I owed you, so now you owe me. Don't screw me over, okay?"

"You have my word. Rach?"

Her jaw was set, but she nodded grimly. "My oath before God."

Dante nodded back. "Good enough. The guy is Aldous Xenon. He hangs around a bodega in Chinatown near Gallery Place. I'll give him your names, tell him you might be coming. If something happens so that you don't need to see him, forget his name. Hell, forget mine, for that matter."

"Won't do that, Dante. Like you said, we owe you."

"So you headin' out?"

"Yeah. After one more cup of real, synapse-jolting coffee." I held up the steaming pot. "Another for you, Rach?"

She shrugged and gave a tight little smile. "In for a penny, in for a pound," she said, holding up her cup.

The car was still on the street, and, what was better, no holicops were stationed at it to gun us down when we showed. We got in and drove far away from the Union Station area, then found an all purpose store where we bought presentable clothing and shoes we thought we could run in. Adequately dressed, we stopped at a pay link on the street and punched in Frank Jersey's code.

Frank does a lot of work out of his home, and he answered after the first tone. He looked like he was alone. I had disabled video input on our end, so he couldn't see me. His voice growled "Jersey," so roughly that it sounded as if it were coming across the timbreless lines of a hundred years ago. He scowled at the blank vidscreen on his end. "Whozis?"

I couldn't speak. Here was a guy who had been at times like my own father, and damn it, I just didn't *trust* him.

"It's Rachel, Frank," she said quietly. "And Gideon."

A deep sigh escaped him, and I saw him sit back in his chair.

"We need to talk to you," she went on.

He bit his lip for just a moment, then held up his hands. "Not here. Don't say anything. Not a thing. Big Boy. Half hour." He leaned forward to pop the link, and the screen went gray, the sound went back to music.

"Big Boy?" Rach asked me.

"Lincoln Memorial," I said. "Frank always calls it that. He'll be outside on the right, the river side. He likes to face-to-face informers there, exchange anything that can't be done on-line."

"What's wrong?"

"I don't know. It feels funny. Like he was waiting to hear from us."

"He probably was. He must know what happened, even if they didn't tell him beforehand. He must have known we'd contact him."

"I want to go now," I said, "get there early, scope the place good, make sure he's not doublecrossing us."

"Gideon, this is *Frank!* He wouldn't do that."

"I hope you're right, babe, because if he does, there's nothing we can do about it but die."

Chapter 4

We got to the Lincoln Memorial in twenty minutes, parked the car near the river, and, staying in the shelter of the trees, walked to where we could see the back of the structure. Everybody looked like typical tourists, since the government workers who mobbed the place at noon were cloistered in their offices at this time of the morning. That made it easier for us to spot possible Hand agents, but nobody seemed to fit the bill.

Then, still keeping in the shelter of the trees wherever there were any, we crossed to the other side of the reflecting pool. From the grove near the Vietnam Veterans Memorial, we checked out the northern side of the monument. Again, nothing *especially* suspicious, though since everything was suspicious, we weren't feeling too reassured.

We watched a mother and father push a toddler around the base of the monument and then haul it up the steps, then watched another mom and dad with a teenager who looked as though he'd rather be somewhere else. The second father took photographs by the score, and the kid's expression showed he was sick and tired of posing. I didn't blame him.

At the foot of the wide steps, a young couple sat, their arms around each other. Every now and then they would kiss, looking around to make sure no holicops saw them. They had the air of a couple on their honeymoon, but I thought that their surreptitious glances might not really be for cops, but for surveillance of those vicious killers, Eshanti and Braque. I pointed them out to Rachel, and we determined to keep a close eye on them.

In another few minutes we saw what we thought might be the blocky, heavyweight form of Frank Jersey walking on the south side of the pool toward the memorial. He was wearing a long, light raduster. As he got closer, the cropped steel gray hair and a craggy face like the bottom of a miliboot confirmed our ID.

We walked toward the monument. Frank glanced our way once only, registered us, then kept walking up the memorial's steps and around to the south side. We followed, sharply eyeing the tourists as we went, feeling naked and vulnerable on the steps.

When we walked around the corner of the memorial, Frank was standing several yards away. The trees were high enough that they hid us from the street and the traffic coming over the Arlington Bridge. It was a good place to meet, although I felt cornered. I guess that's why Frank liked to meet informers there. The place put them in his pocket all the more deeply.

He just stood there looking at us, and I nodded. "Hey, Frank. Thanks for coming."

Frank Jersey smiled thinly, then snaked a meaty hand inside his raduster and pulled out a small but lethal Avenger .32.

I heard Rachel's sharp intake of breath, then my own. I thought about going over the side fast, but knew it would be no use. Frank was combat trained, quick with a gun. We couldn't have gotten to him fast enough to keep him from nailing both of us.

As I waited for the shot and the impact, his hand came up, but instead of pulling the trigger, he flipped the gun over and held it out butt first.

"You're gonna need these," he drawled, and he shook his head disgustedly. "Come on, take it, it's small enough to stick in your pants, assuming you're bright enough not to shoot your nuts off. Got one for you too, Rachel," and he pulled out a second pistol after I took the first. They were sweet, powerful little guns, easy to hide, about a fifth of the size of the Willoughbys we'd used last night.

"Frank, I. . . ." But he cut me off.

"Stick 'em down in there, go on, they're not cold, it's plaz, not metal."

"Thanks, Frank."

"Yeah, yeah, just forget where you got 'em. I got one year left till retirement, and Liz and I want to go somewhere other than Hell. Nah, blouse your shirts down over them. Though I don't know why I'm telling you two how to handle weapons, after that little stunt of yours last night. I never knew you guys were combat ready."

"We weren't," said Rachel. "Just lucky, I guess."

"Takes more than luck to take out a scrub team, missy. You two kicked some ass, though it's not public knowledge. Doubt it ever will be."

"How'd you hear about it, Frank?"

"Hand downed me the scrub team's playback footage just before you called. I hate those goddam trials without juries. Bastards deserved to get smoked."

"We didn't like doing it, Frank," Rachel said. "It just . . . happened. Thanks for meeting with us."

"I've covered your butts for five years. I won't stop now."

"One thing, Frank," I said. "Do you think anybody might have followed you here? You know, looking for us?"

"Shit, sonny, I'm an ARC Captain. My standing orders are to scrub rogues like you myself. Now why would they think we're compadres having a nice meeting at the Big Boy?"

"Okay then, you want to give us the skinny? What was this scrub all about? We've done our duty for Hand and country. This is payback? We haven't done a thing, Frank!"

He smiled, but the hardness of metal was in his voice. "That's probably what a lot of people you fed to the scrubs said."

Rachel's face got red. "They were sinners, Frank. They deserved what they got."

"Oh yeah. Sorry, I forgot that you still believe in the Guiding Hand, missy. You still think being ARC narcs was doing God's work?"

At that moment the sloppily dressed teenager appeared from around the corner, hands in his pockets. Frank gave him a look that would have cooked a potato, and he disappeared fast.

"Okay," Frank said, "you don't have to answer that if you don't want to, but I got one question that I do want answered."

"Go ahead."

His face lost its bluff good humor. "I want to help you two, but I don't want to play games. So tell me, what does the Hand have on you? What did you two do?"

"*Nothing,* Frank!" I said. "Not a thing, except for the few techs we let slide, which you already know about, and . . . well, you know how Rach and I feel about each other."

"That's not enough to get you scrubbed," he said.

"Hell, we know that! So you tell us—you've got to know what they've charged us with, you tell us what we did!"

It was like watching Mount Rushmore nod. "Okay, maybe you know why they really want you, and maybe you don't. But the *official* charges are bullshit. You two are charged with violating the Artificial Realities and Extranoumenal Environments Design, Programming, and Transportation Act. Why? Because you've been dealing in pornovirts—humans doing the nasty with demons."

I thought Rach was going to explode. "Skin dealers? . . . Skin dealers! That's ridiculous! . . . my case history . . . I've burned *libraries* full of porno books and virtuals."

"It's a frame," I said quietly, my mind racing, trying to figure out why.

"Sure it's a frame," Frank said. "Either you two did something else you're not telling me, or there's some political reason they want you whacked."

"Who's *they?*" Rachel asked.

"Maybe somebody in ARC, but more likely some sleazebag in Transgressions or even the Pentagon. They gotta have connections, because they linked you with Beautiful, and that only happens when they're desperate to whack you."

"Who? Beautiful?"

"Yeah. *Mr.* Beautiful. He's a case all right. The guy's a demon who's active among the city's crime families—fancies himself a real *goombah,* y'know?"

"But how can the Hand be involved with him?" Rachel said incredulously. "The Hand is dedicated to wiping out demonic influences wherever they can."

"Dirty politics makes strange bedfellows," Frank said. "They tolerate this scuzzbucket demon among humans, so that they can get rid of some humans they consider demons."

"Like us."

Frank nodded. "Like you, sonny. Want somebody scrubbed, you accuse them of narcotics, porn, or illegal realities. Then you fabricate a link to Beautiful, haul his ass in, he signs a confession implicating you. They let him go on a prearranged technicality, and you wind up dead, or worse."

"So you're saying," Rachel said slowly, "that this Mr. Beautiful fingered us as part of a virtual skin ring?"

"Bingo."

"You know where we can find him?" I asked.

Frank nodded. "Back room of a speak called the Interface out in Foggy Bottom. Another link to that place might interest you two. The owner—a guy named O'Leary—got scrubbed last night too. Only it stuck. They blew his brains all over a store window. His joint's notorious. Lots of disreps

—leftover Sinn Fein hardliners, outlaw techs, you name it. Watch your asses, you go out there."

"Any other scrubs last night?" Rachel asked.

"Yeah. They were out in force. You were the only ones who survived."

"Who were the others? Any pattern?" Rachel's always the organizer.

Frank shrugged. "Only name I recognized was O'Leary, but I thought you might want to check it out. Here's a hard of the list." Rachel read the names, shook her head, and gave the paper to me. I didn't recognize any either.

As was giving the list another sweep, I heard Rachel gasp. I looked up at Frank and saw that he was whipping out another gun from under his raduster. It was much bigger than the ones he had given me and Rach. He was starting to snarl, his lips curling back from his teeth, and I thought, *Jesus, he's gonna kill us after all.*

But then he yelled, "*Down!*" and I realized he wasn't aiming at me but somebody over my shoulder. I crouched and spun around just as the first shot went off, and I saw the punk kid and his "parents" in a tripartite firing stance, the kid prone on the cement, the adults standing side-on, Willoughbys extended.

I heard a whole lot of shots before I could pull out my Avenger. The firefight didn't last more than a few seconds. There was no cover, and a lot of lead flying. Frank caught dear old Dad in the chest, knocking him backward off the balustrade into the trees. Rach and I both hit the mother, my shot in the shoulder, and hers in the neck a moment later.

But the kid was hot. One of his shots *spanged* off my pistol, knocking it out of my hand. When I dove for it, another bullet shrieked past my head, and by the time I grabbed my gun again, a third round had nailed Frank in the chest. He jerked and sat down hard.

Before I could aim, Rachel's Avenger was rattling away. The kid didn't offer much of a target, but Rach hit what was there, which was mostly his head. He didn't fire again.

From the sound of daddy dear moaning in the bushes below, he wouldn't be giving us any more trouble.

But Frank had all the trouble he could stand. He was breathing hard, and a froth of blood was bubbling from his mouth and nose. "Shit. . . ." he muttered. "Aw *shit*, if that ain't the way . . . year to go and lookit this. Liz is gonna be so pissed. . . ."

Rachel held him steadily, but her voice trembled. "Don't move, Frank . . . just don't move, you'll be all right . . ."

"Aw, get outta here, missy. Just kick their asses, goddam lyin' bastards . . . can't do nothin' for me . . . get out now. . . . I'm dead . . ."

And in another three seconds, he was.

I felt like hell, having mistrusted him. I should have known better. Frank Jersey was a straight arrow all the way. I wasn't surprised to find that I was crying.

"Come on, Rach," I said through a rapidly closing throat. "He was right. We've got to go."

She stood up, hissing out an angry breath, her face alive with fury, sorrow, and regret. But there was no time to mourn; and we jammed our pistols into our clothes and ran around the building, down the broad white steps, and through the trees to our car.

The sounds of sirens followed us as we drove away, and as they faded into the distance Rachel finally spoke. "I loved that guy, Gideon."

"I know. I did too. He . . . didn't have to do that. He could've just let them have us."

"No," Rachel said softly. "He couldn't have." She was right. It was the perfect eulogy for Frank Jersey.

I switched on the radio so that I wouldn't have to think for a while, even though the only station available was the Voice of God.

CHAPTER 5

Finding a speakeasy in Foggy Bottom is like searching for an elephant in a haystack—you're bound to come across it sooner or later. But just then we didn't get the chance. As we were heading up 23rd Street toward Washington Circle, the news came on the Voice of God, and yours truly and my sweet Rachel were the lead story, along with the other scrubs of the night before.

It was everything that Frank had said it would be—two rogue ARC agents engaged in the vile business of providing the most disgusting pornography available, men and women mating in unholy lust with demons. That was what they said, "unholy lust." I wonder how they would define holy *lust*.

They left one thing out—that we were still alive. According to the story, we were as dead as Swivel O'Leary, Deirdre

O'Connor, Adam Schonbrun, and the other strangers on Frank Jersey's downloaded list. There was no mention of the scrubbers scrubbed by the scrubbees either—only the report that in an unrelated incident, three agents of the Hand of God had been taken to their supreme reward after being involved in a fatal car wreck. Poor guys. And after the slaughter we'd just left, the Voice would probably report that three Hand agents and one ARC captain were killed in a joint falling-down-the-Lincoln-Memorial-steps accident.

"Lie a lot, don't they?" I said to Rachel.

"Yes. Is this meant to relax us, throw us off our guard?"

"Hell, no. They're after us—that lovely family at the memorial was proof of that." I thought for a moment while hymns in honor of the three departed servants of God played on the radio. "Maybe we should make it harder for them."

"How?"

"Why don't we visit Dr. Clean before we look for Beautiful?"

The suggestion took her by surprise. Dr. Clean runs a back-alley business in cybernetic enhancements near McPherson Square. Though she claims that she doesn't do plazcoz work, more than a few rogues have changed their appearances, thanks to the good doc. She's one of the people we've turned a blind eye of "justice" to, the main reason being that she does a helluva good job.

She's also more ethical than most choppers and provides a good alternative to a lot of the butchers working the street. The way I always looked at it, and talked Rach into, is that if somebody's going to get a flesh job, they'll get one. By leaving the doc on the street, I figure we've saved dozens, maybe hundreds of lives.

And a less philanthropic reason for letting her stay in business is that the doc has ratted out about a dozen major suppliers in the past few years.

We headed east to McPherson Square and parked on 15th Street, two blocks away from the pawnshop Doc's been using as a cover for the past few months. When we rounded the corner and saw the storefront, I knew something had hit the fan. What was left of the front window lay in pieces on the sidewalk, and the guitars, synthaxes, and other instruments on display were cracked, crushed, bent, and twisted.

When we went inside, we didn't even have to push open the door, since it was hanging by one hinge. Dr. Clean was at the back of the store, trying to tidy up what looked like the wake of a tornado.

"Your place was never neat, Doc," I said, "but this is ridiculous."

"Well well," the doc said in her crisp, nasal voice, "Eshanti and Braque. Come to finish what your playmates started?"

"Don't blame us," Rachel said. "What happened?"

"Technology Assessment finally caught up with me. Sent a goon squad over."

"You're lucky," I said. "This was the warning. The next time they close you down along with your place."

"There won't be a next time."

"You going straight?" Rachel asked.

"Maybe, maybe not. You'll never know. I don't want to get set up again."

"You think we caused this?" I said.

"Somebody punched my ticket."

"Well, not us, Doc." I was angry both at what had happened to her and at her accusation. "We stood by our deal with you. Hell, we came here to see if you could help us.

The Hand tried to put holes in us last night, didn't you hear the Voice?"

"They broke my radio too." She gave a shuddering sigh. "Look, I'm sorry, I know you wouldn't sell me out, but I'm a little . . . testy today. I'm going to salvage what I can here, and then I'm heading west. Reconstruct my face, get a new identity, start over."

"Facial reconstruction's what we wanted to talk to you about," I said. "The Hand's looking for us, and we'd be a lot safer if they didn't know who they were looking for."

Doc shrugged. "A day ago I could've done it. Today my equipment is practically nonexistent."

"You know any other choppers who could do it?" Rachel asked. "We'll pay."

"You don't have to pay me for a referral. Come on in the back, let me take a look at your faces, see how hard a job it'll be."

We walked through a beaded curtain into a back room, then went through what looked like a closet door. Inside was a white room just big enough for an examining table and another work table. Cabinets had been ripped off the walls, their contents crushed into unrecognizable bits of circuitry, chips, and resistors. Doc swept away some pieces of debris from the examining table and told Rachel to lie down. She did, gingerly.

Doc switched on a white contour light, which miraculously still worked, and pulled it over the table. Suddenly Rachel's face looked like a relief map of the Smokies, with rills and ridges and crevices everywhere. "I hate this," she said.

"Vanity, vanity," said the doc. Then she grunted, "Hmph," and again, "*Hmph!*"

"What?" I said.

"I can't recommend a chopper to you."

"Why not?" Rachel asked.

"Because the only chopper who would do plazcoz work on you would be a quack. Nobody worth his Hippocratic Oath would put plaz on plaz. Three months from now your face would start to shift, get lumpy—you'd look like you were melting."

Rachel sat up. "What are you talking about, plaz on plaz?"

"You've already had one face reconstructed, Rachel," Dr. Clean said, as though she'd caught Rachel in a very obvious lie. "It can't be done twice."

Rach's hand went up to her face like the doc had told she had leprosy. "I've never had a *thing* done to my face."

"Lie back down." The doc pointed out to me some areas under Rachel's cheeks, at her temples, on her nose and her chin. Under the light they glowed a pale green. "See those? That's plaz deposits. If you never had this done, Rachel, then you must've been born this way."

"I don't understand," Rachel said as she sat up.

"Well, let's check you out, big guy," the doc said, and I lay on the table, knowing that she couldn't find any plaz deposits on *my* face, but fearing that she might.

She did. "You're full of it, Gideon. More than Rachel. You two had better like your faces, because you're stuck with them."

"Look," I said, "could there be something wrong with your light?"

She shook her head. "The goons didn't touch it. Neanderthals never look up."

We said good-bye to Dr. Clean in a daze. I knew that I had never had a facial reconstruction. And if I had had one done as a kid, the deposits would have had to have been added to as I grew older, and that hadn't happened. Rachel felt the same way. It was impossible, and yet we had seen the green glow on each other's faces, and the doc had no reason to lie to us.

We headed toward Foggy Bottom, discussing possible explanations and finding none. If we were stuck with our faces, we would just have to be more careful about who saw them.

In Foggy Bottom, that wouldn't be much of a problem. After the State Department, now rechristened the Department of Universal Evangelism, moved out of the area, Foggy Bottom went back to its original murky, swampy roots. It's got more criminals per square inch than the Congress of a hundred years ago, which is saying something. A lot of them congregate at the speakeasies, which might serve synalk or real liquor, but most often just have homemade beer.

We had no idea where to find the Interface, so I pulled the car over and asked a hard case. "Two blocks down and one to the left," he said. "Steel warehouse door. *But*—you gotta know the password."

"Which," I said, "you are willing to tell for a price."

"I like a guy knows how the world works," he said, and we made the exchange.

The Interface was like most other speaks, with a monster at the slotted door. I gave him the password, and he let us in without checking us for weapons.

The place smelled damp and musty, a pungent mixture of cheap beer and urine. A well worn bar was on the right, its wood made smooth and shiny by years of weary elbows. Mismatched stools ran along it, with only a few occupied. A few tables and chairs were on the left side of the room, and a steel stairway in the center with a chain across it led up onto a walkway with dark doors off of it. Behind the stairway I could see another door. I wondered if that was where Mr. Beautiful was lurking, but I didn't notice much more after that, because a woman at the far end of the bar turned around. It was Cynna Stone. Or her ghost.

She was gorgeous, just like always, but she was also translucent. I could see the faint shape of a row of bottles through her head, a sensation that added nausea to all my other emotions at seeing her again. Right here in front of me was a dead woman who I had loved, alive . . . or half-alive . . . again. Edgar Allan Poe would've loved it.

"If it isn't Mr. Eshanti," she said, just loud enough for Rachel and me to hear. Her smile was as warm and inviting as it had ever been. To look at her, you'd expect her to be a model or an actress. Anything except one of the nation's top experts at destroying things.

"Cynna . . . you look . . . great."

"Oh, my heart would be all aflutter—if I still had one."

"Gideon?" Rachel said. "Who is . . . this?"

"This is Cynna Stone, Rachel."

"Cynna Stone? The bomber?"

Cynna, or the holographic simulacrum that was all that was left of her, made a pouting face. "Ooo, I hate that word. *Demolitions engineer* has a much nicer ring to it, don't you think?"

"You know her?" Rachel asked.

I nodded. "From long ago."

I could feel the jealousy starting to bubble in Rachel, but I didn't want to tell her any more than she needed to know.

I'd known Cynna before I got involved with Rach, but by the time the news came out that it was Cynna Stone who had breached over a dozen branches of the First Bank of God, as well as the Holy Federal Repository for a total of well over a billion dollars in credit, our brief affair was long over.

I had caught the scent of illegitimacy on my lover long before I knew what she had done. Though I was perversely attracted by her air of lawlessness, I was still an agent of ARC. If I'd been sure she was a sinner, I would have had to turn her in, and I didn't want to do that. So we parted, and I never saw her again. Until today.

"This is Rachel, Cynna. Rachel Braque."

"Yes, your partner. I thought you two were now like me." Maybe she didn't like to say *dead*.

I shook my head. "The Hand tried, but we took them out."

"Oh really? Or maybe it's just a set-up—the Voice feeding phony data so you can infiltrate the haunts of the depraved?"

"That's not true," I said.

"I know, I'm just teasing. There's blood on your shoe. I typed it as you came in—O negative. Not your type, even if I was. So the Hand finally realized you weren't a fascist at heart and put out a hit on you, huh? In a way I'm sorry it wasn't successful—then maybe you'd be with the real me, wherever that is."

"Sorry about what happened," I told Cynna.

She shrugged. "It was inevitable. Do what I did, you always figure on slipping someday. That's why I set *this* up." She swept a hand downward to indicate her holographic body.

Rachel cleared her throat. "Are you a hologram? Or an android of some kind?"

"Combination of the two," Cynna said. "The android part moves me, holds all the personality and memory data on three CD's, as well as the holographic file. That's what you see on the outer edge. I might look a little younger than you remember me, Gideon—that's what happens when you don't keep up your holo file."

"How did it happen?" Rachel asked. I could tell any jealousy had faded in the light of the pity Rach felt for what Cynna had become.

"My partner. Good at B&E, but didn't know shit from shinola about bangers. We were using proto-glycerine caps—nitro in gel form. Real unstable. Kinda like my partner's grip. Kaboom." She gave a deep sigh. "But enough about my unfortunate demise. What brings you two fugitives to the Interface?"

We told her then about the porno link to Beautiful, and mentioned the fact that the owner of the speak had also been scrubbed.

"Yeah, Virgil," she said. "He was a weird guy, nice enough, but it seemed as if his head was always somewhere else. Talked to himself, like most heavy boozers."

"Wait a minute," Rachel said, "I thought his name was Swivel."

"Yeah, it was—Swivel O'Leary. But I called him Virgil because sometimes he'd talk to himself in Latin. He didn't get it, but"

"*Latin?*" I said. "You remember what he'd say?"

"Hey, I got chips, not brains, I never forget." Then from what appeared to be her mouth came an edgy tenor voice with a gravel undercurrent. "*Vocabulum est grallae. . . .*"

The voice shifted back to Cynna's. "That's it. The rest was always unintelligible. Hey, you two look like somebody just walked over your graves. What's the deal?"

I forced a smile. "Nothing."

"Yeah, I just bet. Look, what's the next step for you two?"

"Try and get Beautiful to clear our names," Rachel said.

Cynna laughed. "Fat chance. When the Hand smears you, it doesn't come off. You worked for monsters, Gideon. Just a piece of advice. When you finally realize there's no going *back*, think about going *Front*." She gave several overly dramatic winks before I nodded. "They're the only hope, old buddy."

"You were involved with the CFF?"

"Hey, who do you think got the biggest part of the billion I lifted? Just remember they're there. And if you ever need to do any banging—" She smiled discreetly at Rachel. "—referring to demolitions, of course—you know who to come to."

"Thanks, Cynna," I said. "You know if Mr. Beautiful's around today?"

"He's always around if the little shit summons him."

"Little shit?"

"Abonides, this pain-in-the-ass minor demon, sort of Beautiful's social secretary. You gotta go through him to get to Beautiful. Door under the stairs. Knock eighteen times. Three groups of six.

"Mark of the beast," I said.

"Mark of the *doofus*," Cynna replied, and turned back to the bar.

CHAPTER 6

Nobody stopped us as we walked to the back door. I knocked the way Cynna had told me, and the door slowly creaked open. The room glowed red from the torches secured to the wall, but it was too dark inside to see who, if anyone, had opened the door for us. Then a chill went through me as I saw the walls of the room. They seemed to be made of glass, and behind them were the faces of the damned, writhing in torment.

Then I realized that the faces were just painted on, and the sensation of movement had been the result of artistic genius of a dark and twisted sort combined with the flickering of the torchlight. Rachel and I stepped into the room, down several steps, and waited until our eyes got used to the diminished light.

A massive pool table was on our right, and to the left was a huge desk that seemed formed from a single block of reddish wood. On either side of the desk was a tall statue of what I can only assume were demons of some sort. Maybe they were Beautiful's bosses, their likenesses displayed the same way that Hand employees have portraits of Solene Solux over their desk. The furnishings were a combination of old gangster movies and an ancient Middle-Eastern style. "Sumerian?" I asked Rachel.

"Assyrian," she whispered back. I can always count on Rachel for obscure information on the arts. Her brain's like a quick access romdisc. Sometimes she even surprises herself with the trivia she pops up with, especially when she's under stress. If she felt as edgy as I did, she could probably have recited all of Shakespeare. I was glad I had a gun wedged in my pants, even though guns can't harm demons.

"Hey!" Rachel said, and her voice echoed unnaturally in the room. "Anybody here?" she said more softly.

"Hahahahaha!" We both jumped a foot in the air as, from one of the dark corners, scuttled one of the most loathsome little demons I've ever seen. He stood just under three feet tall and was covered with coarse golden hair. He had the prerequisite pair of horns, a pointed little beard, and a misshapen body that ended in goat-like legs. The hooves were encased in shiny patent leather spats, his only clothing except for a black bow tie on a white collar that circled his scrawny neck. His eyes were gigantic. What should have been the whites were orange, and the pupils were black slits, like a cat's eyes, but the nastiest cat you could ever imagine. He had to be Abonides.

He hurried forward as if he was going to attack us, and I yanked out my pistol in spite of myself. He jerked to a stop and held up his furry paws, then screamed in a high-pitched voice that could have shattered glass:

> "What's this! What trouble have I bought?
> Have I copped a fate naughty and full?
> Are you heat or scrubs who want me shot?
>
> I plead you see I'm only dutiful—
> I didn't make the game I play!
> The one you want is Mister Beautiful!"

"I don't believe it," Rachel said. "A demon who speaks in terza rima."

I took my eyes off the ugly troll long enough to look at her in disbelief. "What?"

"A thirteenth century Italian verse form," she went on. "Three lines per stanza, with intertwining rhymes—aba, bcb, cdc—"

Generally I admire Rachel's erudition, but now wasn't the time for a poetry lesson. "Okay, shorty, you're right. Where's your master? We need to see him."

> "See him? Not everyone may.
> Those who do are select.
> Make your bones! You've dues to pay!
>
> I will summon him if I elect,
> But for me to chant and call him hence,
> From you the word I must detect!"

*   *   *

These underworld types, both gangster and satanic, are secretive. They love passwords, codes, magic gestures, all that crap. But today I wasn't in the mood for it. I walked right up to the fuzzy little poet and grabbed him by his beard. "Look, you loudmouthed little shit, I'm Gideon Eshanti and this is Rachel Braque, and we've already paid our dues. Now you summon your master up now, or I'm gonna yank this beard out a hair at a time, comprende?"

Abonides giggled nervously, a sound like cats fighting in a sack, and said,

> "Your brow is twisted, you look tense.
> Your great desire to see my master
> Urges me to quickly fetch him hence.
>
> So screw the word—you want him faster,
> To speak to him as friend to friend.
> I'll call him, though it spell disaster!"

"That's more like it," I said, and released his goatish beard.

"Well done, Mr. Diplomacy," Rachel said.

I scowled at her. "You want to stand around here guessing words all day?"

Abonides ignored our patter and walked to a pentagram, a five-pointed star in a circle, on the floor in front of the desk. He made a few arcane gestures, then actually took his head off. None of our mutual friends have that particular talent, so Rachel and I stared goggle-eyed at the little bastard, while the head, cackling all the time, did a couple of swoops and whirls around the body before it set itself back in place. I assume he was just showing off. Hell, if I could do that, I guess I would too.

Then the reconstituted Abonides levitated until his hooves were a good two feet off the floor. When he'd gotten the proper altitude, he started screaming again, in his less than mellifluous voice:

> "The underworld will part and rend
> A fissure up, from Hell to surface,
> And Beauty rise, though it may be my end!"

A whiff of brimstone more powerful than ammonia hit us, and made us close our eyes and wince. A fountain of fire shot from the floor, and thick, black smoke with snaky tendrils of red billowed out from below, covering whatever the hell was going on beneath it. Then Rachel and I, for the first time, heard the voice of the demon, Mr. Beautiful. . . .

CHAPTER 7

"Uh-hwaaahk, uh-hwaaaaaahkkk!"

After a further series of wet coughs, as the smoke cleared, we saw Mr. Beautiful, fanning the air with one hand, while he held the other in front of his mouth. He couldn't talk for a long time, just kept coughing and spitting gobs of black phlegm that sizzled when they hit the floor, giving us a chance to check him out.

He was no taller than average, an inch or three shorter than me. His horns didn't add to his height, since they came out from the sides of his head and curled toward the front. His face wasn't pretty, but he looked a whole lot more human than Abonides. His eyes appeared normal, although they were bluer than any human eyes I'd ever seen. He was dressed to kill in a shimmery gray sharkskin suit with green lapels and sleeves. A metallic gold vest covered part of his white shirt and black tie. His shoes were so polished he could have seen his reflection if he had looked down.

But he didn't. When the wracking cough stopped, he glared at Abonides, then aimed a kick at the little demon, but just missed. "Abonides! You cowering lickspittle!" He would have sounded like he was sneering, whatever he said. "I told you to go light on the smoke and brimstone and shit when I'm in my human form. This stuff goes right to my freakin' throat, man!"

Rachel and I gave each other a look. This demonic TB case wasn't quite what we had expected.

Abonides didn't seem to like the rebuke. He got an even sneakier look on his face and said,

> "You find it even harsher as of late,
> With human heart and human lung—
> Perhaps you are not one so great!"

But when Beautiful twisted his head and looked down at the demon as though deciding which foot he should tromp him into the earth with, Abonides brought back his ingratiating tone, and turned Beautiful's attention to us.

> "But I speak with too sharp a tongue.
> As your servant I stoop and crawl.
> Here are two with stories unsung!"

"All right, you little putz," said Beautiful, talking to Abonides—but looking at us, "fire up the espresso machine. I want a pot of the double stuff ready for me when I'm done with Gideon and Rachel here." He gave us the glower of a disappointed uncle and waggled a finger at us. His nails were long and had a coat of clear polish.

"I gotta tell you kids I'm not happy, not freakin' happy at all when two of my people are kickin' the hell outta scrub teams in their undies. Howzat gonna play with the dagos and spics and those damn Indians downtown, huh? Now I got every mob in this town handin' me money 'cause I got Mephisto's patronage and a sweetheart deal with the Hand. But you two start blowin' their people's brains out, you know what I'll have? Nada! Freakin' squat, man! Every scrub gun in D.C.'ll be after me!"

We let him talk longer than we should have, but we were stunned both by what he was saying and the proprietary tone he was using with us, like we were his underlings who'd pissed him off. But we damn well weren't.

Rachel finally broke the ice. "What is this? We don't work for you—we've never even seen you before!"

He looked at her sadly and shook his head. "Trouble with the rackets these days is nobody's got loyalty anymore. Hey, Rachel, I'm fightin' a war here. I got enemies on every front and two different planes of existence. Last thing I need's a mutiny by my own freakin' people, got me?"

"No," I said, "we don't 'got you.' You know we're not involved with you. You implicated us because the Hand wanted us scrubbed, but we slipped the noose. And now we're here because we want to know why the Hand wants us dead. We want answers, Beautiful, and we want them now."

His face got cold then, and I don't mean just his expression. I swear I could see frost forming on his cheeks as his twisted smile faded. When he spoke, icicles hung from every word. "Don't push it, Eshanti. Ask Abonides what happens when he pushes me too far. I gotta push back. And it ain't pretty, man."

"You don't scare us, Beautiful. Spill it."

Like I said, he was of average height, but all of a sudden he started growing, like the madder he got the bigger he got, and when he stopped he was a good head taller than me, looking down like he was about to bite my scalp off. Maybe he could have done it, I don't know.

"You making demands on me?" he said, and it took every ounce of guts I had not to shake. "You got rocks big as church bells, boy, but I'm gonna make 'em ring if you don't watch your step!" He hissed in disgust and walked around his desk, seeming to shrink as he went. "Couple of ham and egg grifters," he mumbled, "think they can walk into my office in my speakeasy and give me this shit?" He threw himself into the heavily padded chair and grinned at us.

"You can't intimidate us," Rachel said bravely. I wished she hadn't. I didn't want to see him get big again.

"Yeah, I know, you guys are fearless." He waved an impatient hand and laughed. "Don't gimme that. You've had the late night kick on your door, you know how vulnerable you are." He laced his hands behind his head and looked at the ceiling. The face in it looked back.

"This planet's brimming with fear," he said quietly. "It's everywhere, in everything. In the sweat of anxious transglobe grunts, in lonely beds at four a.m., in skinny chicks with scars taking backhands from their husbands. You two are nothing special. You got buckets of fear in you." He looked back down at us, and it seemed like he had four eyes so that a pair could pierce each one of us.

He spoke so softly we could hardly hear him, but the words dug deeply into us nonetheless. "And I'd rip that fear out and show it to you if I didn't need both of you."

Somehow Rach was able to shake off the hold that Beautiful had on us. "This is useless. Let's get out of here, Gideon."

"Come on, Rachel baby," said Beautiful, and he sounded kinder now, persuasive. You had to hand it to the demons, they could play any role they wanted. "You're not going anywhere. You're still in shock from that nasty old attack last night. Best thing to help you get over it is to plunge yourself into your work."

"I don't have any work anymore. You took care of that."

"Of course you got work, gorgeous—you and the boyfriend. With me. Now you two good little soldiers are gonna help with a little problem I got with Sanguinarius, that rat bastard. Been a stone in my shoe for centuries, and soon we settle all accounts." He jumped to his feet and started pacing back and forth. "Sonovabitch thinks I got my head in the sand, I don't know what he's gonna do with all that ordnance he's stockpiling? That megalomaniac's got this vision of himself straddling the Horse of Death, man, with my head on his sword, and he's leading his army of demons armed with machine guns, bazookas, cluster bombs, hell, he's even invented his own weapons—crazy guns that shoot deadly serpents and hellfire, the guy's a freakin' case!"

Beautiful stopped pacing by the pool table, picked up a ball, and rolled it to the far cushion. When it rolled back, I saw a face on the ball, moving.

"And then his master, Belial, will reward him with chests of gems and chariots full of food and chambers full of plump, naked boys, or some shit like that." He picked up the twitching ball and slammed it into the far pocket, where it whirled into the hole. I could've sworn I heard a thin little scream.

Beautiful fixed us with a glare. "Your tiny little minds can't conceive the desperate grandeur of a demon's dreams. Sanguinarius wants it all, including my head, but I'll be bum-buggered from Dis to Dorchester if that gun-crazy diablo's getting the drop on me!"

I cleared my throat. "How did this thing start between you and Sanguinarius anyway?" Rachel's look said she thought I was crazy to be chatting with this demon, but I just gave her a nod to indicate that I had something in mind.

"Start? Hell, it's always been!" he roared. "It's a vendetta. It's hate! We're demons, hate's our thing, our shtick, our raison d'etre. It's . . . what . . . we . . . do!" Then, almost proudly, he added, "We're great haters."

"So who's Belial?" I asked.

"He's the fat, stupid slob of a demon lord that Sanguinarius serves, just like I serve Mephistopheles. Ah, we were warring over turf when your ancestors were nature worshippers, but finally I got the upper hand. And why? 'Cause I was smart, that's why! Smart enough to get connected with humankind's most potent sinners—smart enough to take human form and become a player in the rackets—smart enough to find out every mob boss's weakness and play 'em against each other like a freakin' maestro. They all depend on me for somethin'.

"But Sanguinarius just thinks he can waltz in with his little weapons and blast his way to victory. That is so like Belial's cadre, man. All muscle and no brains."

I leaned on the edge of the pool table and tried to look more relaxed than I felt. "So what's a smart guy like you gonna do about it?"

"Gonna go to the mattresses, man. Gonna hit him before he figures out how to use his new toys. And you two are my secret weapons."

"Us?" Rachel said.

"Sure. You proved yourselves when you kicked that scrub team's ass. You're ready for the big time."

Rachel looked at me, and I just nodded at her. Play along. See how far we get.

Beautiful grinned. "I want you two to go to Hell."

I hadn't wanted to get that far.

CHAPTER 8

"Hold it," Rachel said. "You want us to kick Sanguinarius's butt? Isn't it supposed to be nearly impossible for a human to kill a demon?"

"Here on earth, sure. Except for the minor demons like Asskisser Abonides here, we're tougher than week-old bagels," Beautiful boasted. "But you ain't gonna be on earth. You're gonna be in Hell, and that means a level playing field. Still, you don't gotta kill him unless you want to. I mainly want you to see what Sanguinarius has got. If I'm gonna put a job on that monkey, I gotta know what he's packin'."

Beautiful stalked over to his desk, aiming a swat at Abonides that the minor demon barely evaded. "Big bastard thinks he's the only demon can score from the military. Hell, I got buyers workin' the streets, M-50 tanks, auto weapons

with armor-piercing bullets, capillary-bursting sonic devices
. . . arms race with me, will he? I'm gonna shut him down."

"You still haven't said what you want us to do," I reminded him.

"I want you to help me take away his edge." He grinned,
showing yellow-white teeth that matched his eyeballs. "He's
whipping on a trio of high brass who used to belong to
those wussies in the CFF. If we can snatch them outta his
hell pit, one of 'em might be grateful enough to steer some
Pentagon hardware my way, enough to outgun that limp-
dick Sanguinarius."

I thought I knew who he was talking about. Generals
Mangini and Tantinger and Admiral Pike had been three of
the Joint Chiefs of Staff. Hand agents had learned that all
three of them were CFF sympathizers. They were gutsy
enough to admit it, and all suffered the same fate, as set
forth by Solene Solux—eternal damnation. The condemned
were given over to demons, and vanished off the face of the
earth, never to be seen again.

"Let me get this straight," I said. "You want us to go to
Hell for you, find out what weaponry Sanguinarius has stockpiled, free three captives, and then come back, right?"

Beautiful smiled and nodded. "That's the drill."

"One thing's missing—what's in it for us?"

He spread his arms, palms up, and shrugged. "Hey, you're
my little worker bees, right? My soldiers, my shock troops,
my em-ploy-ees."

"My foot we are," Rachel said.

"Well, you are, honey, until I say you're not. And if you
scratch my back, maybe I scratch yours and tell certain law

enforcement officials that, 'Gee whiz, I think I made a mistake. Eshanti and Braque? Oh, man, I thought you said Peshoonti and Crock!' Dig? Besides, it's not like you're in any real danger. Hell hasn't claimed you . . . yet. You wanta come back, all you gotta do is think about leaving, and you'll be back."

"We have to tap our ruby slippers together?" Rachel asked.

"Huh?" Beautiful gave her a blank look. I guess his viddisc watching was limited to gangster films.

"So you're saying you'd clear us?" Rachel said.

"Maybe. If you can be cleared after playing shoot-the-hole-in-the-Hand-agents. But I ain't even gonna think about payback until you two mooks do something I might wanta pay you back for, capiche? But hey, don't make any rash decisions. Chew on it, talk it over. You got all the time you want." He plopped himself down at his desk. "I give ya sixty seconds."

I turned to Rachel and we whispered, though I suspected those pointed ears could pick up on everything we said. We came to the conclusion that there was no other option. We had found no leads on earth about why the Hand wanted us dead. Maybe we had to go to Hell to get the truth. And if we could come back if we got into trouble, well. . . .

"All right," Rachel told Beautiful. "We'll go."

"That's my brave little boy and girl!" he said, leaping to his feet. "You kids know what a psychopomp is?"

"Something that conducts souls to . . . to the place of the dead?" Rachel said.

"You got it. Abonides! Get the psychopomps!" The demon scurried off into a dark corner of the room and came back with two helmets you might expect to see in an opera if the costumer was on lysergisynth. "The psychopomps are in the helmets, kids. Just put 'em on, you'll feel those little claws diggin' into your head, and your souls will be ripped from your bodies and enter into Hell." He barked a laugh. "But don't worry—it's not nearly as painful as it sounds. And your earthly selves will be safe and sound right here with me." He leered at Rachel. "Don't worry, honey, I'll keep little Abonides here away from the goodies while you're cookin'. And either one of you tries to job me, you don't get back. I'll leave you there to burn."

Rach and I took a long look at each other, took a deep breath, then put on the helmets. What followed was worse than I could have imagined.

It was like my dream, but different too. This time it was real, and the pain was real, and the nightmare was a nightmare of reality. In my dream, I had fallen into Hell through fire, the dream being a synthesis of everything I had ever heard about Hell as a place of fiery torment.

But this descent into Hell—the real descent—was, even as I experienced it, more real, more in keeping with our times, the way we lived, and maybe even the way we die. It was still hot. The heat singed the hair within my nostrils as I tried to breathe. But it wasn't red-orange, the color of flame.

Instead it was a color such as unbearably hot circuits might have, burning with a cool purple-blue flame, the hue of a dead man's bruises. And instead of tongues of yellow fire, streams of data—numbers, letters, and arcane symbols that belonged only in Hell—streamed past me, biting and ripping at my flesh like living things.

And even my own skin, or whatever memories of it sank into Hell with me, was not what I had always known it to be. Instead of being soft and supple, it was slick and silvery, coated with a constantly-changing surface, not of hairs and pores, but of infinitesimally tiny yet regularly shaped squares, with cilia-like metal threads crisscrossing their surface.

Then it seemed as though I was being sucked through a hose or a tube. It was alive with motion, but not organic, like a sentient but manmade intestine. I don't have the words to describe it. Metaphors fail, and similes stumble. I think even Rachel would have trouble describing it. It was completely alien to any experience I ever had on earth. Let me just say that I was damn glad when it finally stopped.

But before it did, I saw something that I remembered from my dream—the face. Remember that big ugly mother? It was there at the end of the tunnel or tube or whatever the hell it was. And once again it opened its maw wide to swallow me up. I don't know whether I screamed more at the horror of it, or at the fact that my dream had foreseen the reality, and I didn't know why.

All I know is that I got lost in my scream, and I followed the sound and the darkness down until the light came back.

The red firelight of Hell.

CHAPTER 9

We were there, Rachel and myself, wearing what we had been wearing in Mr. Beautiful's office when we had let those damned psychopomps rip out our souls and slamdunk them into Hell.

And this was Hell, all right. There was no denying it. The cries of the damned souls gave it away.

The next clue was the presence of the two middle-aged men, naked and spreadeagled on metal crosses surfaced with barbs.

"My God, Gideon," Rachel whispered, clinging to me. I was no less horrified than she, and I grabbed her just as hard. The men's flesh was pierced in a thousand different places, and they were moaning dully, their heads fallen forward on their ravaged chests.

My first thought was to go to them and get them down from their primitive yet stylish instruments of torture, but when I looked closely, I saw that there were no nails through wrists or feet, no ropes binding them to the prickly metal. They hung there as if by magic, or, I thought with a sickening rush, as though they had been glued there.

"We've got to get them down," Rachel said. Still clinging to my arm, she walked toward the closest of the pinioned men, dragging me with her.

The man's gray hair was cut short, and his face was deeply fissured with wrinkles. The eyes, when he opened them, were even older. "General?" Rachel said.

His moans continued for a few moments, then the words lumbered out. ". . . yes . . . Mangini. . . ."

"All right, General, we've come to help you," I said. "How are you being held up there?"

"By . . . by flesh. My flesh . . . is the cross. . . . "

My stomach churned again and I saw that he was right. His pierced skin actually merged into cold, hard metal. As I touched it curiously, I could feel where the soft flesh become stronger and thicker, until his own body became his implement of torment.

I looked at Rachel and shook my head. "He's right. We can't get him down."

She looked at Mangini with tears forming in her eyes, then at the other man several yards away, and finally turned back to me. "But Sanguinarius can."

I knew what she meant and nodded. Then I looked around, knowing that if we had to confront the demon, it would be better to do so with weapons in our hands.

There was no shortage of them. The huge chamber in which we stood was an arsenal. A phalanx of a dozen tanks stood in neat ranks at one end, and their presence here had transformed them the way Mangini's flesh had been transformed. Their streamlined contours seemed to have swollen into the shapes of faces, bestial and malignant, with brooding eyes that watched Rachel and me as we went from one wooden crate to the next, examining the labels, lifting the lids to peer inside.

Assault rifles, bazookas, canisters of nerve gas, laser rifles, plastique charges, even combat buddies, those little combat androids you wear on your back like a deadly teddy bear—Sanguinarius had it all. I could see why Beautiful was feeling so threatened.

"There's something funny about these weapons," Rachel said, and I knew what she meant. "They're different here than they are on earth."

"And what experience have you had with weapons on earth?" I asked her.

She shook her head. "Yeah, I know what you mean, Gideon. I shouldn't have, but I do. I know weapons the same way you do. Instinctively? I don't know. But I do know that if these things were sent down here from earth, they've changed since they've been here."

"Well," I said, taking an assault rifle out of one of the boxes and slamming a clip full of .144 caliber explosive shells into it, "maybe we'll be lucky and they'll be powerful enough to clean demons' clocks." If they weren't, I didn't know what would be. .144's could open a man from groin to neck if you caught him in the trunk with one. You had to hold the butt against your chest, or the kick would send the rifle flying back over your head. Don't ask me how the hell I knew, I just did.

I also helped myself to a number of the small explosive charges. Rachel armed herself with a laser rifle and set it to charge. Within seconds it was hot, ready to fire a five-minute uninterrupted stream of amplified light that could sizzle its way through flesh and bone like a hot knife through warm yellomar. "Feel more comfortable now?" I asked her as she hefted the gun.

She smiled grimly and nodded. "Let's find the keeper of this hellhole."

We walked back to where General Mangini hung. "Where's Sanguinarius?" Rachel asked him.

He shook his head weakly. "Don't . . . be fools. Get out now... or you'll be . . . like me. . . ."

"Where is he?" Rachel hates to see anything suffer, and suffering greater than Mangini's was inconceivable. I almost felt sorry for Sanguinarius.

"Through . . . that door." The bloody head gestured to a massive iron portal with screaming faces covering its black surface. As we walked closer, we could hear them, like the faces we'd seen on Beautiful's walls. The second crucified victim we passed was either Admiral Pike or General Tantinger, but we didn't stop to chat.

At last we stood at the door, watching the faces writhe and twist. "We go in?" Rachel said.

"We go in," I agreed. We bit down our disgust at touching the faces and put all our weight against the heavy portal, trying to ignore the thin keening sounds that poured from the open iron mouths

As it opened, the door screamed far louder than the faces of which it was made. But louder than the screech of rusty metal was the crump-crump-crump of a combat rifle from inside the room. Rachel and I sheltered behind the heavy door and inched our heads around its thick edge.

This chamber was even larger than the first. The ceiling was vaulted with natural rock, and steam hung heavily beneath it. The source of the steam was a crevice at the far end that ran from one side of the chamber to the other. We couldn't see what flowed through it, but the constant dance of red-orange light and the frequent tongues of flame that licked up over the edge told us that this must be one of the many rivers of fire that tradition has crisscrossing the infernal regions.

Near the edge, crucified on the same X-shaped cross that held the others, was the third of the damned Joint Chiefs. And aiming a monstrously large rifle at him was a demon that could only be Sanguinarius. His broad, scaly back was to us, and a combat buddy perched like an insane, ravenous vulture on his back. In his other hand, the demon held a second gun, larger and heavier than the first.

The roar of the weapon reverberated around the chamber, and Rachel and I watched in horror as two shells tore into the body of the crucified man. The first seared and ripped off his arm at the shoulder, sending a fountain of blood jetting from the gaping wound as the arm spun over the edge of the crevice into the fire below. The second shot, following immediately, caught the man in the abdomen, punching a fiery, foot-wide hole through him, showering the air with blood and bile and tissue that steamed from the flaming projectile.

The man screamed, and as his shrieks subsided, his arm, his bowels, and the flesh over them incredibly grew back, reappeared as if their destruction had been only an illusion. The hole in his torso filled from the ragged outside edges in, and the arm sprouted from the bony, bloody stump. The reconstruction was nearly as horrible to watch as the demolition had been.

The demon laughed, and the combat buddy, with a sinister life of its own, laughed too, a high cackle that prickled the hairs on the back of my neck. The buddy aimed its minicannon and fired it over the top of Sanguinarius's head. The round took off the top of the victim's skull, and the buddy screamed in glee as shards of bone and brain made a gray-yellow cloud.

I nearly retched then, not from the carnage, though that was bad enough, but at the sight of the brain regenerating itself, and the expression on the man's face as it did. He was suffering all the ultimate pain of death, but could claim none of its peace, could only die and be reborn over and over again, in ceaseless torture.

When the skull finished renewing itself, and the skin and hair covered the top of the head once more, both Rachel and I had had about enough. "Hey, ugly!" I shouted, and was both pleased and frightened to see the broad back stiffen.

When he turned slowly around, I saw that my insult was well chosen. Sanguinarius was the most hideous creature I'd ever set eyes on. He was built like a weight lifter, with ultra-defined muscles pushing against his scabrous skin. That skin was decorated by tattoos of military ribbons and markings of rank that crossed his chest and crawled down both arms. Thick vines of bandoliers hung from his shoulders.

His head was ringed with spikes, starting with the two horns that jutted from his forehead like short, stout gutting knives. Spikes protruded from his cheeks as well, rimmed his rock-like jaw, and circled his neck like a slave necklace. Fangs jutted both up and down from his wide mouth, and his large red eyes had no room for mercy in them.

"What's this?" His voice growled hollowly, like a big dog at the bottom of a deep well. "Humans? And with guns?" When he laughed, it sounded like he also had spikes on his vocal chords.

"Let that man go!" Rachel demanded. "And the others too!"

"A fee-male!" He made the word sound dirty, and it riled me as much as it did Rach. "Back to the kitchen, bitch! Or the bedroom!"

"That does it," I heard her say, and knew that Mount St. Rachel was about to pop. "I got a question for you, muscles!"

"Shoot, little lady," the demon said.

"If you're already in Hell, where'll I send you when I kill you?"

Sanguinarius bellowed a name at Rachel that I won't repeat, but endeared him to her even less, and brought up a rifle to fire. We both dove to either side, and the shell flamed between us to strike sparks off the iron door. His size and those thick muscles, along with the extra weight of the bandoliers and the buddy, slowed him down, and we felt like quicksilver as we dodged his shots.

"Die!" he screamed over the gunfire. "Die, die, DIE!" A singleminded sonovabitch. He used both weapons, bringing them up simultaneously, but their heaviness made him take an eternity to aim, giving us more than enough time to evade the flaming bullets.

His combat buddy was quicker, and contributed its share of rattling fire at us, but Rachel's first hit caught the little mechanical bastard right in the neck. The laser burned through it in an instant so that the motion sensors in its beady alloy eyes were ripped from its weapons systems. Now it could only spray bullets blindly, as much a threat to the back of Sanguinarius's head as to us.

I aimed between the big guy's eyes, but was high. My shot gave the coup de grace to the buddy, who exploded in a bright ball of sparks and flame. Sanguinarius roared with the sudden pain and tried to fling the buddy from his back.

But the straps had become tangled with the bandoliers of shells that hung from the demon's shoulders and over his chest, and the more frantically Sanguinarius strove to extricate himself, the more snarled he became. One of his rifles got caught in a bandolier, throwing him even more off balance.

He had stopped firing, and since Rachel and I no longer had to anticipate and dodge his shots, we were able to aim more carefully. Her laser beam caught him across the stomach, and he shrieked and doubled over with pain, a gorgeous sight to see.

I fired then, and the .144 took him in the right shoulder, pushing him backwards. Though it didn't rip him apart as I had expected it to, his retreating stumble was damned welcome.

We kept blasting away, and he twisted, shambled, staggered back with every barrage of laser fire or impact of shellburst. My chest was starting to ache from the recoil of my rifle, but better a sore chest than a hole where one used to be, so I kept firing. We were slowly driving the demon toward the edge of the crevice, and separated further to flank him.

Now he had nowhere to go but backwards. Several times he brought up the rifle that wasn't tangled, and once or twice he even fired it, but he couldn't hold it properly, and the recoil did him more harm than his shots did good. In a matter of minutes he was standing only a foot or two away from the edge of the ravine.

"Let's do it!" I yelled to Rachel, and we moved in, heedless of counterattack. Rachel's laser fire slashed at Sanguinarius's legs and my .144 shells hit his chest and shoulders like heavy fists, and in a few seconds his foot sought a step in empty air. His arms flailing, he teetered for a moment between rock and air, and then he went over, roaring and bellowing all the way down, pulling the triggers of both his guns in a final gesture of rage as he, his buddy, and his weapons sank beneath a river of devouring fire.

Rachel and I looked over the edge. Nothing moved below but the currents of flame, and the bright tongues that lapped upward toward us. "You know," I said softly, "there's such a thing as too much weaponry."

"Amen," Rachel said, then looked around uncomfortably. "If I can say that down here."

"I guess that takes care of Sanguinarius. But we've still got the problem of how we get those three men out of—"

The man on the cross was behind me, and Rachel was looking in his direction as her eyes widened in wonder. I swung around and saw the man slowly slide down the cross even as that cross shrank, changed, and rejoined his body. His wounds vanished, and across his haggard face came a look of peace as he found himself lying on the rock, whole, his pain only a memory.

He looked up at us, and his smile grew wider. "Thanks . . . ." We barely heard the word as it floated out on a breath. He began to grow transparent, so that we could see the rough rock beneath him. His body slowly drifted upward, becoming invisible to us before it might have passed through the vaulted ceiling on its way to . . . where? Earth, I hoped.

Still clutching our weapons, we went back into the arsenal, but Mangini and Pike were gone. Not a trace of them or their crosses remained, not even a drop of blood on the rock floor.

A voice seemed to come from all around us. It was Mangini's voice, but not moaning. It was strong now, with no sense of pain.

"Thank you," it said. "I want you both to meet me back on earth. I can show you how grateful I am. The old Transbiologic warehouse near 21st and L Street. Tomorrow. Nine o'clock in the morning. Again, thank you. From the bottom of my newly freed soul. . . . "

The voice faded and was lost somewhere in the steam high above. I smiled at Rachel. "I guess we done good."

"I guess so." She took a deep breath. "Ready to get out of this . . ." Words failed her. ". . . to get out of here?"

"Am I ever. So what do we do, just . . . think of home?"

She shrugged. "Wishing will make it so. I just hope going back isn't as unpleasant as getting here."

Rachel reached out for my hand, and I took hers and squeezed tightly. Then we both closed our eyes and just thought about going back to earth again.

And it happened. Oh, but it was gorgeous—soft coolness and glowing light and fresh air. We seemed to rise through a funnel of clouds, but the clouds were ribbed and regular in pattern, manmade as opposed to natural.

I turned to look for Rachel, but I didn't see her, nor could I feel her hand. When I looked at where I thought my body should be, I couldn't see myself either. The whole sensation was as though I were out of my body, my soul invisible, rising upward toward a glorious light.

Then, the next thing I knew, I was standing in Mr. Beautiful's office, that heavy psychopomp pressing on my head so that I looked down into the ratty-eyed face of Abonides, who immediately began spouting that terza rima stuff again.

> "Neither one of you a slaughtered lamb?
> It is Sanguinarius who tastes defeat!
> I salute your strength—let's down a dram!"
> "Thanks," I heard Rachel say, "but I'll pass."

CHAPTER 10

I took off my helmet and looked at Rachel. She didn't appear any the worse for wear after our struggle, and I've got to admit that I felt pretty good, considering that I had just been to Hell and kicked a demon's ass.

Abonides plucked the psychopomps from our grasp and stashed them in a dark corner, while Beautiful stood in front of his desk, a scowl on his sour mug, and fiddled with a scepter capped by a silver horned goat's head.

"So?" he demanded, "what happened, what happened?"

"We gave you everything you wanted and more," Rachel said.

"You cut them toy soldiers loose?"

"They're back on earth now, for all we know," I said. "And Sanguinarius is cooking in hellfire."

Beautiful looked at me oddly. "Of course he is, moron. He's a freakin' demon."

I shook my head and yielded to the luxury of looking smug. "No, I mean really cooking. Rachel and I blasted him into a river of fire."

"Blasted him? You like blew him away? Oh, that's beautiful! Two humans takin' Sanguinarius out like the garbage! Belial will need a high colonic when he hears about this!" His face went suddenly grim. "Speaking of Belial, he'll still be able to use all that shit Sanguinarius stockpiled. Did you see his arsenal?"

We gave him a rough estimate of the late demon's arms stock, and he nodded his head, registering every detail. "Bad . . . bad. Man, that's a lot of shit. I wonder how grateful those soldier boys you turned loose are gonna be. I gotta get stuff from them so I can move in on Sanguinarius's turf. Mephisto will think my ass is golden if I can steal G.I. Joe's hell pits away from Belial."

"Mangini's grateful anyway," I said. "We're supposed to meet him at a warehouse tomorrow morning."

"Warehouse, huh? That sounds promising, kids."

Rachel crossed her arms and glared at Beautiful "Now. We've done your dirty work. Will you keep your end of the bargain and clear our names with the Hand?"

"Wha, you think it's gonna be that easy?"

"Easy?" I said. "We went to Hell for you!"

"So big deal, I live there. It's a walk in the freakin' park. So you kicked Sanguinarius's ass, how do I know it's gonna do me any real good? For that matter, how do I know you ain't bullshittin' me? All I know, you coulda hid in a closet and wished yourselves home the first time you even saw him."

"We're not lying, damn it!" Rachel said.

"Hey, did I say you were? Just that you could be. Tell ya what, you two kids go see Mangini tomorrow, he agrees to supply with some matériel, then I see what I can do for ya."

"That wasn't the deal," I said.

"I make the deal, punk. I want you to do a little work for me, you do a little work for me. Sanguinarius wasn't the only badass wants me dead. That pornhound Asmodeus would like to star me in his very own snuff film, with my 'nads in a jar, the kinky bastard."

"Asmodeus?" Just what we needed, I thought. More demons.

"Now don't tell me you never heard of that guy, Eshanti. You never been to a stag party where they show those cheesy movies that get the boys hot and sweaty so's they gotta stick their hands down their pants just to 'straighten things out'? Asmodeus is the no-talent prevert who makes them films."

Beautiful spat in disgust, hitting an even more disgusted Abonides on the cheek. The little demon wiped it off, but it left a scar.

"That schmuck Asmodeus comes off like he's an artiste. But he's afraid to try for me. Hell, I keep my standing in the mobs because they're all too afraid to try for me. Still, I show one sign of weakness and they'll be on me like rabid freakin' hellhounds, man. So I gotta get armed! Now you get your asses over to that warehouse tomorrow and get me some shit!"

"But—"

"That's it, that's all!" He stepped into the center of the pentagram on the floor, stamped his right foot, and vanished in a thick, black cloud of smoke. I thought we could hear him coughing from somewhere far below us.

> Abonides grinned, and said,
> "Plunge ahead! Never retreat!
> The master plots and works his magic —
> With your help, his rule will be complete!"

I just looked at the little prick. "Aw, bite me," I snarled, and shoved him out of the way as we left.

It was fairly late, so we drove back to Dante's, where he fixed us a quick and easy supper of pan-fried quails and refried beans. He'd been surfing the nets ever since he woke up at five in the afternoon, but hadn't come across anything other than the official and erroneous reports of our demise.

"Oh yeah," he said, "there was some other weird report about an ARC captain who went nuts and shot down some tourists from Omaha at the Lincoln Memorial. Wounded the father and killed the mother and the little boy—seven years old. Man, what a shame."

"Closer to seventeen," Rachel said. "Holy Youth Legion, probably."

"Wait a minute—you know about this?"

"The ARC captain's name was Frank Jersey, right?" I said.

"Uh, yeah, I think so."

"He didn't go nuts," Rachel said. "He was trying to save our lives. The typical all-American family was with the Hand and were trying to kill us."

"Wow! Look, you guys, could I load this on the nets? I mean, would it get your asses in any deeper than they already are?"

"Just hold off for a while, Dante." I said. "We're still trying to find out just why we're targeted, and the lower profile we can keep the better. We'll tell you when to go public with it, if ever."

"We're not ready to cut all ties to the government yet," Rachel said.

Dante shrugged. "Your call. But I think the government's decided to cut them with you."

CHAPTER 11

Neither of us slept very well, so we had several cups apiece of Dante's hot, black, real coffee the next morning. It gave us enough zip to delete our grogginess so that we felt almost human as we drove over to 21st and L.

The warehouse was hard to find, since the letters above the large door that read Transbiologic Supply were nearly worn away. They had first been scraped over, probably by Solene Solux's troops years before, after the Artificial Realities Act passed, and companies like Transbiologic were declared illegal. The baking D.C. summers and the freak storms that become less freakish every year had deleted most of what lettering remained. The Hand says that the crazy weather—along with the quakes that dumped half of Japan in the ocean, leveled the hills of Frisco, and submerged Ellay—isn't due to the depletion of the ozone layer, which has got to be thinner than the Hand's excuses. Instead it's the judgment of God, a manifestation of His anger at the technological sins of our forefathers that created the Acti-deck mutants and their kind. Personally, I think that's a crock, though Rachel feels there may be something to it. I think we cause our own problems, both as a society and as individuals. But maybe I'm wrong. I used to think we created our own hells too.

A smaller wooden door was part of the larger door of the warehouse. After looking up and down the street to make sure we weren't being watched, we knocked. The door clicked, and I pushed it open.

Inside, the only light came through a skylight caked with years of grime and pigeon crap. To either side, the vast warehouse was filled with boxes covered with dusty tarps. I hoped they were weapons that would make Beautiful happy enough to give us the skinny on our guilt. I'd pretty much given up on reinstatement after the corpses we'd left behind us, although Rachel hadn't. She still wanted to go back to the government she served so well. I told her it was possible, but I knew it wasn't. I hated lying to Rachel.

I thought I saw a wisp of smoke drift up at the far end of the room and pointed it out to Rach, but she'd already noticed. We walked towards a shabby metal desk with a high-backed chair behind it. The chair's back was to us, and the smoke—cigar, from the scent—drifted up over.

"General Mangini?" I said. "We're here."

The chair spun slowly around and we were surprised to see, not Mangini, but the demon Sanguinarius, smoking a fat cigar, and grinning at us with bared fangs, through which the smoke drifted like escaping souls from behind hellish bars. "You . . . you're dead!" Rachel said. "We nuked you!"

"Hey soldier," the demon said in his gruff, growly voice, "How do you think you get to Hell? You gotta be dead in the first place."

"But where's Mangini?" I asked. "He told us to come here."

"I haven't been apprised of his whereabouts," Sanguinarius said, "but it was me who told you to show up here." He spoke the last few words in a perfect reproduction of Mangini's voice. "Come now—didn't you think that 'from the bottom of my newly freed soul' was a bit thick?"

"But we saw you die," I said. "You fell into that river of fire, and. . . ."

"Soldier, I swim in fire. I'm a demon. I live in Hell. Is the big picture being airlifted into your brain's landing field?" He took out his cigar and blew a blast of smoke at the ceiling. A small rocket of blue flame followed it. "I gotta hand it to you two. You may be rookies, but you handled me like seasoned vets." He frowned, and his heavy eyebrows met in an angry V. "I ought to be mad at you for releasing my prisoners of war. But I was so impressed by your military prowess that it was almost worth it. Good mercenaries are hard to find."

"We're public law-enforcement officials, not mercenaries," Rachel said.

"You're mercs all right," Sanguinarius said. "And mercs can go from one side to the other. That's what you're going to do right now, and help me pay back Pazuzu."

"Who's Pazuzu?"

"Pazuzu, soldier, is my primary enemy. You know him as Mr. Beautiful, but Pazuzu has been his name for the past several millennia. He picked up that handle back in the Assyrian campaign."

"Assyrian, huh? Explains his tastes in decorating," Rachel whispered to me. The demon either didn't hear or ignored her.

"You can't trust Pazuzu. The only reason you did that little job for him was because he has something you want, doesn't he?" Rach and I looked at each other but didn't speak. "You actually think he's going to give it to you? Fat chance. I'll tell you the way of the underworld—you want something out of Pazuzu, you have to have something on him. Now. How strong are your allegiances to him?"

"Nonexistent," I said.

"Good. That'll make this easier. Now. As you no doubt have learned, Pazuzu likes to play mobster."

"Like other demons like to play soldier?" Rachel said.

Sanguinarius scowled. "Watch your mouth, private, or you'll find it sewn shut with hungry maggots in your cheeks." That shut us both up. "Pazuzu, like all demons, has his own hell pit. He uses his to secrete hostages and stolen goods for the mob. Kidnap victims sometimes, but mostly negotiation hostages." He must have seen my puzzled expression, so he explained.

"When warring mobs agree to peace talks, each gives a high-ranking member to Pazuzu to insure good faith in the negotiations. He's got a couple now from the Marto and Salinas families. But the hostage I'm interested in is a kidnap victim the Marto family's holding for ransom—Krystal Getty."

"The heir to the Getty fortune?" Rachel said. "I didn't know she'd been kidnapped."

Sanguinarius smiled, and his fangs seemed to lengthen. "If you don't hear or see it on the Voice of God . . ." He said God in such a sneering, surly tone that, according to Solux's Sententia, he should have been struck dead on the instant. ". . . it doesn't happen. But this did happen, and if anything were to happen to the girl—like if she were to escape? Pazuzu's standing with the mob would be greatly undermined. The Martos might even decide to terminate him. With extreme prejudice."

"What are you getting at?"

"What I'm getting at, soldier, is that only two trusted lieutenants of Pazuzu would be able to enter his hell pit to perform this mission." He spread his arms wide—eight feet from claw tip to claw tip. "And as the fortunes of war have delivered two such humans into my hands, I would be a foolish general indeed not to press the advantage."

I folded my own, far shorter arms and tried to look stern, but it's a tough trick when you're facing down an eight foot tall demon. "I'll ask you what I asked Beautiful—what do we get out of it?"

"First, you get a chance to doublecross a demon who has every intention of doublecrossing you. Second, you get into the good graces of the most heavily armed demon in or out of Hell, and third, you get to leave this warehouse alive." He shouted into the shadows all around us. "Alpha Company! Battle formation!"

And from those shadows came over a dozen demons of different sizes and degrees of hideousness. One thing they all had in common was highly powerful weapons, all of which were pointed directly at Rachel and yours truly.

"You two soldiers have already proved to me that you've got a lot of guts," Sanguinarius said. "Please don't make my troops splash them all over this armory."

He reached beneath his desk and brought out a pair of psychopomps. These were even gaudier than the ones Beautiful had, with metallic wings and a lightning bolt symbol on either side.

"Don't just stand there, soldiers," he said. "Grab your gear. Full metal helmets, equipped with psychopomps ready to draw your souls down to Hell!" He laughed. I didn't think it was all that funny, and neither did Rachel.

"What about weapons?" I asked.

Sanguinarius waved a hand casually. "You'll have what you did when you, uh . . . temporarily neutralized me. That should be enough, don't you think?"

Rachel couldn't resist. "You were pretty easy to handle. What if we meet some real tough guys?"

The demon snorted, and a little burst of fire shot out his nose. Then he sniffed and said, "Pick up those helmets, soldiers, before I do something I won't be sorry for."

We picked up the helmets, took a deep breath, and put them on.

"Advance! To Hades!" Sanguinarius shouted. "Attack!"

CHAPTER 12

No matter how many times a guy took this trip, he'd never get used to it. It was just as sickening and appalling as before, and I was plenty glad when the sensation stopped, and we were back in Hell.

We hadn't been around the nether regions much, but I'd have been willing to bet that Mr. Beautiful's Hell pit was the armpit of the whole place. The fumes from two large vats nearly knocked us down as we took our first breaths. Imagine a hot attic full of dead things. Now dump in a load of sewage. Stir well, baste in ammonia, and you have the recipe for what Mr. Beautiful was storing in two metal vats. Rachel and I took short, shallow breaths through our mouths, but the stench was still hard to bear.

The decor matched the smell of the place. A sickening purple-black, the shade of vomited-up prunes, was the color scheme, brightened by the glowing green coming from the vats. A few torches, held by severed arms nailed to the walls with foot-long spikes, provided the only other light. At least we had the guns that we had used on Sanguinarius, and we put them over our backs on their straps of scaly leather.

When our eyes grew accustomed to the light and fumes, we saw a table nearby. At it sat two men and a demon.

"Are those men playing cards with a pig?" Rachel said.

The thing sitting with them did look pretty porcine. It was a fleshy pink, covered with bristly hair, and so fat that if you shot it three times you could have gone bowling with it. Its nose was a snout, and it held its cards and a black, ropy cigar in bristly appendages which sprouted from its hooves. "I think it's one of Beautiful's associates," I said. "The handsome one."

Just then the pig-faced demon spoke in a wet grunt.

> "Prepare your bets, my friends. Chance is the law.
> The name of our next game is five card draw.
> We all are equal when the game begins,
> But screw integrity—the cheater wins!"

"Judas priest, more poetry," I said. "That terza rima stuff again?"
Rachel shook her head. "Iambic pentameter."
"Great."
Just then Pigboy looked up and started spouting verse again.

> "A pair who leave their home and daily bread
> To wander through this land of woe and dread!

You tread on fiery ground that angels fear.
How brave! How bold! And what doth bring you here?"

I looked at Rachel, Rachel looked at me, and then I started lying. "We're, uh, jobbers for Mr. Beautiful. He's got us running aphrodisiacs from . . . from Dis to Dorchester, and he had us stop off to see how things were going here. Check on the hostages, you know."

"They are, as you can see, filled full with zest.
Unlike most others, each is but a guest.
And boss Pazuzu! Hale and hearty fellow!
Will not he come himself? Could he be yellow?"

I figured if I was working for him, I ought to defend him against such slander. "Oh no, just busy, you know?" I looked at the two men sitting there in their t-shirts. One of them was in his forties, with black hair and a thin moustache. The other was older and bald. Both were sweating heavily. The stench from the vats and the heat made me feel a little clammy myself.

"How you guys doing?" I said.

"Losin', whaddya think?" said the older man with a distinct Mediterranean accent. "Who are you two?"

"I'm, uh. . . ." I thought frantically for a gangsterish name, but the only thing I could come up with was: "Fats . . . Fats Monahan."

"One of the mick families, huh?" He looked at me curiously. "So why they call ya Fats? You ain't fat."

"You're not seein' everything," Rachel said so suggestively and out of character that my jaw dropped. "I'm Mona."

"Hey, Mona, how you doin', keed. I'm Del—Delmonico Ferlinghetti."

"I've heard of you," Rachel said. "Aren't you a capo in the Marto family?"

"Hey, baby, you get around. And this here," he said, gesturing with his cards to the younger man, "is Carlos Portillo. This pig thing winnin' all the hands is Chamo."

As Chamo dealt the next hand, I saw several cards come from the bottom of the deck. I leaned over to Ferlinghetti and whispered, "I think the pig thing cheats."

"Hell, I know. Everybody cheats down here."

"You've been here before?" Rachel asked.

"Every time we try to make peace with the spics." Portillo looked up darkly at the Italian. "Same old thing—we make peace, everybody's nice, then somebody pops somebody else, and it's time to negotiate again. And we sit here and play cards so everybody upstairs stays honest."

Portillo finally spoke. "This is the last time. I don' come down here no more. This guinea's at home here, he got no soul . . ."

"Ah, get outta heah . . ."

"But me, I can' take it. Used to be you got a hostage, you treat them like a guest. But they treat us like dirt. I'm always thirsty, always hungry, no matter what I eat or drink. And the smell from this toxic waste is terrible. But what they doin' to that poor girl, Madre de Dios, it's a true sin."

As if on cue, a choked, high-pitched cry came from the other side of a stone wall near one of the vats. "Krystal Getty," Rachel said quickly.

"Si. We Portillos kidnap somebody, we never have this Beautiful take care of them. He is a brute. All he like is the torture."

Rachel and I walked to the wall and looked around it. A girl, probably around eighteen, was strapped into a heavy wooden armchair. A leather strap was around her neck. Its ends went behind the chair and were attached to a piece of wood that had been twisted to tighten the strap. The girl could barely breathe. The more she pushed against the back of the chair, struggling for air, the tighter the strap became.

"Help me. . . ." Her voice was little more than a whine. The strap made it nearly impossible for words to squeeze through the narrow channel of her throat.

"God," I said, and I felt Rachel's hand tighten on my shoulder. We tried to loosen the strap right away, but as soon as we touched it Krystal surged forward, and we heard the sickening crack of a ruptured vertebra, followed by what the girl could produce of a scream, high and pinched and nightmarish.

"We need a knife," Rachel said, and we ran back to the card players.

"Man, if I could win just one hand. . . ." Ferlinghetti wailed as he tossed his cards onto the table.

"That girl's neck is breaking!" I said, "We've got to cut her free right away!"

Pigboy started in again:

"With my garotte my skill is past reproach.
To torture flesh and bone I need no coach.

So revel in the sound of her neck's crack,
For this is Hell, and it will just heal back."

"My God, Gideon," Rachel said. "He's breaking her neck—
over and over again."

"This isn't what Beautiful wants," I said.

"Pazuzu's orders were quite vague and few—
Bind her tight, and all else may I do.
Her eyes may weep, her dainty blood may spill,
Her neck break o'er and o'er till I've my fill."

The girl whimpered again, and I couldn't take any more.
"Beautiful wants her cut loose," I said. "Right now."

"Hey," said Ferlinghetti, "you can't do that. My family's got
a ransom on her."

"Screw the ransom," I said, unslinging my assault rifle and
pointing it at Chamo. Rachel did the same with her laser
rifle. "Cut her loose."

Portillo made a sudden move, and I swung my rifle in his
direction. But he wasn't attacking. Instead he had taken a
long switchblade from his trouser pocket, clicked it open,
and jabbed it down so that its point stuck in the surface of
the table.

"That knife, she'll cut through anything," he said, with a
smile at me and a sneer at Ferlinghetti.

"You dumb spic," the older man said. "That dumb-ass
deed will throw back negotiations between our families for
months—and we'll be down here all that time!"

Portillo shrugged. "At least I won't have to hear her scream-ing anymore. Besides, I love to watch you dagos lose at cards."

Rachel pulled the knife out of the table and went back to the girl. The wooden garotte fell to the floor with a clatter, and after a few moments Rachel came back.

"The girl's gone," she said. "I cut her free, she turned her head back and forth and smiled, like everything was work-ing okay, and then she vanished. I guess she's back on earth by now."

> "Getty is freed? What perfidy is this!
> My master will bind me in fires of Dis!
> You turncoats! You work not for my dread boss.
> Bring back the girl, or your souls are the loss!"

I'd had quite enough out of this poetry-spouting pig. Be-sides, you don't threaten me unless you've got a bigger gun than I do, and Pigboy didn't. So I stuck the muzzle of my rifle right between his beady little eyes, so he could see the big hole where those .144 caliber slugs came out, and I gave him some poetry of my own.

> "I want you to shut your freakin' mouth,
> Before your brains go north and your chin goes south."

Pigboy shivered and moaned in fright, and I looked proudly at Rachel. "Well?"

She shook her head. "Burma-Shave," she said.

Another poetic term I didn't know.

CHAPTER 13

When we got back, Sanguinarius was more than happy to see us. "A fine job, soldiers! Your mission was accomplished satisfactorily. The prisoner of war has been freed, and was found wandering about the streets. She has since been returned to the arms of the loving—and *grateful*—Gettys, and my enemy Pazuzu has been disgraced in the eyes of the six families."

I didn't like to ask it, but I did. "I suppose it would be asking too much for a show of gratitude from our commanding officer?"

It was incredible how quickly he could stop smiling. "And the official specifications of that gratitude?"

I tried to speak his language. "Classified information on the reasons behind the military execution attempts on the lives of my fellow soldier and myself, *sir*."

He liked that *sir* bit, but not enough. "As you said, soldier, that material is classified, on a need-to-know basis. Your need is not strong enough."

"In other words," Rachel said, "you don't know why they wanted to scrub us either."

He stiffened. "That information is not pertinent to our current objective."

"Well, it is to ours, *general*." She made the title sound just a tad sarcastic. "So what you're saying is we get nothing out of bringing down Beautiful for you?"

"You get what every soldier gets—the satisfaction of knowing that you have done your duty."

"I thought that was for God and country, not for butt-ugly demons." I had the feeling Rach was going a little far. After all, Sanguinarius's demons were still holding weapons on us. Butt-ugly they may have been, but they were also deadly.

"All right then," said Sanguinarius. "You also get to keep your lives. Does that satisfy you? If not, say the word, and I can end them both with a single command."

Rachel opened her mouth, but I blurted out, "That arrangement will be fine, *sir!* Request permission to stand down!"

"Permission granted."

I took Rachel by the arm and we walked out the way we had come. She started to pull back, but I whispered, "You want to get us both killed? Let's just get out of here."

"Oh . . . *hell!*" she snarled, loud enough for only me to hear.

"Been there, done that."

When we were safely outside, I said, "A little dangerously feisty in there, weren't you?"

"I'm just sick and tired of running errands for these ugly, role-playing idiots! We went to *Hell,* Gideon! *Twice!* Once for a demon who thinks he's the King of Chicago, and again for a General Patton wannabe. And we don't know a thing more than we did before! I've had it with these stupid demons—I want to try and contact ARC."

"Contact them how?"

"I don't know—just *link* them, tell them who we are and that we want to know what the mixup is."

"But if the Hand still wants us dead—and there's no reason they shouldn't—they'll be able to trace us within seconds. They'd get us, Rach."

"Let's find a pay link, keep the car running. We can tear off as soon as we suspect anything."

It would be dangerous, but what else could we do? "All right. Let's go."

There was a link a few blocks away. I used my credit so they'd know it was really us and not a hoax, and punched in ARC HQ's code. A comgen voice greeted us in the name of the Imperator.

"This is Gideon Eshanti and Rachel Braque," I said. "We want to—"

The voice cut me off. It had already relayed the names to the mainframe and received back the data. "Gideon Eshanti and Rachel Braque are deceased."

"We're not deceased. You can tell that from my voice print."

"I repeat, Eshanti and Braque are deceased."

"Okay then. But if they *weren't* deceased—a hypothetical algorithm—what would be their status?"

There was no pause at all. "They would be enemies of the state and of God, and would be judged and executed on sight."

"By whose orders?"

There was a longer wait than before, maybe three seconds. "By order of the Imperator, Solene Solux."

God, I thought. On the Imperator's direct orders. "And what was their crime?"

"Violation of the Artificial Realities and Extranoumenal Environments—"

I broke the link. We didn't need to hear the rest. It was the same crap Frank Jersey had told us about.

We ran to the car and pulled away. Two blocks from the link, we saw an official Hand vehicle, siren wailing, heading for where we had just been.

We drove aimlessly for a while, then Rachel said, "Let's go see Graziella."

Graziella Flynn was a deckmate of ours, and the closest thing to a friend that Rachel had. "Why, Rach? You heard it—the orders came from the Imperator, not some mid-level flunky. What good can Graziella do us, even if she is your friend?"

Rachel's voice was tight, barely under control. "I just . . . need to talk to her. To know that the whole world hasn't turned upside down, that somebody still believes in me . . . in what I am. What I was."

It was nearly lunchtime, and Graziella always ate outside in pleasant weather. ARC headquarters were located in the former Air and Space Museum, shut down years before because of technological sins against the state and God, and

Graziella usually could be found dining *al fresco* at the Hirschhorn Garden of Sacred Sculpture.

We parked on Independence Avenue, and walked, heads down as if in thought or prayer, through the crowds of clerical servants that thronged the area. Graziella was sitting alone, eating a sandwich on a bench near the statue of the apotheosis of Saint Newton.

Rachel walked slowly toward her, while I stayed further back. "Graziella?" she called when she was several yards away.

Graziella looked up and smiled in recognition. Then, instantly, she remembered that her friend was a friend no longer, and her face went white. Her sandwich fell off her lap as she stood up and screamed at the top of her already shrill voice, "Enemy of the Hand and of God!" Then she pointed straight at Rachel.

I had a funny feeling we weren't going to get much help from Graziella.

Already people were starting to heed Graziella's call. Several men and women began to move to intercept Rachel as she started back toward me, but when she whipped out her Avenger, they backed off fast. Your usual desk worker isn't so quick to become a martyr to his faith. Though we have firsthand knowledge of Hell, nobody's seen Heaven yet.

"Come on, Rach!" I yelled. "Run!"

She beat it towards me, I grabbed her hand, and we ran down 7th Street. Already we could hear the whine of whistles behind us. I just hoped we wouldn't hear any shots.

Heavy footfalls joined the whistles as we jumped into the car. I coded the ignition, hit the ped, and we shot down the street. I took every twist and turn that I knew about and some that I didn't, and in another fifteen minutes we were parked in a dark alley near 10th and M Streets.

"Wow," I panted. "With friends like that . . ." I gave Rachel a half smile, but wasn't surprised to see her blinking back tears. That was rough. Rough and nasty and dirty. The kind of system where you get ahead by betraying your friends isn't any kind of system at all. It's a rat warren where the ones who bite fastest with the sharpest teeth get the cheese. I didn't want any part of it, not any more.

Truth to tell, I hadn't for a long time. It was ironic, but maybe getting scrubbed was the best thing that ever happened to me. I felt pursued, harried, in danger of my life, but I also felt more alive than I had in years.

"You okay?" I asked Rach.

She nodded, her lips clamped together.

"Rachel," I said softly, "I'm going to tell you something I told you before. Maybe this time you'll believe me. There's no going back. There is no place for us anymore in ARC or in any government controlled by the Hand of God. There's no mistake. They want us dead. And no matter what we do or how hard we try to explain, they won't be happy until they kill us." I took her hand. "There's only one way left. And that's the underground."

The tears were coming now. I saw them sparkle as she looked at me. "Gideon," she said, "everything I believed in, everyone I trusted. Is that all gone?"

I nodded slowly. "But what you believed in was never there to begin with, Rach. At least not in the Imperator, and not in the Hand of God. But we can still believe in each other. And maybe we can still find some people in this . . . godly but godforsaken country to trust."

She nodded. "All right. It's the only thing we can do."

"Then it's agreed? We'll go see this Aldous Xenon that Dante told us about?"

She took a deep breath, then nodded sharply. "Goddamn right," she said.

It was only a mildly heretical oath, but for Rachel, it was a start.

CHAPTER 14

Washington's Chinatown is small but secretive, and I knew that none of the residents would be particularly helpful to an Afroid and a Euroid searching for somebody on their turf.

I linked to Dante's apartment for more information. "The bodega is the Black Swan," he told me. "It's written in ideograms, but there's a picture of a black swan on the sign— even you can't miss it, Gideon. It's right off Gallery Place. Xenon knows you're coming."

"Thanks, Dante."

"Say, uh, you decided to go public with this yet?" I looked at Rachel and she nodded.

"Might as well. Go ahead and put it on the underground nets. Tell them everything we've told you. We might need all the help we can get before . . . well, we just might."

"Don't sweat it. This gets out, you'll be as close to heroes as we got these days. Later."

I closed the link, and we headed to the Black Swan. Like Dante had said, it wasn't hard to find. The Hand had identified the owner as Buddhist by stenciling two circles, the top one small, the bottom one larger, on the window. I looked at the symbol that demeaned the founder of a faith and frowned. "Why do they call it a bodega if it's in Chinatown?" Rach asked me.

"*They* don't call it that. The non-Chinese call it that. Or rather the Hand does, and everybody else does what they do. Every ethnic store's a bodega, whether it's Indian or Chinese or Lebanese. Any little store whose owner isn't Hand of God is a bodega."

Even though the day was sunny, the store was dark and gloomy, pretty much the same as it must have been a hundred years ago. There were all sorts of foodstuffs in there—the real things too, not synthetics. What they were I couldn't have told you, and I probably wouldn't have eaten most of them unless you held a gun to my head. I thought it was a wonder that the Council of Purity hadn't shut down places like this long ago. Probably because they were Buddhist. They didn't care what anybody ate who wasn't Hand of God, and I'm sure that was quite all right with the Chinese.

An old man with a thin wisp of a beard appeared from out of the shadows and said something in Chinese.

"Aldous Xenon," I said. "Man named Xenon. We look for him."

The old man shook his head and jabbered some more Chinese. Suddenly Rachel started speaking to the man in a language I had never before heard her use. I can only assume it was Chinese, since the old man jabbered to her now, complete with gestures, and she jabbered back to him, nodding and bowing with her palms together. Then the old man bowed deeply to her, and she led the way out of the store.

"What was that all about? I didn't know you spoke Chinese!"

Rach shook her head in confusion. "I didn't either. It just came to me. When he spoke, I understood what he was saying, and I knew what he meant." She looked at me in near panic. "What's going on, Gideon? Why are we . . . finding out all these *things* about ourselves that we never knew before?"

"You never took any sleep courses, did you?" I asked.

"Of course not. They're illegal. And besides, they don't work."

"Neural jacks?"

She ran her fingers through the back of her hair. "They're illegal too. Besides, you've been over every inch of my body, Gideon. You ever find any?"

I grinned. "Maybe you've got a Chinese lover."

"Hey, I had enough guilt in our relationship—I couldn't have handled two men."

"Chalk it up as a mystery then—along with our weapons expertise and facial surgery experience. There's more to us than meets our eyes, apparently."

"It's not funny," she said. "It's terrifying."

"And that's why I'm joking. So I don't feel so damned scared." I tried to throw off the eerie feeling that Rachel and I were strangers, even to ourselves. "Let's find this Xenon."

Rachel led the way to the outside staircase the old man had told her about. It was more a fire escape, really, clinging to the outside of an old brick building that may have once been a warehouse.

The rickety stairs and the rotting wooden door were only camouflage, though, for a very high-tech screening system. As I raised my hand to knock, an electrovoice said distinctly, "You have weapons. Do not enter with them."

"Um . . . where can we put them?"

"On the top of the steps. No one will disturb them."

We didn't like the thought of losing our punchy little friends, but we obeyed. When we straightened up, the door was open. "Enter."

There was a short entry-way inside. The door closed behind us, and we pushed open the door at the other end, leading us into a large, high-ceilinged loft so cluttered that only an impact grenade would help straighten things up. There were fiberboard boxes everywhere, many empty but some sealed. Machines whose purpose I could only guess at stood like metal sentinels, and a long counter littered with machine parts ran the length of one wall. The whole place was lit by industrial xenon tubing, and the only decoration was a picture of a horned demon's skull, well-rendered for being applied directly to the wall, I thought.

Leaning against the long counter was a tall, sepulchrally thin man. He must have felt safe with us, for he was unabashedly smoking a cigarette, a crime that could have earned him a year in prison—five if he had a packet with more. His hair was a bright red-orange, and he wore a tight gray and blue spansuit that made him look even thinner. He was paying only partial attention to us, his chilly gaze fixed somewhere in the middle distance.

"Looks like he's writing a poem in his head," Rachel said softly to me.

"Or thinking real hard about how to kill somebody," I said. Then I spoke to Xenon, trying to break the spell he seemed to be in. "Gideon Eshanti. And this is Rachel Braque. Dante said he told you we were coming."

"Yes. I asked him to send you," Xenon said in a reedy tenor voice. The sibilants hissed like angry snakes. "A couple of renegade ARC agents might prove . . . useful." He blew out a stream of smoke and pursed his lips. "'ARC agent'—sounds a little like *archangel,* doesn't it? Archangels are supposed to be the chief or principal angels in the pantheon, capable of far greater deeds than the other angels. Do you think you can prove to be archangels for our cause, Gideon Eshanti and Rachel Braque?"

I wasn't ready to become a full archangelic recruit until I found out a little more. "Maybe," I said. "Dante thought you might be able to help us."

"Oh, there's no doubt we can do that," he drawled, then took another slow inhale of the cigarette. "The question is, can you help us?"

His relaxed manner annoyed Rachel. "You said yourself you could use a couple former ARC agents. Yeah, we can help you. Some."

Aldous Xenon refused to be rushed. He stubbed out his cigarette in a flat container into which he had been tapping the burnt ashes, then lit another, sucking in the smoke as though it were a great luxury. "Some? We don't want some, my dear. We want all. Contrary to what you might think, the resistance is not staffed by part-timers working their way through school. So don't tell me you can help 'some.'"

"Take it easy, pal," I said. "Rachel just has a little trouble with the concept of total war against the people she gave her heart and soul to."

For the first time Xenon became animated. "Well, you'd better reclaim that soul fast, Ms. Braque. Because you were working for a system as corrupt as any in history, and possibly worse since it claims that its tyranny is divinely inspired." The smoke came out through his nose in a furious rush. "And that drags true faith into a dung-heap and soils everything that real religion stands for."

He sighed, and a half smile came over his face. "You'll have to forgive my preaching," he said. "It's only natural. I come from six generations of Lutheran ministers, all of whom would have disowned me if they knew the . . . *acts* to which I've been driven.

"But it's not just Protestants doing the protesting. The Roman Catholics have kept their priesthoods going underground, the Jews their synagogues . . . the resistance is made up of people from all faiths, including the Eastern religions as well. And we even have our share of atheists and agnostics, who would be scrubbed instantly were their true feelings known. Solene Solux's amendments to the Constitution of this country have destroyed it, but not beyond redemption. We want to take it back for the people, and not just the Hand of God—*all* the people. So that they can believe whatever they like and pray to whatever God they choose."

For a moment he smiled self-consciously. "Okay, sermon's over. I tend to run off at the mouth if I don't watch myself. That's why I work alone most of the time. The other reason is that it keeps me expendable. If this whole thing were a setup—and don't think I'm not considering that possibility—if you were to betray me and turn me in to the Hand, the Front would survive. So I can afford to take the risk of assuming you're sincere. So you tell me. Do you want in or not?"

Rachel was strangely silent. "We want in," I said. "There aren't any more excuses for Solux."

"You speaking for Rachel?"

"No," she said. "I'll speak for myself. It all depends on what you want us to do."

"I thought I made myself clear. No ifs. All or nothing."

She nodded curtly. "Then I'm in. What do we do?"

"I want you to strike a blow at the Hand. It's a small thing, but it will have a great impact. And you've got the kind of background inside the government that might enable you to succeed. I need you to plant a small mechanism on a car."

"Could that 'small mechanism' be a bomb?" I asked.

"No. It's a homing device."

"For a bomb."

"Maybe."

"Whose car?" Rachel said.

"Who else? Solux's, of course."

I couldn't believe it. "You're going to try and kill the Imperator? Are you crazy? She's got so much security around her it's suicide to even think about it—literally. I've heard rumors she's got psionic bodyguards."

"She does," Xenon said. "Three of them. That knowledge cost us the lives of two freedom fighters."

"Her car's going to be guarded as well as she is. And even if you got through, wouldn't they scan it for every type of device imaginable?"

"*Demolition* device, yes, but not necessarily a homing device. They've put most of their effort into guarding the building the car is in, figuring if the compound is secure, so is the car. But there's a lot of traffic in and out of that building. And anybody with a Level Four security pass can get in there."

"Yeah, well, we don't *have* a Level Four security pass."

Like a magician, Xenon reached behind him and came up with a small plastoid card. "You do now. One of you, anyway. Rachel, you'd be the better choice—except for Solux's top mechanic, Jo Boyle, most of the people in the building are men."

"I'd blend in better then," I said.

"Yes, but Rachel could, well, get places you might have trouble with, um. . . ."

"What you're saying," Rachel said with more than a trace of disgust, "is that I bat my eyes and cock a hip at the *boys,* and I can get in."

"With a Level Four pass, yes, that's what I'm saying."

Rach shook her head. "Some things never change. All right, but I'm doing this under protest."

"If you get out alive," Xenon said, "it will be duly noted."

CHAPTER 15

I think I had the toughest part—the waiting. I love Rachel, even more deeply now that our lives are in danger of ending any hour.

Xenon insisted that she take public transportation, so I couldn't even drive her to the building, wherever it was. He would only tell her the location, because he didn't want me getting last-minute qualms and running off to be the hero.

At least she was going in well supplied. Xenon took her photo, sealed it under the type of impervious plastic the Hand uses on all their security passes, and modified the cellular scan so that it would match both Rachel and the parts-delivery man whose corpse they had taken it from last night.

Xenon guaranteed that it would get her in. Planting the device and getting out again was Rachel's problem. Even if she made it out okay, I was sure they would still find the device, and I said as much to Xenon.

"You're wrong, Gideon. They won't find it. The anti-scanning shield cost us dearly. It contains no demolitions and emits no radio waves. It's virtually undetectable."

"Then how does the damn thing work?"

"It hums in response to the vibration of the electric engine. That means we can use a resonance impactor."

"A smart bomb," I said.

He nodded. "It homes in on the particular frequency of the little hummer. There's a Front cell only a block away from the building. They've got a sensor there, and they'll know as soon as the car is driven outside whether it's working or not."

"Is that where the bomb is too?"

"No. There are cells with sensors at various places in the city. The one with the bomb is located along Solux's usual motorcade route. It'll be launched when the car is at a place where there's minimal danger of harming bystanders. We want Solux dead, but nobody else if it can be helped."

"And if it can't?"

"Gideon, the only way anybody is going to be safe again in this country is if the Imperator goes. Snakes rarely regrow their heads. But if a risk has to be taken, we'll take it."

"And Rachel's taking one of your risks right now," I said bitterly.

"One of *our* risks. Did you think you'd just sit around safe houses all day and twiddle your thumbs? I've risked my life over and over again, and your time—and Rachel's—is only beginning. Now give me some peace, please. I'm trying to get some work done."

Rachel came back several hours later. When the sensor sounded I nearly jumped out of my seat, but Xenon stopped me as I started toward the door. "I need to scan her first," he said. "And to see if she's brought anyone with her."

"Rachel wouldn't betray us. Never."

"You know how . . . *persuasive* the Hand can be."

She appeared just then on a vidscreen, looking relieved and confident. "All right," Xenon said. "She's clean."

The doors opened, and in another few seconds Rachel was in my arms again. "Thank God you're back," I said, but all Xenon wanted to know was if she had accomplished her mission.

"Yes," she said. "It's on the car. The pass got me in fine, no problem."

"So how did you get past Boyle?" Xenon asked.

"I didn't even see her—she was in a meeting with some mechs about engine improvement or something. But three of her . . . associates were working on the car."

"And?"

"*And* I did what you suggested. I flirted." Rachel's face registered loathing and a trace of self-hatred. "I gave them the cover story, that I'd just started working for the parts company, and I couldn't *believe* that I was actually near the Soleneozine, and could I just see it, please, I'd heard so much about it."

"They went for it?"

"Yeah, and they almost went for *me,* too. I nearly had to fight them off. When I asked them if I could look underneath, since my main interest was in exhaust systems, they scampered to bring me a dolly. I palmed the device, wheeled under, and tenderly patted the tailpipe, remarking what a round, firm piece of equipment it was. Get the picture, or do I have to make myself any sicker?"

"So it's on," Xenon said. "Securely?"

"I assume so—it's your magnet. They mentioned they're taking it for a test drive today."

Xenon nodded. "Yes. It should be right about now, in fact." He went over to a deck and hit a few keys. The screen glowed, and he kept tapping silently, then looked up. "I'm in touch with one of the cells with a sensor. We'll know in a few minutes if it's tracking properly."

We waited for what seemed more like hours than minutes, but finally Xenon smiled at us, his lips compressed. "They've got it. It's tracking. A very nice job indeed, Rachel."

He logged off and sat back in his chair. "So I'll tell you what you need to know. But before I do, you might want to take off that contact mike inside your collar."

Rachel reached up and ran her fingers around the inside of her blouse collar, then stopped. She plucked something away from the cloth and held it out for me to see. It was a metal disc no thicker than a Reed dime, and a quarter-inch in diameter. The underside was barbed so that it would cling to cloth. As we looked at Xenon uncertainly, he reached into his ear and removed a small receiving device I hadn't noticed before.

"You were listening," Rachel said. "You heard everything I said."

"And everything that was said to you," Xenon said. "It was the only way to make sure you weren't a traitor. Even then, I couldn't be sure no one might follow you back here. But if they had, they'd be here by now, so I won't need this any more, either." He removed from his pocket a small hand remote.

"What was that for?" I asked.

"That was to use if we had any unwanted visitors from the Hand."

"And what would it do?"

"It would ignite the two pounds of plastic explosive under the counter." He lit a cigarette and drew in the smoke deeply. "If it makes you feel any better, I would have waited until the Hand agents were all in here with us."

"Oh yeah," Rachel said with a tremor in her voice. "That sets my mind at ease all right."

Xenon looked at her with sleepy eyes. "Dying's not that bad, you know. A whole lot of my friends have already done it. After a while it gets to be like an old friend."

"'Half in love with easeful death,' huh?" Rachel quoted from something. "It hasn't been all that close a chum to me until lately, Xenon, and I can stand to wait a good long while before getting to know it firsthand."

"Here's hoping that'll be the case," Xenon replied. "Now, as for the Citizens' Freedom Front—which, I also hope, will be able to pull this country back from the living death in which it now exists—the first thing to do is to tell you how to get there."

"I thought the CFF was *everywhere*—at least that's what they want us to think," I said.

"Oh, we are everywhere. Just like the Hand. But there is an underground headquarters, you know, located beneath the British Embassy." He paused a moment. "You don't look surprised."

"I'm not," Rachel said. "The Brits make no secret of not approving of Solux's regime—they haven't for years."

I nodded in agreement. "We've heard more than one rumor about the Brits being connected with the CFF, but diplomatic immunity is still strong enough to keep the Hand from overrunning the British embassy—without definite proof of their cooperation."

"Well, you have that proof now," Xenon said. "I've just put the fate of the underground in your hands. That's what happens every time someone new joins. But be warned. If anyone in the CFF discovers you intend to sell them out—or even strongly *suspects* you of it—you'll be dead before you even hear the shot or see the knife."

"Only a pretty ineffectual underground," I said, "would do things any other way."

"There's another thing," Xenon said, "that I'd like you to remember. When I bring you in, you represent me. If you are executed as traitors, even mistakenly, then I too am a traitor. My life's in your hands, understand?"

We both nodded.

"You know where the embassy is?"

I nodded. "Mass Ave., up by the Naval Observatory."

"Right. But you *don't* go up to the front door. There's a secret entrance that is truly underground. Wait until dark. Use the abandoned subway entrance near the corner of Belmont Road and Massachusetts, where the Islamic Center used to be. The locks on the door are real, but the hinges are fakes. When you get down to the bottom of the stairs, hop down onto the local tracks. Don't worry about the third rail—it's been dead for decades. Start walking northwest.

About four-tenths of a mile, you'll come across a door to your left. It's marked Maintenance 98-C." He handed me a key. "It's locked, but this will open it. The back wall of the second room is a fake. Move the cabinet and just push on the wall; it'll yield. Then close it. It's a fifty-yard walk to a door leading into the embassy cellars. I'll let them know you're coming."

"Sounds easy enough."

"Oh, it will be. Except for the rats and the skells and the bands of feral cats. Oh, and the sinkholes, of course."

"Of course," Rachel said. "You wouldn't happen to have any electric flashes, would you?"

"And a couple of flamethrowers?" I added.

CHAPTER 16

Xenon did have electric flashes, though, and it was a good thing. The abandoned stairway was as black as pitch, and it was only going to get darker. He had also supplied us with extra rounds for our Avengers and given us a surprisingly good meal, cooked by himself in a little kitchen just off the loft. I finally got to eat some of the things I had only goggled at in the bodega below, and they weren't bad.

What *was* bad, however, was the smell blowing up the stairway we were descending. It wasn't as bad as the reek of Beautiful's Hell pit, but worse than anything you'd expect outside of Hell. The stench of urine and feces was the worst. It seemed as though decades of skells, those walking skeletons that live as outlaws in the abandoned subway tunnels, had used this particular station as their *pissoir*. The rats and cats had done so too.

Rachel and I each held a flash in one hand and a pistol in the other. Xenon had warned us not to shoot the embassy guards once we got into the private tunnel, but he also told us to have no hesitation about shooting *anything* else before we got there. "Give them the chance, the skells will kill you. Then they'll take whatever you have, maybe have sex with your bodies, and then most definitely eat you. It's that simple. So don't give them the chance."

We didn't intend to, but almost anything could have been down in those tunnels. Rachel didn't talk to me, nor did I to her. I think she shared my feeling that even the slightest whisper would be overheard in the vast echoing space.

Of course the darting beams of our flashes were signal enough to any hungry skells or rats or cats that dinner was on its way. The rats and cats needed no light, and we'd heard that the skells' eyes have adapted to the darkness so that they're huge, popping out of their sockets. That would be a damned unpleasant thing for our flashes' beams to fall on, and I know I tried hard not to think about it. But the more you try not to think about something, the more vividly you see it.

The stairway led down to a platform. Our light only revealed more puddles and piles of feces, and torn posters on the walls with Hand of God censorship stamps over the offensive parts. For booze and tobacco ads that was pretty much the whole image. Same with movie ads that suggested any sex or violence. The only ones that had survived the censors' rampage were a few inoffensive clothing ads where the models were completely and heavily clothed—of course—and some food ads.

A few posters had been ripped from the walls, and when I glanced at one of the slashed and wrinkled balls of paper, I found that it advertised for a computer company called IBM, one of the firms bankrupted by the government during the technological purge following the election. I kicked it over the edge of the tracks. Something scuttled, and I heard a small splashing. Whatever it was, it was moving away from us. Just how I liked it.

"Well," I whispered to Rachel, "shall we?" My voice sounded infinitely small in the darkness, but I felt as if I had just struck a huge gong, alerting all the hungry subterraneans that we were there. Rachel nodded, and we walked to the edge of the platform.

It was only a four-foot drop to the tracks, but it looked like miles. I went first. Taking deep breaths, thankful to leave the worst of the stench on the stairway and platform, we headed down the tunnel. Or up it. Like that creek without a paddle.

Xenon hadn't been kidding. There were sinkholes, big ones. But none so big that any of the rails had sunken into them. Most of the time we walked by the side of the track, but when we came to water, we hopped up on the previously-deadly third rail and walked along it like a balance beam. Only thing was, if you fell off you lost more than points.

I slipped once, but Rachel grabbed me right away and I was able to regain my balance. Good thing. I'd felt my foot go into marshy, soupy ground. It might not have dragged me down, but I'm glad I didn't get to find out.

We were maybe halfway to where Xenon had said we'd find the maintenance room when I became aware of the cats. The hair stood up on my neck. Now don't get me wrong—I like cats one or two at a time. But it's different when you're underground in the darkness, and you hear the pad-pad-pad of soft little paws trotting along somewhere near you. It's far worse than the quick scuttling of rats. That gentle padding sound slowly begins to multiply, until you know that there must be dozens of cats around you, cats so hungry that a pack of them is bold enough to tackle anything they might be able to eat. We could see only the tunnel ahead of us, so we knew the cats were all behind us.

"Rach?" I whispered.

"Just keep walking. Don't run." I guess she was afraid I was going to panic, and she wasn't far off the mark.

So we kept walking, and finally I said, "Look, let's just stop and see what they do." We slowed, and the cats slowed. The soft rushing sound grew softer. We stopped, the cats stopped. We started walking again, and so did the cats.

"I can't take much more of this, Rach. Maybe if we swing around with our lights, we can scare them away."

"Okay," she said, in a voice so shaky that I knew the little kitty-cats were getting to her too. "If that doesn't work . . . you think a shot would scare them?"

"Sure," I said confidently. "They probably don't hear loud noises down here. On the count of three, right?"

I counted to three, and we swung around with the beams of our flashes shooting down the tunnel the way we'd come.

"Holy shit . . . ," I said, but I don't think the second word got out. There were literally hundreds of pairs of eyes gleaming yellow and green in the light. The cats were spread out across the track bed. They were either too light to be sucked down into the ooze, or they knew the safe places to walk. Confronted with all of those tiny glowing circles, I wondered if there were a Hell pit in which this was the torture, ending, of course, with all the cats leaping on you and tearing you to bits.

"I hope they scare easy," Rachel said, sounding amazingly calm.

"Yeah," I agreed. "We don't have enough bullets for all of them. Man, I wish Xenon had had that flamethrower." Maybe it wouldn't have worked. The lights sure didn't bother them. I noticed one cat actually batting at the end of the beam as I moved it around. Cute.

The closest cat was ten yards away. He wasn't cute. He was a monster, a gray tiger whose back was probably a foot off the ground, and that's a *big* cat. His fur was standing up so high that it probably added a few inches to his height. One baleful green eye stared at us, but the other was just a dark hollow. His ears were laid back to his skull like they'd been taped there, and I could see he already had his claws unsheathed.

"Nice puss-puss . . . ," I said, trying to be friendly. But I heard in reply a noise that sounded like my stomach growling after too much Mexican food. It was the lead cat, of course, rumbling his little anthem of hatred for all the others to hear, as though they needed further enraging.

"I don't think he likes *puss-puss*," Rachel observed, and I had to agree.

"What about *Killer?*"

"Or *Rowdy?*" she suggested.

"I like Rowdy. Rowdy's good."

"No, Rowdy's very bad. I think he's the King of the Cats."

"Shall we shoot Rowdy?" I asked.

"Well, we'd better do something, because I don't think these kitties are going to want to listen to us discuss names much longer."

"They might get mad if we shoot their king," I said.

"Then why don't we fire a shot in the air. Scare them off."

To think was to do. I pointed my pistol over the cats' heads and pulled the trigger. The noise was deafening. It reverberated through the tunnel, and I scarcely heard the bullet whine off the concrete ceiling.

And what did the cats do? What we had wanted. No sooner had I fired than old Rowdy whirled and ran the other way. So did the rest of the cats. It was like watching a big multi-colored thick carpet hump and roll away from you.

But the kitty carpet stopped too soon for my taste. They were scarcely twenty yards further away than they had been before. Rowdy was the first to realize that he hadn't been aerated, and he stopped and whirled around. He growled, and it was a lot louder now.

"Rowdy's pissed," I said, and Rachel and I started backing away from the slowly-reforming battalion of cats, which was a dumb thing to do, since we didn't have eyes in the backs of our heads. Naturally, it wasn't long before I tripped on something and nearly fell.

I shone my light down quickly to see what it was. The beam was only on it for a split second, but the sight registered all too well. We'd finally found a skell—or rather a skell's skell. We'd never know if the rumors about the bulging eyes were true, since they appeared to have been nibbled daintily out of each socket. In that brief moment, I could see where pointed teeth had scraped away the muscle.

Bad kitties.

"I've got an idea," Rachel said, when she saw what I had tripped on.

"Please. Mr. Bones and I will be glad to hear it."

"I think we ought to shoot as many of them as possible. Just stand and fire and pick them off, including that big one."

"Why? I like cats."

"Because maybe they'll start gnawing on their fallen comrades, and that'll give us enough time to get away."

It sounded better than nothing. "Okay. When we run, why don't you take the lights and let me reload both guns."

"They're that persistent, huh?"

"I suspect."

They were coming toward us again, faster now, and we stopped, held out our lights in one hand and our pistols in the other, and started shooting. Most of the cats suddenly vanished into the darkness at the side of the track, but there were too many of them to miss completely, and several went down screaming. I had aimed for Rowdy, but as soon as the gun came up he had vanished, swallowed up by his courtiers.

We each fired a full clip of sixteen, and when the slide stayed open after the last shots, we turned and ran like hell. Like a relay team passing the baton, I gave my light to Rachel and she palmed her Avenger to me. I loaded fast, trying to keep my footsteps within the beams of light, all the time listening for the soft footfalls of the disappointed cats who didn't get to their cannibalistic feast fast enough.

It didn't take them long. Only this time we didn't hear just the little kitty footsteps. They were howling now, a spine-chilling combination of meows and hisses and screams that left us in no doubt of their intentions.

I had just finished ramming fresh clips into both pistols, when I glimpsed something shiny up ahead. "Rach! Over there—to the left!"

It was a round aluminum doorknob, and we went toward it with all the passion of knights after the Grail. I fumbled in my pocket for the key Xenon had given us. There was a clatter at my feet, but I kept running for the door. "What was that?" Rach asked.

"I just dropped your gun."

"*My* gun?"

Now we were close enough to see the door. *Yes!* 98-C, all right. If it had been *97-C,* we'd have been cat food. As it was, it was close enough. I tried to jam the key into the lock, cursed, turned it around, and tried it again. It fit, and I twisted it and the knob at the same time, pushing Rachel in ahead of me and turning around to close it behind us. . . .

. . . Just in time to see old one-eyed Rowdy come flying though the air, claws and fangs extended, straight at my face.

I slammed the door shut just in time, and the thud as the King of the Cats smashed into its hard surface was one of the most rewarding sounds I've ever heard.

My relief was so great that I half giggled. "Aw, poor puddy tat bump him nose. . . ."

"Cats . . ." Rachel mumbled, breathing heavily. "Just cats. . . ." She shook her head as if to clear it, then shone the light around the room. All that remained in it was a large cabinet against the back wall. "That must be it. Let's move it."

It slid away easily, and the false wall opened to our push. "You know," I said, "with those watch-cats—and the skells and the rats and the sinkholes, how many people could even get this far?"

"Close the wall anyway. Xenon said to close it." I closed it.

The tunnel we were in now was earth, shored up with alumiron beams. It was narrow, and the ceiling was so low that I couldn't walk erect, but at least there weren't any cats. The smell was gone too. Nothing but good clean dirt. "All tunnels ought to be like this," I said to Rachel, but she didn't respond.

We had gone scarcely ten yards when our lights—both of them—started to flicker, then dim. In another five seconds we were in a darkness lit only by the red memory of lights still in our eyes.

"My God," I said. "You think both our batteries could die at once?"

"No. It must be their security. An energy draw—probably takes the juice out of electroweapons too."

I hissed in a breath as a cat's eye seemed to open up ahead and look at us brightly. But then I saw that the eye was a round hatch, and the upright slit of a pupil was the figure of a man standing against the light behind him.

"What are your names?" a voice boomed out so loudly that I figured it had to be amplified. The man was very definitely holding a weapon. With the light behind him, I couldn't see his face.

"Rachel Braque!" Rachel called.

"And Gideon Eshanti!"

"Empty your weapons. Then throw them toward me."

I took the clip from the remaining Avenger and tossed it and the gun in the direction of the man. They landed in the dirt, and I winced. The pistol had served us well, and I hated to see it treated so badly.

"You have two weapons," the man said. "Where's the second?"

"We lost it on the way in," I shouted. "Fighting off the cats."

"Come in with your hands on top of your heads." It seemed unnecessary, but he was holding the gun.

The man moved aside, and Rachel and I stepped through the hatch into a typical cellar room with block walls and tube lighting. Two other people, a short man and a tall, thin woman, were there, both heavily armed. Their faces bore the unmistakable message that if we so much as burped, they would be glad to toast us. I smiled, but it didn't melt their hearts one bit.

The short man patted me down while the woman held his gun, and then he did the same for her while she searched Rachel. "Clean," said the short man.

"So far. Strip 'em and scan 'em," the man behind us said. He stepped in front of me then so that the light was falling on his face rather than obscuring it, and I suddenly looked into a pair of eyes that were so shockingly familiar I thought I was peering into a mirror.

CHAPTER 17

Or so it seemed for a long moment. Then the sensation went away. But while it lasted, it was so strong that I *knew* I had seen this man before, and not just casually.

He cocked his head. "Why are you looking at me like that?"

"I, uh, thought you looked familiar."

"And do I?" His tone suggested that it would be a good thing for me to say no. Since he had the gun, I said no. Maybe I was just so glad to see human companionship after our affair with the felines, that anybody with two eyes and a furless face would have looked welcome and familiar.

"Well," he said, "after Vivid and Ronald get through looking you two over, I'll talk to you some more. When you see me next, I *will* look familiar, because then you will have seen me before." He gave me a cold smile and a nod and left the room. He might have been a smartass, but I felt like an idiot just the same.

Good old hospitable Viv and Ron led us out of the room and through a labyrinth of corridors. Then we separated— boys in one white, metal-tabled room, girls in another. I don't know what Viv did to Rachel, but I hope it wasn't as rough as the strip search and scan ham-handed Ron gave me. My doctor had never been to some of those places.

I was feeling a little sore and walking a little bow- legged when I rejoined Rachel. Her cheeks were red and her jaw was clenched, but she didn't seem damaged. The Doctors Kildare led us up a short flight of steps and down another hall, and all of a sudden we were in the embassy, in one of its more secluded wings. The walls were painted a dark blue, and the furnishings were nearly as rich. Sev- eral paintings hung on the walls, a mix of landscapes and muted abstracts.

The man who had opened the hatch for us sat on a sofa. He didn't look up from the sheets of hard he was examining when we came in, and he didn't get up when he saw us. He was Afroid and wore a white jump and tinted glasses, prob- ably intended to make him look even meaner than usual. He still looked familiar to me.

"Well well well, Eshanti and Braque." He said it the way you'd say *Dogshit* and *Owlcrap*. "So you're the rogue ARC agents who've got the Five Fingers shakin' like palsied old women."

"That's us, chief," said Rachel, who does not suffer sarcasm gladly. "You gonna thank us for doing your job for you?"

"Hardly. And my name's not chief. It's Derek Literati. Now you've gotten this far, Senator Burr wants to see you."

"Senator *Erin* Burr?" I asked.

"That's right, Eshanti. She's the shadow leader of the CFF. And I'm warning you—either of you make one false move near the senator, I'll kill you."

"We're on the same side, hard guy," Rachel said.

"Maybe so, maybe not." He stood up. Damn, he was tall. "All I see is two ARC agents standing in the heart of CFF headquarters, and that doesn't strike me as real smart on our part."

"Hey," I said, "we took out a scrub team, after all."

"Yeah." He nodded, and the muscles in his face tightened further. "That makes me even more suspicious."

"Now you're penalizing us for being good fighters?" Rachel said. "I thought we passed our initiation when I helped Xenon set up Solux's car. I mean, Solux is our old boss, you know? The Imperator? The leader of this particular country? And we're helping in an attempt to kill her? What more do you want?"

"I want Solux dead. Maybe then I'll trust you. Come on."

He led us to an ornately panelled door and knocked, then opened it. Inside was a large conference room, dimly lit by hidden track lights. Behind the large conference table, and in front of a large holomap of the world, stood Senator Burr.

She was a surprisingly short woman, yet her compact frame seemed to hold a titan's reserve of energy and power. Her hair was pulled back severely in a bun, and her clothes were simple but fashionable. She didn't smile, and looked like she hadn't for a long, long time, but she came around the table and shook hands with each of us. Literati looked like he was ready to jump us if we squeezed too hard.

"Ms. Braque, Mr. Eshanti . . . Aldous Xenon briefed me about your midnight visitors. Never trust animals that eat their young—or a government that shoots its own people."

"It didn't improve our opinion of them any," I said.

"I can understand that. But you haven't been able to discover why you were targeted?"

"They brought false charges against us," Rachel said. "But as for the real reason, we don't have a clue. All we know is that we don't trust the Hand anymore. If they'd do this to us, they'd do it to anybody."

"You've learned a lesson," the senator said, "that a lot of people have known for years." She turned away from us, looking blankly at the map but not seeing it. "I was one of the first to realize it. I'd been a senator for three years when the Hand came to power. After six weeks I resigned. They passed so many amendments to the Constitution that it wasn't the Constitution anymore. When the states voted to roll over and give up power to Solux, that was the beginning of the end. And when Congress in effect repealed the entire Bill of Rights, there was no hope left."

She whirled around quickly and fixed us with her gaze. "No hope except for the CFF. We've tormented the Hand for a dozen years now, and we won't stop until this country is free once more. Oh, of course Solux says it *is* free—but only free to follow the will of God as pronounced by Solux. And if one chooses not to do that, one is either sentenced to Hell, or, in their parlance, 'remanded to the direct custody of the vengeful God.'"

"We'd prefer not to go either route," Rachel said.

"But are you ready to fight to see that no one else has to?"

"Yes," I answered. "Solux is the real evil in this country, we know that now."

"And you, Rachel?"

"I'm with Gideon."

"All right then, I'm going to trust you."

"You won't regret it," I said. "Desperate people make loyal allies, and we're nothing if not desperate."

"If you've been to Hell," she said, "I'm sure that's true. And that's why I felt you could be of value to us."

"Because of our experience in Hell?" Rachel asked.

"Yes. Let me give you the background." She sat in one of the chairs at the conference table and beckoned to us to join her. "Our current attempt to . . . eliminate Solux is not our first. Our most ambitious and, I'm afraid, reckless attempt took place six years ago.

"As you know, Solux spends most of her time in a sanctum in the Pentagon. We have agents there, more than the Hand would like to think about. None very high up, but a great many in the workaday jobs, typical government drones. Only these drones are our eyes. Acting on their information, fifteen of our finest agents undertook a guerrilla raid on the building, the objective being to kill or capture the Imperator.

"Heavily armed, they made their way along air ducts and secured hallways, but they never made it to Solux. Marcus Vanders, the leader of the commandos, informed us on wireless transmission that they had come across something so . . . significant, so disturbing in its implications that he wouldn't explain it over wireless. Whatever it was, it caused him to abort the mission.

"Unfortunately, they never made it back here. The Imperator's troops cut them off, and the last we heard from Vanders, they were engaged in a running firefight. He confirmed eight members of the squad dead before we finally lost contact with him. That means that seven of our best fighters could be prisoners of the Hand."

"They'd hold them prisoner illegally?" Rachel asked.

"To Solux, the only law is the law of God, which allows him to do whatever he wishes. We know that there are areas in and beneath the Pentagon where political prisoners are being held in some fashion. They could be there. But there's another, more appalling option."

"That they could be in Hell," I said quietly.

"Yes." The senator nodded. "That's what I fear most. Hell is an actual place, I realize that. But I can't help but think that the supernatural aspects of it have been exaggerated by the Hand to force the people to its will. For all I know it could be another country. The one thing I'm sure of is that it's better to have a clean death and take your chances with the afterlife than to be sentenced to Hell by Solux."

"You have a pretty unorthodox view of Hell," Rachel said.

"Well, enlighten me," Burr said with no irony. "You've been there. What is it like?"

We told her as much as we knew, how people like us and Beautiful's hostages and the three joint chiefs could, under the right circumstances, go in and out of Hell, not painlessly, but readily enough.

"There's something I don't understand, though. In the Getty case, the girl is back with her family, with no recollection of how she got there. But this is the first I've heard of Mangini, Pike, and Tantinger being freed. When did it happen?"

"Yesterday," I said.

"If that were the case, one of them surely should have been in touch with us by now. All were loyal to our cause."

"Sanguinarius might have tricked us again," Rachel said. "We thought we had killed him and we hadn't—maybe we didn't actually free the three chiefs either."

"All these theories are beyond me," I said. "I just know I was there and it's as real as this place."

"If you should ever return," Senator Burr said, "and have the unexpected leisure to look around, keep on the alert for these people." She handed me a list of seven names. "These are the missing commandos. We don't know if they're dead or alive, in Heaven or Hell. But we'd *like* to know. They were good comrades."

"Yes, they were," Literati said quietly. We had forgotten he was in the room.

"Well," I said, "it's possible we could make a return trip. We're still trying to figure out why we—and the people who were successfully scrubbed that night—were targeted."

"We've begun our own investigation of that," said the senator, noticing our looks of surprise. "You didn't think we were going to let you just waltz in here without making sure the whole thing wasn't a set-up, did you? In this short time we've only been able to look into one of the victims—James Hennelly, who worked for New Corporeal Biologics."

The name was familiar from the list Frank Jersey had given us, but we hadn't known what business Hennelly was in. "The meats company?" I said. "The Hand forced them out of business years ago. The market in synthetic flesh was one of the first things they outlawed."

The senator nodded. "That's true. But as you know, there's still an overseas market for synthetic organs, and NCB was—still *is*—supplying them illegally."

"That would be plenty for an arrest and a jail term, but probably not enough to get Hennelly scrubbed," I said. "He into anything else?"

"One of our agents talked to his partner, who swore that other than their meats activities, Hennelly was clean, at least for the five years they'd worked together."

"Nothing peculiar or quirky?" Rachel asked. "Something that might clue us in to other reasons Solux might have to clean his clock?"

"Quirky. . . . ." Senator Burr looked questioningly at Literati.

"Yeah, there was one thing," he said. "Seems the guy had a penchant for Latin."

"He spoke it?"

"Just a phrase. *Vocabulum est tabula* something or other, the partner never heard any more than that. He asked him what it meant, but Hennelly would just brush him—" Literati must have seen the look that Rachel and I gave each other. "What's with you two?"

"We've heard the phrase before," Rachel said. "Or one like it."

"Where?" asked the senator.

"In our dreams," I said. "Seems that a few of the folks targeted had the same—or slightly different—Latin phrase in their heads. Weird, huh?"

"Maybe it means you know more than you think you do," Senator Burr said. "Something the Hand doesn't want you to know?"

"Possibly," I said. "But we have no idea what it is."

"Hopefully you'll find out." Senator Burr stood up. "So what's your next step?"

Rachel answered for us. "Since you've already looked into Hennelly, that leaves us three people who were scrubbed that we need to track down. Find out why."

"And if they knew any Latin," the senator said.

"Yes. That too."

"Derek, get Rachel and Gideon a list of the victims."

"We have a list of the names," I said, "but we don't know where to find them."

"We do," said Literati. His voice sounded no warmer than before. "Follow me."

Senator Burr shook our hands again. Politicking dies hard, I guess. "Good luck to both of you. And let me know if you find out anything new about our missing commandos. Or Solux. And, in spite of his protestations, his *beloved* Hell."

We said goodbye and followed Literati into a smaller room with several computers and a wall full of disk cabinets. He sat down, whacked a few keys, and a printer spat out two sheets of thin paper, one of which he handed to each of us. "Easily foldable and digestible," Literati said. "Though there's nothing there the Hand doesn't already know."

"Well, we'll be sure to give them your name," I said, just trying to get a rise out of the guy.

It worked. He looked at me like killing me would be too quick. "We don't joke about that kind of thing here. Things are too serious for that. Too many people dying. People you know. People you like."

"I'm sorry," I said, and I was. He looked angry, but there was loss in his face too, and I wondered how many of his friends had died over the years, working for the Front. "Things have been so grim that I guess I try to . . . fight it off with jokes. Not always appropriate."

He smiled, just a little. "You remind me of Marcus. He was the same way. Never could take anything seriously. Didn't stop him from being a good soldier, though. Maybe you're right. Maybe we need more of that."

"You knew Marcus Vanders?" Rachel asked.

"Knew him? Hell, we were brothers—in everything but blood. Marcus's mom and dad died in an autobus crash when he was twelve. He moved in with my folks and me. We've been like that ever since, right up until he . . . disappeared."

"You ever . . . go after him?" I asked.

He shrugged, but it wasn't as casual as he had intended it to be. "This is a war. People get killed. We don't have the leisure to chase down our casualties. Now look, you two. . . ." He seemed anxious to change the subject. "You're in the Front now. That means that if you get caught, all our lives depend on your keeping quiet. The Hand's got tortures like you wouldn't believe. Like a good *religioso*, Solux got a lot of ideas from the Spanish Inquisition. And how could the Hand condemn people to Hell if there weren't a symbi-otic relationship between the two? So take these." He gave us each a hard-surfaced capsule.

"Poison?" I asked.

Literati nodded. "You'll never know what hit you. Take your own chances with Heaven and Hell, because there's only one option if you're caught. And this way you won't inform on us. Bite down and you're in lala land for good."

"Thanks," Rachel said. "I guess."

"Sleep here tonight," Literati said, "and you can leave in the morning before daybreak."

"We go out the same way we came in?"

"Yeah. Too big a risk otherwise. The Hand watches our doors round the clock."

"We had a problem with some hungry kitties on the way in," I said.

"Don't worry. We'll arm you when you leave, give you hand flamers. Cats are scared as shit of those."

"Why couldn't Xenon have given us some before we came in here?" Rachel asked.

"We figured if you *really* took out a scrub team, a few hundred cats shouldn't pose a challenge. And if it did . . . then we were well rid of you."

"And," I said, "you'd save a *bundle* on cat food this week." He still didn't laugh.

CHAPTER 18

Again, no mad eve of passion for my love and me. Instead we spent what was left of the night chastely in separate alumiron bunks, sleeping the sleep of the dead, like any good soldier. General Sanguinarius would have been proud of us.

"Sir. . . ." The word stirred me from sleep, and when I drowsily opened my eyes, I found myself looking at a nightmare.

Red glowing eyes stared at me from the ends of metal stalks, like a robot beetle. The thing's head was shiny metal, with a crestlike ridge of darker alloy. The arms and most of the body were metal as well, but what was most shocking was that the lower half of the face and the chest from sternum to waist was composed of what looked like living human flesh.

I sat up with a gasp, nearly skewering my face on the thing's protruding eye stalk, which seemed to glow brighter in alarm at the near miss. My heart was pounding, and I felt suddenly dizzy. "Judas *Priest!*" I said.

"My a-puh-puh-pologies, sssir," said the critter in a quavery tenor. "I duh-did not mean to stuh-startle you. But it is time fuh-for you and your compuh-uh-*annn*ion to leave."

After a few blinks to get the sleep-film off my eyes, I saw the thing more clearly. It was a meat all right, a multi-server unit, if I remember the meats bust of three years ago correctly. He looked like an early model. The skin of his jowls was lined and wrinkled, and the muscles of his chest, out of which poked a potpourri of metal pipes and hoses, sagged like an old man's. He smelled like a combination of machine oil and sweat, an unwelcome bouquet for an early riser like myself.

"You've got to be kidding," I heard Rachel say from the next bunk. "Is that what I *think* it is?"

"None other," came a feminine voice from the doorway. Vivid, the woman who had "welcomed" us yesterday, stood there, the light behind her. "What's wrong? Never seen a meat before?"

"No," Rachel said, and I could hear the revulsion in her voice. Outlawed hi-tech, even outdated examples, is still a brave new world to us in many ways. "Where on earth did you get it?" The thing straightened up, and I could see a series of boxlike chambers going all the way around its waist.

"Charles is a farm boy," Vivid said. "I found him when I was with a Front cadre in the Midwest. Meats never sold well out there, and he nearly drove the hayseeds psycho who had the guts to buy him. But they couldn't destroy him, and they didn't want to keep him, so they dropped him off on an abandoned farm. I found him while I was skidding east and took him with me."

Rachel was up now, moving toward Charles like he might bite her. "Look at that—the control panel rises and falls as he respirates. Doesn't he spook you?"

"No, but maybe that's because we're sorta family. I did my fetal time in a Fecund 5088." Rach and I had seen an inoperative model one time in the Forbidden Technology wing of the Smithsonian, the Hand's chamber of horrors. At the time we thought it was a monstrosity, since that's what the identifying voice chip said. The thing looked like the upper torso of a pregnant woman, with bioengineered fetal chamber. Half of its head was machinery, and tubes ran out of (or into) the nipples, with probes and sensors piercing the abdomen like a pincushion.

"Good lord," Rachel murmured in response to Vivid's admission. "Are you . . . all right?"

"Sure. A womb's a womb—how much do you remember about your mother's? My folks were c-space jocks, virtual pilots for Ascot Texture Mapping. They were gonna make millions comgenning the future. They wanted kids, but Mom didn't want to lose her place in the c-space rotation, so a colleague pulled some strings and got them nine months of time in a 5088."

"That's horrible," Rachel said.

"Horrible? Far from it. It worked fine. It just proved the female womb was replaceable, and that's why it scared everybody."

"I'm sorry," Rachel said. "You may be absolutely normal, but I still think that gestating in a machine is . . . ." She couldn't find a strong enough word.

Vivid only laughed. "You and two hundred million other Americans. Pulling the plug on New Corporeals was one of the Hand's most popular moves."

"And rightfully so," Rachel said. "Putting a halt to the meats was one of the good things the Hand did for this country."

"Bullshit. A little extra moral certainty at the cost of our freedom? That's a high price, and it's the one we've had to pay the Hand all the way down the line. If you want to go along with them in regard to meats, you have to go along with everything else as well." She cocked her head. "Maybe you don't belong in the Front, you feel that way."

I sat up. I had been quiet through the argument, but now I had to speak up. "Is the Front going to tell us what to feel too? What to believe? What to think? Rachel can't help that she's repelled by meats. That's how she's been taught, and even though we know our teachers were wrong, those attitudes take time to change." I got up and walked over to where Rachel sat on her bed. "We can't help the way we feel. But the more we learn about the technologies the Hand banned, the more we'll be able to accept what we've been taught to believe is evil. I want to learn, but I don't want to be forced into accepting your ideas any more than I wanted the Hand to force me into renouncing them."

Nobody spoke for a long time. Vivid was right from her side, we were right from ours, and the middle knew that we were equally full of crap. Good old Charles represented that middle as he spoke:

"Thuh-this is all very fuh-fuh-fascinating, but the fact re-muh-muh-muh-*mainnnns* that Mr. Eshanti and Ms. Buh-raque must be out of here before duh-dawnnnn."

The three of us laughed in spite of ourselves. "Well," said Rachel, "I like his practicality anyway!"

Charles, who turned out to be an excellent cook, prepared a delicious omelette for our breakfast, and we were also treated to real coffee, not as good as Dante's but rich and caff-packed just the same. Vivid restocked us with new Avengers and ammunition, and took us to the hatch. Flamers in hand, we set off down the tunnel to the maintenance room.

We opened the door gingerly, but no kitty cadres were waiting on the other side. After only a few minutes of walking down the tracks, however, we heard the first soft footfall behind us. I didn't waste any time, but turned around and pressed the flamer's trigger. I was rewarded with a bright bolt of electrical fire, which sizzled everything within six feet of where it hit. A dozen cats squealed, jumped, and ran in the opposite direction. We had no trouble after that, and came out onto the streets in the pre-dawn darkness.

Rachel and I sat in the car and ran down the list of three names unaccounted for—Adam Schonbrun, Deirdre O'Connor, and Brian Avery.

"Schonbrun worked for Eschatology Inc. down near the Watergate," Rachel said. "I did some data tracking on them last year."

"I think I remember you talking about that—they the Dante Mapping people?"

Rachel nodded. "They use research into death and the afterlife as a cover, but their main interest is in mapping

Hell. It's illegal, but pretty harmless. More quackery than anything else. And from what we've seen of Hell with our own eyes, they're way off base. Might be best, though, if I checked them out on my own. They know me, and if I brought a partner along, it might be harder to get any skinny on Schonbrun."

"You're welcome to them," I said. Dante Mappers always struck me as too goofy for words. Why anybody would want to map a Hell that everybody else in the country wants to avoid is beyond me. I turned back to the list. "Two other names. Brian Avery, who lived over near McPherson Square in a communal house with a gang called the Clean Machine."

"Sounds sanitary."

"The last one is Deirdre O'Connor. And look who she works for."

Rachel blew out air and shook her head. "Another demon."

"Yeah. One we haven't met." Behind O'Connor's name on the list were the words, *Amo-Amas-Amat Films (the demon Asmodeus)*.

"The porno king Beautiful told us about. Well, I'm not going there alone, Gideon."

I agreed wholeheartedly. "From what I've heard, I might not be safe by myself either. Why don't I drop you at the Dante Mappers, and I'll check out this Avery, then swing back for you. We'll go to the film place together."

Eschatology Inc. turned out to be located in a shabby office building in a neighborhood gone to seed, but Rachel had her pistol and her wits. Still, I waited until she was inside the building before I drove away to McPherson Square, fifteen blocks east.

I had to ask around the street before I found the Clean Machine's house. It was down a narrow brick alley, snugged up against another equally shabby house across a small circular courtyard. On the front of one house was scrawled *DEADLY 7* in spray paint. Three kids wearing leathovine jackets and vests sat on the steps, openly smoking cigarettes. Apparently the police didn't wander back into this rat warren very often. Nobody was in front of the other house. I pointed to it and asked the three wannabe-toughs, "Is that the Clean Machine's place?"

They didn't answer at first, just looked at me like I'd said something bad about their mommies. Then the biggest of the kids, wearing a vest that left his muscular arms and chest bare, stood up and sidled towards me. His face was pale and pimply, and his rasta'd black hair shot out in greasy spikes. He smiled what he must have thought was a particularly sinister smile, showing me an array of green and yellow teeth.

Then he spoke. Just two words, and the second one you, but they would have been enough to get his mouth locked in a cybercell for a year per word.

"Just asked a question," I said. I didn't want to get into a fight. Far be it from a fugitive cop killer to want to draw the attention of the police. I turned and walked toward the other house, figuring to knock on the door, but I felt a steely hand clamp down on my shoulder.

My new friend said those same two words again, and I turned around and looked at his smiling face. "You said that before," I told him politely. "Now if you have anything to add, go ahead, but if not, I really have other people to see and things to do."

The speech didn't impress him. He recited his litany once more, louder this time and with a longer pause between what were apparently the only two words he knew. And I'm not so sure that he understood them.

I looked at the two boys sitting on the steps. "Is there something he wants? A bone? A pat on the head?"

The taller of the two, who had been combing his hair ever since I entered the alley, spoke. Although his vocabulary was more expansive, he didn't sound much smarter than his friend. "He don't want you should go see the Cleans."

"Well, I hate to disappoint such an eloquent young man, but I'm afraid I have to." And I turned and started to walk away. Again I felt the hand on my shoulder, again I heard the first and most unpleasant of the two monosyllables. But I didn't hear the second. It got stuck in the kid's throat, along with the edge of my right hand.

I tried to pull the blow a little, since I never thought that profanity was a killing crime, but the kid was closer than I had figured, and I hit him harder than I intended. He went down like somebody had yanked the bricks out from under him, flat on his back. On the way down, his hands shot to his throat, and he coughed a thick gobbet of blood. I had a hunch I had busted his larynx, and felt a lot guiltier than I should have. After all, if that was all he ever said, a crushed voice box wouldn't be much of a loss.

The two other alienated youth were on their feet in a flash and came straight at me, one with a pig sticker he pulled from a boot, the other with the teeth of his metal comb held out like a straight razor. I lost no time in pulling out my little 16-shot pal. "Hold it, gentlemen. Don't . . ." I looked at the choking kid on the bricks. ". . . what he said . . . with me. Just take your friend and go inside and seek proper medical help. And if the doctor asks what happened, you tell them that his electric razor slipped."

The blade and the comb disappeared, and they lifted their charming companion to his feet. He was still hacking away, but he would live, more's the pity for the planet. I waited until they were inside their roach hole before I went up to the other door.

I didn't even have to knock. The door was opened by a young girl who looked like she'd just stepped out of central casting for *farm girl, Oklahoma, innocent, sweet.* "Come in, brother, come in, quickly, before the forces of sin muster against you."

I thanked her and came in. Who could refuse an invitation like that?

"I watched you from the window," she said, "as you did battle with those who mock goodness. You surely must have had the Lord on your side."

"The pistol didn't hurt." I looked around. It was clean all right, and shabbily genteel. Like a lounge area in a university dedicated to turning out preachers, there was nothing to show that anyone was having any fun. "Maybe you could answer a few questions for me, Miss. . . ."

"They call me Temperance," she said. "Some of us here name ourselves for the great virtues and try to live up to them. Unlike those across the courtyard, who model themselves after the seven deadly sins."

"Ah, uh-huh. Where's everybody else?"

"In prayer and meditation, or out doing good in this sinful world, trying to keep the powers of Hell at bay, and doing the work of the Hand of God." The Hand, eh? I knew I was going to have to watch this one. "It is my turn to humble myself and watch the door, to see that no sin creeps in."

"Well, I'll try . . . not to be sinful," I said lamely. "Listen . . . Temperance, I need some information on someone who was involved with your group. His name was Brian Avery."

Her face grew long, and I thought I caught a tear in her eyes. "Oh yes. Poor poor boy. He struggled manfully against sin, but he must have failed."

"How do you mean?"

"Why, the Hand sent him two nights ago to the judgment of God. They would not have done so had he not been deserving of a swift death."

My neck felt suddenly hot. "You don't think they might have made a *mistake?*"

"Such judgments are said to come directly from the Imperator, Solene Solux. The Imperator would not judge wrongly. Solene Solux receives all guidance from God above."

I had heard this kind of crap before, but I liked it even less now. Still, I swallowed my anger at this mindless girl in front of me. "And what do you think Brian Avery's sin was?"

"I don't know," she said. "He seemed to walk in the ways of goodness and righteousness. I saw no sin in him, only the successful struggle to escape it and do good."

"Was he ever involved in . . . illegal technology? Anything to do with forbidden—" I stopped short at the shocked look on her face.

"Oh no," she said with so much sincerity that I believed her implicitly. "Brian never had anything to do with anything like that. None of us ever would."

"Okay. Sorry. Did he . . . speak Latin?"

"Latin?"

"The language. Did you ever hear him say any words in Latin? Like *vocabulum est* . . . anything?"

She looked at me as though I were crazy. "No . . . never."

"How about while he was sleeping?"

"We do not share sleeping cells," she said, as though I'd insulted her. "But my cell is next to his, and I never heard him say anything at night except for his prayers."

"Okay. Tell me, where did they . . . send him to judgment?"

"Oh, here. They came in and went upstairs and sent him to judgment in his bed."

"Nobody tried to warn him?"

"Of course not. Christopher was at the door. He allowed them to come in. And the rest of us waited until the judgment was over."

"Did you know who they were coming for?"

"Only Christopher. They asked where Brian was and he told them."

"And none of you did a thing."

"No—they were the Hand of God. They do God's will. They root out sinners and send them to judgment. Surely you understand that. You are an American."

"Yeah," I said, feeling ashamed and angry and infinitely sad. "Yeah, I am. Just one more question—how old was he?"

"Brian? He was seventeen."

Seventeen. That was no way for anybody to die, let alone a seventeen-year-old kid who was trying to be as good as he knew how, while his so-called friends watched and remained silent as his murderers gunned him down. I thought about the Deadly 7 across the way, and then about the Clean Machine, but I was damned if I could decide which one of them was worse.

CHAPTER 19

Rachel was on the corner where she was supposed to be at 11:00, and she smiled grimly at me as she got into the car. "*Vocabulum est acquirer,*" she said.

"Thanks, and same to you. More Latin, huh?"

"That's right, and more illegal shenanigans too. While most of the Eschatology people are involved with borderline activities, Schonbrun handled the outlaw stuff, mapping Hell, or his version of it, like Lewis and Clark on a good day. And did he mumble a Latin phrase from time to time? *The word is acquire,* or *get,* whatever that's supposed to mean. And what was Brian Avery's favorite phrase?"

"Our *Father,* far as I know."

She looked at me doubtfully. "In Latin?"

"No. No Latin at all. And as far as I could tell, no link to outlaw techs, either real or Hand-fabricated. The kid was a saint. And his saintly little friends just let him be martyred without so much as a peep." I looked out the window. "He was only seventeen."

"That's terrible," Rachel said softly as she took my hand.

I tried to throw off the lousy feeling. "Yeah, it was terrible all right. And it's also terrible that the links all stop with the kid. He just doesn't fit the pattern that fits us and everybody the Hand *did* get that night."

"So now what?"

"Deirdre O'Connor, I guess. We've been accused of making porno, so I guess we'll find out what our purported business is all about. The CFF lists the location just off of Union Square, but there's a question mark behind the address."

"That makes sense," Rachel said. "A strictly illegal business would have to move around. Let's just hope we get there before he changes location again. I wonder what this O'Connor did for the demon?"

"You probably don't want to think about it too much."

"You're probably right."

The address near Union Square was an office building two blocks away from Dante's apartment. The building had seen better days. There was no doorman behind the marble counter, and the computerized directory had long since been stripped for parts, so that businesses in the building had to rely on an old-fashioned contraption with plastic letters that slid into slots on the black cloth board.

There weren't many businesses left in the place. Most of them had generic-sounding names like Universal Export, Excel Products, and Epitome Parts. Some may have been legit, but I suspect most were fronts for various illegal operations. From the piles of plastic letters in a cardboard box under the signboard, I figured they came and went pretty rapidly.

Amo-Amas-Amat Films was there, only missing several letters so that it read, "AMO mAs mAT FiLMs 7c." The elevator was out of order, so we found the stairs and started climbing. The demon's office was at the end of a long hall, which was lit only by windows at both ends. Apparently, either the landlord had forgotten to pay the power bill or he didn't give a damn about the seventh floor. Amo-Amas-Amat seemed to be the only office in use there, and that's not entirely accurate if *in use* means lit and occupied.

The translucent glass door showed no light behind it, and in the semi-dark hallway we could just make out the sign with the company's name on it in gothic letters. It had been taped to the other side of the door so that you could read it through the glass. Had it been back another few inches it would have been nothing but a muddle of letters.

"Should we knock?" I asked.

Rachel shrugged. "He's a demon. Maybe he can see in the dark."

So I knocked, but there was no answer. Then I tried the ancient brass knob, but the door was locked. My eyes had adjusted to the darkness by that time, and at the bottom of the translucent panel, just a foot above the floor, I noticed a cardboard clock whose whiteness had faded with years to a yellow cream. Beneath the printed letters, *"Back at . . ."* Red plastic clock hands pointed to 8:30.

I pointed it out to Rach, and she nodded. "Makes sense, I guess. After all, demons come out at night, right? You want to break in?"

"Break in? Living on the wrong side of the law has made you pretty daring, babe. But frankly, I don't know what good it would do. We want inside information on an employee, and that's the kind of thing that only her employer is going to be able to tell us."

"And that's Asmodeus," she finished for me. "So how do we kill six hours?"

"Dante's?"

"He'll be sleeping. And I'm not tired."

"We'll wake him up. Find out if we've come up on the nets."

And that's just what we did. Dante was sleeping all right, but he woke up fast when we gave our names on his com. He was beaming when he let us in.

"We making any noise on the nets?" I asked him.

"Are you kidding? Boards are texting mad about you two—you're legends in your own time."

"Great," Rachel said. "Why don't we just hang targets on our backs?"

Dante waved a dismissive hand. "Don't go casters up on me. It's all vaguery and e-jabber. Besides, wireheads would never rat on you. On the contrary, you got a real fan base. I've turned up half a dozen images off the boards that are supposed to be you."

"Any real?"

"Nah, all false sightings. I'm doing my bit to feed the goat, sending out my own faked photos of you under different e-accounts."

"Feed any bullshit to the rumor mill?" I asked.

He laughed. "I've maxed it with top-shelf disinfo. Told them you two were running whiskey in the Dust Belt, that you were in deep freeze in a Front safehouse in Cameroon . . . even sent one out on AnarchiNet saying you'd converted and joined a Hand mission working the Wyoming communes. Hey, you live on the lam long as I have, you can human engineer with the best."

"Thanks, Dante. We mean it."

"No problem. Gives me something to wake up for in the evening. So what's been happening at your end?"

We filled him in, and his eyes widened as we told him about linking with the CFF. He threw up his hands and said, "Don't tell me where, man. I don't want to know. I always thought I'd be shitty under torture. They give me a taste of the wire, and I'd spill my guts."

"Don't worry, I wasn't planning to tell you any more." Rachel and I were sitting on Dante's sofa, nestled against each other. It was the first chance we'd had to relax since the whole thing started, and her warm body next to mine felt pretty nice. I could tell she had similar ideas, and even Dante, who's thick about matters of the heart, got the idea.

"Well, uh, look," he said, "I need to run out for a while, get some, uh, food and stuff, y'know? You guys are probably whipped, so why don't you logoff for a while, use my bed. Hey, I'll be out for an hour . . ." I raised my eyebrow at him and frowned. ". . . or two." I smiled then, and he grinned back. "Anything you guys are hungry for?"

I looked at Rach and she looked at me, and we both looked at Dante.

"Well then," he said, a pink flush suffusing his cheeks, "I'll bring back some pizza."

After he left, Rachel and I made love. You remember what I said before about danger being scary, but not erotic? I was wrong. Not knowing what's around the next corner, and whether or not you'll be alive tomorrow at this time really does increase the intensity, once you're rested and not expecting scrub teams to blow you away while you're in *flagrante delicto.* I had loved Rachel and she had loved me for a long time, but we never loved each other as deeply as we did in that sweet hour at Dante's. I'll remember it for the rest of my life, however long that life might be.

We didn't sleep afterwards. I just wanted to lie there with her and make the time last, commit every detail to memory—the softness of the worn sheets, the blades of afternoon sun cutting through the closed shutters, the hum of the cool-air system, the feel of Rachel's dear flesh under my fingertips, and the way our sweat held us together. I had never loved her more, and I prayed to a God that I still believed in to let us come out of all this alive.

We were up and dressed a long time before Dante came back. He didn't show until six, and even then seemed embarrassed to disturb us. He cooked us another terrific meal, and we ended it with another pot of his hot, black coffee, which would keep us plenty awake for whatever the evening held with Asmodeus.

It was 8:00 when we got back to the office building that housed Asmodeus's operation, thinking that it might be a good idea to watch him as he came in—*if* he came in like a mortal instead of just suddenly appearing. The building seemed just as deserted as it had before. It was a good deal darker, since the sun was down, and only the streetlights coming through the narrow windows supplemented the minimal lighting inside. Still, no doorman, no security that I could see. Anybody could have waltzed in, smashed open Asmodeus's door, and helped themselves. Surprisingly, though, we didn't see or hear a soul. That is, until we found the man in the stairwell.

We had decided not to wait for Asmodeus in the lobby, but in the stairwell, so we could see who came in with him. If it looked like nasty business, we could keep going up to the eighth floor and wait until they went through the door to the seventh, then retreat.

So there we were, climbing the stairs, nearly to the seventh floor, when all of a sudden I'm looking into the barrel of the biggest damn rifle I've ever seen outside of Hell. The bore is monstrous, a good inch across, and it's got a round magazine that I figure must hold close to two dozen shells, any one of which might pack enough punch to take down an elephant, if you could find one. This was the gun that made them extinct, a Tarbell 3000 autoload, and it looked more and more like it was going to do the same for Rachel and me.

"Are ya *with him?*" a thick, plummy voice said in a stage whisper so loud that it echoed in the stairwell for a good ten seconds.

"With who?" I said, my attention fixed so intently on the big, dark, deadly eye that I didn't see the man holding the gun.

"With *Asmodeus!* That bastard from *Hell!*"

The context told me the correct answer. "No," I said. "No, we're not with Asmodeus."

"But you're *waitin'* for him, aren't ya?"

"Yes, we are." I tried to look at Rachel, and could see from the corner of my eye that she was as transfixed by the gun as I was. Maybe that was why she wasn't joining in the conversation.

"What's yer business with 'im, then? You goin' to join in his vile depredations, goin' to be in one of his *mooo-vies?*"

Finally I saw the face behind the gun, and saw that whatever sanity remained in it was fleeing quickly. The pale blue eyes looking down at us were wide, and flecks of white spittle dappled the corners of his gaping mouth. He was gripping the stock of the rifle so hard that his knuckles were white, and the finger on the trigger was trembling. "We're here to help you kill him," I said in as dull and flat a tone as I could muster.

His mouth fell farther open then, and his eyes glazed over as if he had received too much information for him to process. It lasted only a second, but that was all the time I needed. I snatched the rifle backhanded, pushing the muzzle up. I expected it to go off, but it didn't, and I whipped it around behind my back.

His eyes blazed then, and he came down toward me fast, but Rachel stepped between us, putting her right leg between his, grabbing his forearm and twisting him across her pivoting body, so that he hit the stairs hard on his back. A yelp of pain escaped him, but Rachel held him down, her knee on his sternum, her forearm on his neck, ready to press down hard on both areas and snap his neck over the edge of a step if he tried to fight.

"Behave," she said. "I suspect we're on your side."

He nodded, his eyes wider than ever. "All right," he squeaked. "Let me up . . . please . . . I'm choking."

Rachel eased off her neck press, but kept her knee over his chest. "Who are you?" she asked.

"Sterling . . . Dean Sterling's my name." He smiled then, and I knew that he was, if not totally crazy, at least a few chips shy of a full memory. "I'm a *hunter!*" he said proudly.

"And what do you hunt?" Rachel said.

"Demons," he answered. "They're the only thing *worth* hunting. I hunt them, and I *kill* them."

It was hard to take him seriously. He had to be in his late fifties, a stringy little man, scarred and haggard in shabby clothes worn thin at the elbows and knees. He looked like he'd fallen between the cracks of life and then, to add insult to injury, they had slammed shut on him. His broad dialect told me that he'd probably come here in the Aussie migration of thirty years ago, when the Mareeba virus had ravaged a continent, and the U.S. had allowed in that lucky five per cent in whom the tiny killers could find no foothold.

"Are you with the Hand?" I asked.

"The Hand? Of God? Oh no. They're bad, I don't like them . . . they let things *happen* to people. Things that shouldn't happen. Kids shouldn't have to. . . . "His gaze grew faraway then, and I thought I saw a tear in his eye. "Drew . . ." he said.

"Drew?" said Rachel quietly. "Who's Drew?"

He shut his eyes as though he were either trying hard to remember, or trying harder to forget. Then they snapped open again, and he immediately seemed as though he had regained his senses. "Drew," he said coldly, "was . . . *is* . . . my daughter. A girl, just a little girl. So young for something like this."

"Like what? What are you talking about?"

"Let me sit up . . . catch my breath . . . and I'll explain." Rachel took her knee away, and Sterling sat on a step, his back against the wall. Even in the near darkness, his eyes seemed to burn.

"*Amo, amas, amat*—you know what that means?"

"I love, you love, he loves?" Rachel said.

"That's right. Love. He names it after love." Sterling shook his head savagely. "But it's *not* love, it's got nothing to do with love. It's got to do with hate and death and humiliation." He wiped the sweat from his forehead. "These kids . . . they want to get into the movies, they don't know any better, they hear about him and come to him and he tells them that he'll make them big stars, all they've got to do is pay their dues. And by the time they see what their dues are it's too late, too bloody late."

"The demons, you mean?" Rachel asked.

"Yes. Demons and worse. Beasts, monsters, *abominations* they make them mate with. And the so-called Hand of God allows it to happen!"

"What about your daughter? Drew." Rachel's voice was calming.

"She came to him. She heard about him from her *friends*." He spat out the word. "And he promised her things, and told her that he would mold her career, but that she had to start out at the bottom. She started at the bottom all right—in his Hell pit. In his *snuff* movie."

"She's dead?" I asked quietly, not wanting to set him off.

"No. Others died, but not her. Still, her *mind's* dead. All she says is . . . what she said in the film. Filth. She just looks right past me and says these things over and over again, even when I'm trying to feed her, to keep her alive. . . ." He must have seen the glance that passed between Rachel and me. "You don't believe me?"

Before we could protest, he reached under his light jacket, and I immediately raised the muzzle of the Tarbell. It was in his face when he took out the vidviewer, and he froze, maybe seeing death coming and realizing that there would be nobody left to care for his daughter.

But I put the gun down when I saw that he had no weapon. "Look," he said, holding out the viewer. "If you don't believe me, look for yourselves!"

The machine was an older one, thicker and wider than the card models they sell today. There was a disc in it. The label read *To Serve the Horned Ones*. I aimed it at the cinder block wall of the stairwell and pushed *play*. Sterling didn't look. He closed his eyes and pressed his hands over his ears.

I had seen human/demon porno before in the performance of my duties, but this was by far the ugliest. In the ones I'd seen, the humans seemed to be enjoying what was happening to them, or at least were able to act well enough to be convincing. But this was different. The girls were young, probably in their late teens, and the plot, such as it was, centered around abuse and torture. The screams were real, and so was the agony. So, I think, were the deaths. I don't want to talk about it any more than that. I feel dirty just thinking about it. It was the worst thing I've ever seen. It made me want to kill Asmodeus as much as Sterling did.

I shut it off, and Rachel and I stared at the blank wall, trying to make the images leave our memories as well.

"Drew," Sterling said huskily, "was the redheaded girl."

I heard Rachel choke, as though trying to keep from vomiting, and I was glad she succeeded, because I would have been next.

"Will you help me?" he asked. "I've been tracking him for so long. He never stays in one place . . . but finally I've found him." He looked up at us, his eyes pleading. "Please . . . will you help me?"

"This has to stop," Rachel said. "We'll help you, but we need to get some information from Asmodeus first—about someone who worked for him."

"Then you'll help me?" Sterling said. "You'll help me kill him?"

"Demons are supposed to be impervious to bullets," I reminded him.

"Nothing's impervious to *that*," he said, pointing to the Tarbell I was still holding.

"Maybe you're right," I said. It would be damned interesting to see, anyway. I handed him the weapon. "Don't do anything until we come out. Then we'll back you up, I swear it."

"Asmodeus won't live through the night," Rachel said. There was an edge to her voice I'd never heard before.

Just then there was a heavy bang down below, and we heard footsteps and voices. It could have been anybody, but the quick clattering of hooves told us that at least one demon was among those coming up.

"Come on," I said, and we tiptoed up the stairs to the eighth-floor landing. As the voices below came closer, we were able to distinguish three of them, one slow-talking female and two males. The door to the seventh floor opened and closed, and the voices faded.

All this time, Dean Sterling had been trembling so violently that I was afraid he might hurl himself down the stairs, blasting away with the Tarbell. But I kept a hand firmly on his shoulder, and he stayed where he was. "All right," I said when the three had gone. "Let's go down. Sterling, stay here. We'll get you when we come out. Don't come in unless you hear shots, or hear us yelling for help. All right?"

He nodded. "I swear it. On the life of my daughter."

We left him there and went down the stairs, through the door, and along the dark hallway. A light was coming through the translucent glass, and I noticed a crack in the glass near the bottom that had been invisible before. I peered through and saw a demon who could only be Asmodeus, with a smaller demon and a woman whose air of sluttishness told me that she was an acting prospect, if not already on the payroll. None of them were armed. The office was functional and nothing else, with a few hellscapes hanging on the walls. I looked at Rach, she nodded, and I knocked on the door.

The smaller of the demons opened it. He was a three-foot high assortment of yellow and black carapace and claws. "Enter, and welcome! I am Rutterkind. And what are your names?" He had fawning servility down to a science, but at least he wasn't a poet.

"Rachel. And this is Gideon." Asmodeus was touring us with his eyes, taking rest stops along Rach's body. He stood seven feet high, and everything about him said bull, except the ring was in his right nipple instead of his nose.

He was covered with bristly red hair. Mirrorshades were propped over his horns and somehow balanced on his wide, bovine snout. His prehensile hooves held a riding crop that went with the rest of his leather\horsie\whip-me-beat-me outfit, which included a mesh sash, a huge pentagram belt buckle, and thigh-high black boots. His only other garment was a soft leather codpiece that, in his oversized case, might have been better called a whalepiece.

Before he could say a word, the woman sitting on the desk looked in our direction and brought her arms together. Her huge breasts, barely covered by silver breastplates, created a cleavage easily deep enough to swallow Rutterkind. "Hello, *gorgeous*," she said in a voice that dripped of pralines and magnolias, but her eyes were as deep and empty as bottomless wells. It had been a long time since she had felt anything other than the need to obey. She reminded me of a puppet, and I figured Asmodeus pulled the strings. "Wanna be in pictures?" she said dully. "Haven't chosen my co-star yet. . . ."

Why not play along? I thought. At least it would give us a reason for being there. "Well," I said, "as a matter of fact I was thinking about—"

"Not you, beefcake," said the woman. "I was addressin' the young lady here."

"That'll do, Grinda," Asmodeus said in a quick, punchy, street-wise voice. "So, you two, you wanna be stars, that what you want? You wanna be up on the big screen, that why you're here? Talk to me, kids, time is money."

"Well," Rachel said, "my friend and I here—"

"Oh, so that's it? This side of beef is part of the package, we got a package deal here? What's the skinny, doll?"

"We're looking for work, and Deirdre O'Connor said you might be able to help us."

"Deedee! Oh yeah, a great gal Friday. And Friday *night,* you know what I mean. Pretty. Very pretty before those Godboys got done shooting her up. We got a small but appreciative audience for piecework, but there weren't even enough pieces left for a short subject, you get my drift. Well, that's all flesh under the bridge. So what's your experience? Nah, don't tell me. I can tell just by lookin' that you're hot. You got good bone structure, know what I'm sayin'?"

He looked at me then, right at my groin, and I felt like a piece of meat. "And you, Mr. Beefcake, don't worry, we'll get special effects to take care of you."

When I looked at Rachel, she was smiling, just a little, in spite of herself. "So you can use us?"

"Oh yeah," said Asmodeus. "Use and abuse—but only if you're versatile."

"And what does being versatile entail?"

"Exactly." The demon grinned. "Tail. Hooves. Horns. You name it, dollface."

"This isn't just straight smut then?" Rachel said.

Asmodeus shot a quick look at Grinda, who waved a hand carelessly in the air as if on cue. "Relax, darlin'. They're just like us 'ceptin' they don't hide it. They're raw lust, sugar, droolin', snarlin', cloven, hopped-up flesh hounds." With every word she spoke less animatedly. I wondered if Asmodeus had her on drugs.

"So whaddya think? You in, babycakes?" Rachel nodded, and the demon looked at me. "What about you, porkchop? It's a different ride for the men. You ever worn a bit in your teeth before?"

"I think I can handle it," I said coldly. "But look, Deirdre was a friend of ours—"

"Yeah? Never heard her mention you, Gary."

"That's Gideon. We'd sort of lost track of her, and we just want to know if—"

"Hey hey hey, we can talk old dead friends later, right? I gotta get down to the set, and I want you two to come with me."

"You mean do a film—*now?*" Rachel said.

"Nah, hey, not if you don't want to. But I'm shootin' a feature right now, thought you could visit the studio, y'know? Check things out, see for yourself it's not as bad as you mighta heard."

I looked around. "So where's the studio, the first floor?"

"Basement, tubesteak. All the way down to Hell."

"Hell?" I looked at Rach, and her expression seemed to say not *again*. . . .

"Demons are the real stars. Gotta film 'em in their natural habitat, right? Besides, you got nobody pokin' their heads in when things get a little . . . noisy. Rutterkind. . . ."

The little troll produced two psychopomps from behind a desk and held them out to us. "Place these on your heads, if you please. They will enable your—"

"We know the drill," I said. "But look, before we go, we were wondering if Deirdre ever—"

"*Hey!*" Asmodeus whipped off his mirrorshades so that we could see his piggy eyes. "First we go to Hell, *then* we can talk Deedee, got it?"

I didn't want to, and neither did Rach, but we had been to Hell before and survived. There was no reason we couldn't do it again. And we needed the information on O'Connor. Maybe, if we played our cards right, we'd even be able to do some snooping around for Senator Burr's lost commandos. "Okay," I told Asmodeus. "But just to look, right?"

"Absofreakinglutely. You don't like what you see I'll have you back here quicker'n you can say red *shower*."

I thought about asking what a red shower was, but figured I was better off not knowing. We put on the helmets, I took Rachel's hand, and we waited for the psychopomps to do their occult work.

CHAPTER 20

Third time may be the charm, but not where going to Hell is concerned. Once more, it felt like the synapses were being stripped from my brain and replaced with strands of razor wire. And that was the *pleasant* part. It's no wonder everybody in Hell seems slightly nuts. Getting there is half the agony.

When we opened our eyes again we were standing next to Asmodeus and Rutterkind in a film studio, which is to say that there were lights and two cameras. But the set was hardly conducive to lust. It was a playground, with a sandbox, swings, and a sliding board. Then it hit me that some warped, demonic, and even vaguely human minds could find arousal in such a setting, and my stomach felt even sicker than it did on the trip to Hell.

I became aware of soft grunting behind us, and wet slapping sounds. Rachel and I turned around and saw several demons performing unspeakable acts on each other and two human women and a man. The few clothes remaining on the humans gave the illusion that they were children in the hands and claws of the far larger demons. The women's hair was in pigtails, and all three had been shaven clean of any body hair. I was relieved that no real children were here, but that relief lasted only until I heard the man moan in pain.

When I looked at Asmodeus again, he must have seen the disgust and hatred in my eyes, for he grinned so that his fangs actually locked for a moment before he forced them apart with a twist of his jaw. "Take it easy, pal, it's all effects. Trust me, they don't feel a thing. It's called *acting,* right?"

"Why's that man moaning then?" Rachel asked. Her voice was as shaky as mine would have been.

"Aw, he's hammin' it up, doesn't want to do the part the way it's written. Some performers you gotta stroke all the time, pamper pamper, stroke stroke, all I do around here. Be right back."

"Gideon," Rachel said quietly, "let's get out of here, I can't take this."

"We've got to find out about O'Connor first, Rach. Then we'll leave, just think our way out of this cesspool."

Asmodeus shambled over to the groaning man. The demon leaned down, so that his huge face was next to the man's pale, gaunt one, and growled a few words that we couldn't hear. The man stopped groaning. His eyes, and those of the women, were hollow pits. All that seemed to dwell in whatever was left of his soul was pain.

Asmodeus came back smiling. "Everything's copacetic now. I just gave him another half point of the net. Don't know why I'm so good to these people. So whaddya think? Ready to start emoting?"

"I'd like to know about Deirdre first," I said.

"Oh yeah, Deedee. So whaddya wanta know?"

"Did she ever . . . mutter anything to herself in Latin?"

"Latin? Oh, you mean that dead language the Enemy used to use, like *corpus delicti* . . . hey, that gives me an idea— what about a necrophiliac romance called *Corpus Delectable?* Whaddya think?"

"Sounds good," I lied. "But what about the Latin?"

"Oh, Deedee, yeah, yeah, she had this thing she said now and then, I always kidded her, sayin' she wasn't tryin' to *exorcise* me or nothin', you know? It was something like *vocabulum est janua* something-something, I don't know. So, you happy now?"

"Yeah," I said. "Thanks."

"Ready to get to work? Get crackin', so to speak?"

"Well, actually, I think maybe we ought to go back to Earth and talk about contracts a little."

"Contracts? Hey, we don't need no stinkin' contracts, we're ladies and gents, we trust each other, am I right?"

"Sure, but . . . our agent thinks it's very important to have everything in writing—keeps us out of trouble if there's ever any legal question that comes up."

Asmodeus nodded shrewdly. "A contract, huh? All right, beefcake, that's what you want, that's what you get. Only here in Hell, our contracts are written in blood." He turned to the demons. "Ukobach! Ribesal! Buer! Leave those has-beens!

We have new performers, fresh meat! Let's be sure to draw plenty of blood while we take our pleasure of them—they like a nice, long heavily detailed contract. Lights!" The set was suddenly flooded with bright red, nearly blinding Rachel and me.

"Camera!" We heard the clatter of Rutterkind's claws and some other demon's hooves as they ran to the two cameras.

"And . . . *action!*"

The demons threw the humans from them and began to come toward us as we backed away. Their intentions were all too clear. It was impossible to tell what were horns and what were other, only slightly less hard, protuberances.

Rachel and I backed toward the rear of the set, but they were all around us now. There was nowhere to go, and not a weapon in sight. Asmodeus himself was in the lead. He had torn away his mirrorshades so that his pig eyes stared lustfully at Rachel. But I didn't feel forsaken, since a large, barrel-shaped beast was heading directly for me. They moved slowly, anticipating the warped pleasure they would soon be taking from us, along with our sanity.

"Being this is your first part," Asmodeus snorted, "I'm gonna give you something easy. Just show me some pain, got it? We'll work our way up to agony and misery and madness later." He ripped off his mesh sash and unbuckled his belt so that the codpiece fell away, and we both hitched in a breath. "Like what you s-s-s-see, little lllllll. . . ."

His words seemed to catch in his throat, and suddenly he and all the other approaching demons stopped, but not voluntarily. It was as though they were held in a force field of some sort, and their growls and roars and snorts *stuttered,* became punctuated with rattles and glitches and crackles, like syspeakers fading in and out.

Then the demons, the cameras, the lights, *everything* but Rachel and me, began to shimmer and tremble, as though on the verge of falling apart or vanishing.

And that's precisely what happened.

I was transfixed as Asmodeus, directly in front of me, lost his sharp edges, became less real. The textures of his multicolored, bristly hair became smooth, the color less scaled, until he was a solid, uniform red. Then his head, his horns, arms, legs, hooves, all disconnected from one another, remaining where they were in relation to everything else, but *simplifying* themselves into rudimentary shapes, breaking down even further until I recognized them as polygons. Asmodeus had become nothing more than a series of vertices filled by a solid color.

Then he became even less. The color faded, leaving only thin lines showing the shape of the demon's body. I could see *through* him, as though he were a hollow robot made of wires.

This *deconstruction,* for lack of a better word, had also been happening to the other demons, and to the cameras, lights and sets, even the floor and walls and grotto-like ceiling. For another moment, all that was left was a series of white lines twisting against blackness, and then even those faded, leaving us in the deepest darkness I have ever known.

I heard Rachel's voice then, flat, with no echo, as though we were in a padded closet. "Gideon?" It sounded as though she was right next to me, but when I tried to reach out for her, I couldn't touch her. In fact, I wasn't even sure that I was controlling my hand. I couldn't feel it moving through the air. I tried to touch myself, but again there was the same terrifying feeling of senselessness, as though I was bound in an SD tank.

"I'm here," I said, relieved to at least hear myself. "But I don't know where *here* is."

"I can't feel anything," Rachel said. "Or hear a thing except for you. Could this be . . . the Limbo of the Roman Catholics?"

I didn't have time to answer, because a yellow-white light was starting to appear in front of me, and I thought for a moment that we might have died down there in Hell, and this was a glorious light coming to take us to some other afterlife.

But the light broadened and broke itself apart to form letters. Dumbfounded, I read, *ALL WILL BE EXPLAINED. ACCESS GARAGE.*

As disoriented as I was, the words confused me even more, as though they were in a foreign language. *Access garage?* In my mind—or maybe in reality, for I had no idea what was real and what wasn't anymore—I saw a garage door with a *Limited Access* sign on it. Was that what the words meant? Or was it a garage where you parked accesses? Or was it. . . ?

And so my mind ran along, playing with the words, and understanding nothing, until the glowing letters faded away into darkness again, and the darkness faded into a light that I realized was touching my eyeballs through my closed lids, and I opened them to find myself on earth again, with two dead demons and a dead woman at my feet.

CHAPTER 21

"I got 'em," Dean Sterling said, and he sure as Hell had.

There was nothing left of Asmodeus's head but a steaming ruin. If it had been bones and brains and blood, I would have looked away fast. But I couldn't look away from this. It wasn't hot blood steaming in the cool air. Instead it was black and acrid smoke, smelling of charred circuit boards and hot wires. The inside of the demon's skull was filled with metal and dead silicon.

"Androids," I heard Rachel say, and when I turned to look she was there next to me. I put my hand on her to make sure, then I looked back down at the floor.

A few feet away lay Rutterkind. Another blast from the Tarbell had taken him in the chest. The bulletproof Kevlar that had formed his carapace had been no match for the rifle's punch. Something was still working inside his head, which continued to twitch in a regular pattern, the mouth opening and closing, though no words came out. Among the shattered boards I saw the mirrorlike gleam of data disks in the rubble of his torso.

The woman, Grinda, was the worst to look at. She had been a human, not an android, though that might be arguable, considering what she had become. "I didn't want to kill her," Sterling said, "but she pulled that little gun out of her purse, woulda shot me, but I had plenty of time for the others first. She was slow, powerful slow, like she really didn't care." His story was confirmed by the Cobra .32 in what was left of her hand.

"How did it happen?" I asked, still looking at the ruined android bodies of the demons, unable to believe what they were.

"I couldn't wait," Sterling said. "I come up to the door, looked through a crack in the glass. Asmodeus put those helmets on you, and then in a minute or so he and the little one start shaking and trembling in a spasm, like they're . . . well, you know. I was afraid they were going to kill you or something, so I kicked the door down and . . . well, you can see what I did." He looked down at Grinda. "I shot her last. I told her to put it down, but she didn't."

I pointed at the psychopomps, now lying on the floor. "How did they get there?"

"After I shot these bastards, I talked to you and shook you, but you didn't do a thing, so I pulled them off your heads and dropped them on the floor. That's when you woke up."

I admit I didn't get it right away. "And these two," I said, looking at Asmodeus and Rutterkind, "they were here all the time?"

"Every second."

I knelt and picked up one of the psychopomps. It was padded on the inside, and I ripped the cloth away to reveal a bird's nest of circuitry and wiring and a network of ultra-thin needle respondrills that would easily pierce the padding and sink into the skin and skull of the wearer without his even being aware of it.

"My dear God," I whispered.

"A wireless deck," I heard Rachel say over the sound of the blood rushing through my head.

"I didn't know there was such a thing," Sterling said.

"There is now," I said.

"It all makes sense," Rachel said slowly. "The demons being androids . . . the sound starting to go, and then the visuals. . . ."

"You remember," I said, starting to warm to what seemed so impossible, so unbelievable, "when they broke apart, they became *polygonal*, and then—"

"And then *wireframe!*" Rachel finished for me. "Oh my God, Hell is . . ."

"*Virtual!*" We said it at the same time and then laughed together, not because it was funny—it wasn't—but because I don't think either one of us was willing to comprehend it. We laughed in disbelief and embarrassment, the way two kids would if they walked in on their parents making love, or their minister taking a dump. It wasn't supposed to *be* this way.

But it was.

I whirled on Sterling. "When we went under the helmets, Asmodeus was still here, right?" He nodded. "Doing what? Walking? Talking?"

"He was talking to these two," Sterling said, nodding to the bodies of Rutterkind and Grinda.

"But he was with us in Hell," I said.

"They were multitasked," Rachel said in surprise.

"Sure. Not even demons can be two places at once. He was already short-circuiting when you came in here, right?"

"Yeah, that's why I came in. But Hell . . . you can't mean it. Virtual? You're sayin' it doesn't exist?"

"Oh, it exists all right, only not down there, but up here, and it exists because *somebody* made it." I turned to Rachel, as excited as a kid just figuring out a new toy. "And somebody got into the system while we were there and crashed it."

Rachel nodded, her face lit up with the fascination of forbidden truths. "The same person who sent us the message."

"All these years," I said, "Hell, virtual. What a scam. That goddamned Hand of God. That bastard Solene Solux."

"The government," Sterling said, looking down at the defunct androids, the dead woman. "The stinking government . . . their fault. My Drew. Their fault. Damn Solux. . . ."

Rachel put a hand on Sterling's shoulder. "Maybe if you can show her that . . . that none of it was real, that it was all virtual, maybe she'll get better."

Tears pooled in his blue eyes. "It *was* real," he said. "Her pain was real. And their Hell—the Hand of God's Hell—that's real too."

"You're right," I said. "As long as the pain is real, Hell is real. Until the people kill the demons. Until they tear Hell down."

Sirens screamed somewhere out in the city. Maybe someone had heard Sterling's shots. "Let's go," I said, grabbing the decks we had thought to be supernatural psychopomps and handing one to Rachel. "We're going to need these."

"'Access garage,'" she quoted to me, and I nodded and ran out the door with a barked command to Sterling to follow us. Now he was a killer too.

CHAPTER 22

We got out of the area before the holicops came. We asked Sterling where he lived, and he gave us an address up near The Good Physician Army Med Center, where they kept his daughter. He lived in a one-room apartment nearby.

"Be careful," I said when we dropped him off. "You have the most dangerous piece of knowledge a person can have in this country. It's more than enough to get you killed."

He shook his head vigorously. "Don't you worry—I won't talk." But as he walked away mumbling to himself, I wondered.

"He's crazy," Rachel said as we pulled away.

"Yeah," I agreed. "But he's one helluva shot." That made me think of his Tarbell, and I glanced into the back. The big-bored gun was still there. We decided that returning it to him was just too dangerous. Besides we might be able to use the cannon before all this was over.

It was midnight when we got back to Dante's. He was, predictably, surfing the nets, and grinned as we came in. "Hey, Robin and Marian!"

"Wrong," I said. "Marian didn't kick ass."

"Okay, Pancho and Cisco then. The undernets are singin' your praises. You're the hottest thing since that ten-year-old kid who downloaded the link to Solux's private mailbox last year."

"Well, I hope we don't follow in his footsteps." The kid had disappeared, and word was he'd been condemned to Hell for his hacking abilities.

"What the hell are *those?*" Dante said as we pulled the psychopomps from the plastibags we'd stored them in.

"You tell us." Rachel handed him the one I'd ripped the lining from.

It didn't take him long. "Decks," he said. "This is *awesome.* Actual wireless decking units—where did you get them?"

We told him about going back to Hell, the lockup of the system, the message we had received, and what we now knew Hell really was. "It's not real," I finished. "It's an enormous and unbelievably complex virtual reality. All these years of terror and suffering—they've been founded on a monstrous lie."

"Those bastards," Dante said, still looking at the psychopomp. "They outlawed all this shit and then worked on it themselves."

I had to smile. Dante's point of view was that of a frustrated techie. At heart, he was as political as a romdisc.

"So you gonna jack into this thing?" he said, holding up the helmet. "Visit this garage?"

"Wouldn't miss it," I said, looking at Rach. "One for each of us." We fit the padding back into the psychopomp. "So how does this work?"

"Just like your deck on the job, man, only you don't have to hook up neural conduits. Just put it on, and the respondrills should do the rest. When you're linked, just say the word garage. That ought to access it."

"Are we going to feel that horrible sick feeling again?" Rachel asked.

"Beats me. Maybe that's just a part of the Hell program. But you won't know until you try."

I nodded and held the psychopomp over my head. Rachel did the same. "See you there," I said, and she smiled bravely and nodded. Then I set the helmet down firmly in place, trying not to think about the extremely thin respondrills working their way through my skull and into my brain.

This time wasn't bad at all. I was at Dante's one second, and the next I was in the sensationless darkness that Rachel and I had visited before. I or something in my mind said "Garage," and I was there. Oddly enough, the sudden light didn't blind me, and the first thing I saw was Rachel standing right in front of me. She jerked in surprise, and I took her hand, which felt absolutely real. Then we looked around.

The old-fashioned parking garage looked unfinished, and now I could plainly see that it was a computer construct. Most of the chamber itself was completed. The textures of decades of dirt and grime were rendered with masterful realism, right down to a tongue-in-cheek *Level 666* in chipped paint on the wall.

But certain spots on the ceiling were incomplete. Several solid-color polygons conjoined crudely, and other sections of the ceiling were nothing but red wireframe. The dozen or so cars in the garage also existed only as wireframe models, not even positioned correctly. Some were angled oddly, and others were elevated, as though their artist had just set them anywhere in the composition.

In all this visual madness, we heard no sound except our own breathing. Then we heard steps echoing and coming nearer. Around the corner walked a man dressed in a belted trench coat, with a gray fedora pulled down so that we couldn't see his face. He stopped ten feet away and lifted his head slightly to reveal his face, if it was *really* his face. He was handsome, I suppose, if a bit nondescript. He was of medium height and built well, the kind of guy who works out regularly.

"You came," he said. He sounded glad.

"Yeah, we came, all right," I said. "When a Hell pit locks up, when demons turn out to be androids, and when we find out our key into Hell is really a decking unit, we get real curious. So what's the deal here? Who are you? Have we walked—or *decked*—into a trap?"

"No, no trap," he said quickly. "As for who I am, just call me Deep Throat."

Deep Throat . . . a parking garage . . . it reminded me of something, but I couldn't think of what until Rachel spoke. "You're into American history," she said. "The reporters who brought down Richard Nixon in the Watergate affair got their information from a man they called Deep Throat—"

"Who they met in a parking garage, yes," the man said. "Forgive the. . . unfinished nature of this WELL. I spent most of my time cloaking it from Hand detection. They would have no mercy if they found me responsible for an illegal data cluster. But I'm hoping that this meeting in a garage, over a hundred years after the original Deep Throat, will be the start of another . . . coup."

"Okay, so you're Deep Throat, if that's what you want to call yourself," I said. "But what are you? Why did you contact us, and how much do you know about all this?"

He thrust his hands deep into his pockets and started to pace slowly. "I contacted you through the Hell system because it was the only way I could get to you without being discovered. I work in the Pentagon as part of the Hell maintenance team. I make backup files of Hell pits."

"Then it *is* virtual," Rachel said.

"Yes. It's the greatest lie in human history, Rachel. It's entirely computer generated." He ran a hand across his mouth. "From the start, the Hand knew their greatest weapon was fear. They'd seen how politicians in the past two centuries, from Germany in the 1930's to the leaders of Congress at the turn of the last century, used fear to gain their ends—fear of crime, fear of poverty, fear of people not like themselves. If tapping into those fears was so successful, wouldn't it be even more successful to tap into *centuries* of fear and superstition, exploiting humanity's tribal horrors and most primal fears?

"They spent billions of dollars. The military and the CIA had already stockpiled immense research on the subject, and transglobal CEOs and ruthless secular politicians willingly backed them." Deep Throat laughed bitterly. "They thought they could share in the Hand's rule, but once the gates of Hell opened and Kevlarite-coated demons stalked the country, Solux swept *all* the non-believers into prison before they could reveal the truth. That was the first night of the scrub teams. The first of many."

It was almost too much to believe, but we'd been prepared for it. "So why us?" I said.

"Because I saw a chance in you two. I've been following your activities by monitoring ARC data. I know that you, like so many other innocents, have been framed, but I don't know why. I also know from the undernets that you two have been the only ones who have survived long enough to link up with the Citizens' Freedom Front."

"And you want to get to them through us," I said, feeling my temper rise. "Infiltrate them—destroy them!"

"*No!*" he said. "I want to *help* them—and you."

"Why?" Rachel said, and I could feel her doubt. "Why turn on your masters?"

"Because I see what they *do!* I see it every single day, and it makes me sick in my soul." He crossed his arms, locking his hands tight. "I was a believer once. God forgive me. But I believed that Solux's measures were severe, but fair and necessary. But now . . . working where I do, seeing what they've done—and in the name of *God*—I just can't do it any more. I know that the real evil is Solene Solux. But walking away isn't enough. I've got to do something to stop it, and I can't by myself."

"You crashed the Hell pit," Rachel reminded him.

He shook his head in confusion. "I know, but not on purpose. I only wanted to contact you—the lock-up was . . . an unexpected side-effect."

"Which proves that their system, as incredible as it is, is also vulnerable," I said.

"That's what I'm hoping. If it can be damaged, maybe it can be crashed entirely, I don't know. What I do know is that you'll need a far more gifted programmer than myself to do it. I'm even limited as to how much I can find out. The Hell staff works and lives in the Pentagon. My movements are constantly monitored, but I'll do what I can. The more that you and the CFF can find out about. . . ." He trailed off, his eyes vacant.

Rachel took a step toward him. "What is it?"

"They're dowsing," he said, his voice taut. "For WELLs. I have to get out now, fill the WELL. You too."

"But—"

"Go! Think yourselves back. I have the codes of your decks, so I'll contact you again. Now *go!*"

He vanished as though he had never been there. "Let's go!" I said to Rach. I thought about going back to Dante's, and instantly we were there. I imagined that I could feel the respondrills pulling out of my head, but they had probably retracted the instant I'd thought myself back. We tugged our decks off our heads, while Dante watched us like a cat watching pigeons.

"What was it like?" he said. "What did you see?" We told him, and he hung on every word.

"Incredible," he said, walking quickly to his deck and sitting down. "I can't wait to get this on line, it's gonna change the damn world—"

He started to punch a few keys, but Rachel hit his power button and the low hum of his machine died away as the screen went blank. He looked up at her, half angry, half puzzled.

"You try to down that info," Rachel said, ice in her voice, "you even think about it, you're a dead man. Your techie urge to tell all could *blow* it all. You think the Hand isn't tapped in to the undernets? You think that three seconds after your post they won't know everything? They'll put intrusion countermeasure electronics around the Hell program and the entire Pentagon—Ice colder and thicker and tougher than you can even imagine. And how long do you think it would take them to dowse out Deep Throat's WELL? Once they have it, he's dead. Or virtually damned. No, Dante, not a word. The only way we can take them is by surprise. You understand?"

He looked up at her, and I could watch him realize the truth of what she said. Slowly, he looked down and pushed himself away from the machine. "I'm sorry," he said softly. "I didn't think. You're right. Don't worry, Rachel. Not a keystroke. I swear." He smiled crookedly. "So how are you gonna . . . take 'em?"

CHAPTER 23

Before he had been interrupted, Deep Throat had started to say that the more we were able to find out about something, the better position we'd be in. The *something* had to be the Hell program. And the program was somehow datalinked to the demons, since Asmodeus and Rutterkind had started to short out when their Hell pit locked up, before Dean Sterling had turned them into bargain parts. So Rachel and I agreed that the best place to start trying to get the lowdown on the structure of Hell would be with a demon.

We were on speaking terms with only two demons. One was Sanguinarius, who was protected by his demonic cadre, and the other was Beautiful, who had only that poetry-spouting runt Abonides as a bodyguard. Want to guess which one we decided to see first?

It was an hour before dawn when we walked into the Interface. Having seen the power that Sterling's Tarbell had over otherwise bulletproof demons, I had the long gun under an ankle-length coat of Dante's. The duster was tight through the shoulders, but I wore it open, and held the gun against my left side.

The place was nearly deserted. The bartender sat behind the bar, his chin resting in his palm, watching us through slitted eyelids. A man and a woman sat in a booth. The man looked asleep, and the woman was concentrating ferociously on her beer, looking at something I couldn't see. Cynna Stone wasn't there, and I didn't see anybody else I knew.

"Beautiful in the back?" I asked the bartender.

He nodded sullenly, then added, "He got company."

We walked up to Beautiful's office door. I listened for a minute, but couldn't hear a thing. Nobody could see us from the bar, so I took out the Tarbell and slowly turned the knob. Rachel slipped her Avenger into her hand. It might not do any good against demons, but it would take care of any hostile human visitors Beautiful might have.

The latch clicked, and I slowly pushed the door open, not seeing anyone inside. Then, as my eyes grew used to the dim lighting of the office, I saw something lying on the floor near the pool table, and realized that it was Mr. Beautiful. More accurately, it was his body. From the neck ran a labyrinth of wires and cables. I didn't see his head.

The door was suddenly ripped from my fingers and pulled inward. I stumbled, but brought the Tarbell up, and felt the barrel ram into something soft that grunted. Then I looked into the black eye of a machine pistol that was pointed directly at my brainpan. Fortunately, the person holding it had the muzzle of *my* gun pressing insistently against his guts.

"Don't do it," I said, "or we both die."

I slowly and gingerly straightened up, looking at the man who held a gun to my head. He was very tall, and what I could see of his face under his slouch hat was swarthy and mean. He held the gun on me with a steady hand. My Tarbell didn't seem to faze him, but it must have, since I can't think of any other reason he didn't just blast me.

Behind him was another man, shorter and hatless. He looked distinguished, with iron-gray hair, moustache, and beard, but his eyes were pouchy, and he seemed no happier than the first guy. He was pointing his own pistol at Rachel. From the corner of my eye, I could see her Avenger pointing back at him.

"We seem to be in a stand-off," the gray-haired man said in a tense, jagged voice.

"You got that right," I said. "So how do we break it without all of us dying?"

"Depends on what you're doing here. What do you want?"

"We came to see Beautiful."

"You stooges of his?"

"We're not anybody's stooges," Rachel said. "What are you two doing here? Did you kill him?"

"Manny did," the gray-haired man said, nodding at the man whose gun barrel was making me cross-eyed.

Then it hit me who the gunman was. Manny. Manuel Salinas. Top button man for the Salinas family, and one of the mob's most cold-blooded killers. He was reputed to have no fear of dying. I couldn't say the same for myself. My fear had just increased by a gigabyte, and it popped out in conversation. "So, uh, are we going to keep talking indefinitely with guns to each others' heads?"

"I don't have a gun to my head," said Salinas in this creepy, whispery voice, like there was no soul behind the words. "I have it to my belly.

And I've got a Kevlarite vest on."

It looked like we were getting into a dick-measuring contest, and I had to make him think that mine was a lot bigger. "This is a Tarbell 3000 autoload," I said, "and it will eat through your Kevlarite just as easily as it'll tear through your guts."

There. That'd show him.

"And this is a Walker PR .57 with explosive loads," he whispered back. "It will turn your head into a cloud."

That was pretty good, but if he had intended to shoot me, he would have already done it. I hoped.

"Hey, Gideon!" came a familiar voice from somewhere down around floor level. "Cut this 'mine's bigger than yours' crap and shoot the sonsabitches! Rachel, blow away Marto right now!"

"Beautiful?" I said.

"Yeah, hell, who else? Plug 'em! Plant 'em! We'll bury 'em in Arlington! No, no, we'll be just like the dagos and dump their bodies right next to where the freakin' Kennedys used to be!"

"Where are you?" I said, unable to track the voice.

"Behind the goddam pool table, all right? Now *shoot these shitheads!*"

"I thought you didn't work for him," said the gray-haired man, who, I knew now, was Secedine Marto of the Marto crime family.

"We *don't*," I said. "He just thinks we do."

"So what'd you come here for?"

"Information. How about you two?"

"Vendetta," said Marto. "This bastard's been scamming us for years and we've been thinking he's untouchable because he's a demon. Well, he screwed up once too often."

"What'd he do?"

"He let Krystal Getty get away, the lousy shit."

I didn't say a word. I didn't even look at Rachel. It appeared Sanguinarius's plan to discredit Beautiful had worked all too well.

"So Manny and me," Marto went on, "we come to see him. Manny ain't a Marto, but the demon here's holding a boy from each of our families in Hell while we negotiate. And after Manny hears about the Getty broad, he don't wanta have nothin' to do with the demon either, so—"

"Stop callin' me the demon!" yelled the unseen head. "I'm *Mr. Beautiful,* dammit, I'm the *numero uno* crime kingpin in this burg, and I'm gonna see you, ya wop, and you, ya spic, with your freakin' heads decoratin' my bedposts before I get through with you!"

"I wanna kill it, Marto," said Manny. "I wanna blast that damn head."

"Not yet," Marto replied. "Not till we find our boys."

"Wait a minute," I said, finally getting it. "You're looking for your two men?"

"That's right."

"I think we can find them for you," I said, and slowly lowered my Tarbell from Salinas's middle. It was a real relief. That gun is heavy.

Salinas kept his pistol trained on me for a few more seconds, then dropped it to his side. Rachel and Marto then lowered their weapons simultaneously. "Why didn't you say so?" Marto said. "Now where are they?"

"You freakin' *traditore!*" Beautiful yelled, and I walked behind the pool table to look at him. His head was there all right, tilted so that the weight of it rested on his left horn. Within the gaping hole of the neck was a complex assortment of circuitry. The mouth was snarling at me, spitting curses.

"Not so Beautiful now, are you, Pazuzu? Just another noisy head."

"Screw you! You were only too happy to suck up when I was on top! One little freakin' setback, and then you find out who your real friends are . . ." He kept talking while Rachel joined me.

"His identity chips must be stored in his head," she said.

"Disks in the torso like the other one," I said, glancing at Beautiful's headless body. "There's probably an access panel under the clothing."

"Hey . . . *hey!* You two wanna stop talkin' about me like I'm not here?"

"Where's Abonides?" I asked.

"Little fart took off soon as these two goons came in," Beautiful said. "Gutless coward, leaving me here alone with these two slabs of grease."

"Ah, shaddup, head," Salinas said, and kicked Beautiful's noggin across the room, with Beautiful cursing all the way. Salinas laughed a cold little laugh and grinned at me. "Nice shot, huh? I wanted to take him in the neck because I figure everything's softer there, y'know? That explosive load just snapped off his head like a dandelion. It was gorgeous. I gotta admit, I had a little help, though. I'm thinkin' about pullin' down on him when he starts spazzing out on me, shimmyin' and shakin', and I figure now's the time."

"And what time *was* the time?" I asked him.

"What, Secedine, about nine, ten o'clock? We been here all night, I lost track."

"Yeah, tennish," Marto said.

"Same time Asmodeus went haywire," I said to Rach. "They must all be networked."

Marto tapped his pistol against my shoulder. "Look, I don't know what the hell you're talkin' about. But I'm sick of waiting. Manny and me been looking around here all night for something to try and get Delmonico and Carlos out of Hell, and haven't found squat. Now if you can't turn them up for us like you said, we're gonna get back to that standoff again. Only this time we got the drop on you."

"They're not *in* Hell," I said. "Oh, their minds are, but not their bodies. My guess is they're around here somewhere." I figured that Beautiful had kept mum all this time despite their threats, but maybe somebody else knew Beautiful's secrets, someone who we already *knew* could be threatened.

"It's a damn shame, Pazuzu," I said to the head, "that you gotta take this rap all on your own." Beautiful muttered something ungentlemanly, but I went on. "Yeah, here you are, a real smart guy, all semi-detached, while that little servant of yours gets away scot-free. I bet he's laughing his ass off right now, nice and toasty in some other demon's Hell pit. He sure played you for a sucker."

"Sucker?" said the head. "All I gotta do is summon that little putz, and he's in as deep shit as I am!"

"Bull," said Rachel, catching on fast. "He got away free and clear. You couldn't get him back if your . . . head depended on it."

Whatever skin color enhancement hardware Beautiful was running still worked, because his cheeks got red with synthesized fury. He somehow took a deep breath without lungs, and spewed out a stream of what might have sounded like Latin if the priest was drunk and from some country with a lot of consonants in its name.

Apparently it was a summoning incantation—or code, as I now knew—since smoke started billowing in the middle of the pentagram on the floor, and when it cleared there stood none other than the quivering little demon Abonides. I lost no time in grabbing his skinny arm so he couldn't dash away.

"All right, Abonides, you see your boss?" I said, and he nodded, trembling. "Well, these two gentleman will do far worse to you if you don't tell them exactly where Ferlinghetti and Portillo are—and don't give me that Hell crap. We know the truth about Hell."

> "If you would enter Hell's quite earthly halls—
> I mean no disrespect by saying this—
> To do so you must quickly break your balls."

"You filthy midget," said Salinas, advancing on the little demon with his gun pointed straight at him. "I'll bust your balls with a bullet!"

"Wait a minute," I said, holding on tight to the squirming demon. "Let him talk."

"So filled with fear am I that I must piss!
I would not lie! So fill your pockets —
Then break your balls and enter the abyss!"

"I warned you, goat-boy!" said Salinas, aiming his pistol. He was so quick that neither Abonides nor I could react, and the explosive round made a mess of machinery out of the demon's head. Sparks flew, and circuits shattered. I was lucky I wasn't cut. What was left of Abonides stood upright a moment longer, then fell over with a clatter. "I had just about enough outta him," Salinas explained.

"Ha!" yelled Beautiful. "Now you'll never know shit, you dumb spic button man! Shoot first, ask questions later, huh?"

"No," I said. "We got enough. I can find them for you now, Marto, but I want something in exchange."

"Beside your lives?" said Marto.

"That's right. We want Beautiful's body."

Marto raised an eyebrow. "That piece of junk?"

"Call me a piece of junk, will ya, you dago schmuck!—"

"It's a deal," Marto said.

"Fine. Now, either one of you shoot a good game of pool?"

"I was brung up in a pool hall," Marto said.

"Good. You want to set up six balls for that trick break, the one where each ball goes in a different pocket?"

Marto looked at me curiously again, but shrugged and arranged the balls on Beautiful's pool table.

"Eshanti, you traitor!" Beautiful shouted, "I'll getcha for this!" Only Salinas's threat of another drop kick shut him up.

"Okay," I said when Marto was done. "Break the balls."

He did so with a fluid and economical motion. The balls entered the six pockets of the table simultaneously, and Marto straightened up as though that was exactly what he had expected to happen.

What he didn't expect, though, was that the portion of the floor where the pentagram was would slide away like the hidden door to some torture chamber in a medieval dungeon. I led the way down the revealed flight of stairs into a dimly lit stone cellar. There, at a large computer console that was probably a node of the Hell server, Ferlinghetti and Portillo sat unmoving, psychopomps on their heads.

"Delmonico! Portillo!" Marto called, but the two men didn't respond. "What the hell is this? What'd that goddam head do to them?"

"Don't blow your motherboard, Marto," Rachel said. "Your men are fine. Just turn off the power on this thing, and take off their helmets."

He did as Rach suggested. In a few seconds the men's eyes opened, and in another minute they were standing up, wobbly-legged and not seeming to know what had happened to them. We helped them up the steps, and at the top Marto and Salinas each took over the care of their respective lieutenants. "I swear to God, Manny," Marto said as they went out the door to Beautiful's office, "I ever get involved with demons again, just shoot me, please."

"It would be my pleasure, Secedine," Salinas replied, and then Rachel and I were all alone—with Mr. Beautiful's head.

CHAPTER 24

"Don't just *stand* there, you two! Pick me up and let's go find me another freakin' body!"

"Quiet, Beautiful," I said. "We'll have you out of here fast enough. Rach, clean the disks out of his chest while I find something to carry his head in."

"Right," she said. "I'll go over the rest of the torso too, to make sure we're not missing anything."

"Yeah?" said the head. "Better check in my pants too, sweetcakes, know what I mean?"

I shook my head in disgust and went back into the bar. The bartender had an old bowling ball bag that he used to store bar snacks. I bought it from him, cheap, and went back into the office. Rachel held up five silver disks. "That's it," she said.

"Hey, dollface, you didn't check *everywhere*."

Rachel looked at Beautiful with a chilling contempt I was glad she had never used on me. "Don't tell me what I already know."

"What's that, baby?"

"Your brain's in your crotch."

That shut him up, at least long enough for me to pick up his head by the hair and stuff it into the bag.

"Holy crap!" he yelled. "It smells like dead *fish* in here!"

"I know. That's where the bartender kept the herring treats. Try not to breathe. That shouldn't be hard for an android." I zipped the bag completely shut. Beautiful continued to complain, making a buzzing sound inside the bag. I unzipped it an inch and spoke into it. "Keep your mouth shut, and I'll keep it open two inches. Otherwise, it's the herring farm, pal. Deal?"

"Goddammit, I don't make deals with assholes! You're gonna be feelin' the heat, Eshanti, soon as I get some arms and legs back!"

"Hold your breath," I said, and zipped the bag all the way shut again.

The sun was shining as we left the Interface and got into the car. I put the Tarbell in the back seat and Beautiful's head on the seat between us, ready to grab it if we had to move quickly.

"The embassy?" Rachel asked, and I nodded.

"We'll see what they're able to make of the disks and what's inside Beautiful's head. The fact that Hell is virtual is going to hit them like a bombshell."

"It changes everything, doesn't it?"

"Damn near." I took her hand. "Except for my loving you."

She squeezed back and we kissed. The bag buzzed again. Apparently Beautiful's aural receptors still worked fine. I started the car and we headed north.

We'd only gone a few blocks when the traffic slowed, so I turned on the Voice of God to see if it was reporting any traffic locks. Instead, I broke in on a live broadcast.

". . . and is reported now coming down Pennsylvania Avenue. The Imperator is riding in the state vehicle, garbed in the robes of Holy Office, and is waving to the crowd, smiling that small shadow of a smile that belongs only to those who have communed personally with the Lord. Crowds are thronging the streets and. . . ."

"Oh hell," I said.

"Imperator's Day." Rachel finished my thought. We had been so busy the past few days that we had forgotten about it. The most important holiday of the year, except for Christmas, Easter, and the 4th of July. It commemorated the day the Solux had received "divine guidance" to establish the Hand of God party—actually the first day the power-pig had gotten the idea of how to scam an entire nation of chickenshits desperate enough to look for an instant savior. The motorcade took her from Washington Circle down Pennsylvania Avenue to the Capitol, where she would address the nation on whatever moral burr she had up her ass this year.

If she made it that far.

"The homing device," Rachel whispered.

We were starting to move again now, and about ten car lengths ahead, right where we would enter Washington

Circle, I saw a whole phalanx of holicops redirecting traffic down a side street. Maybe they didn't have us tagged yet, but driving past several of them would be pushing our luck too far.

"We're getting out," I said, and Rachel's curt nod told me she agreed. I edged the car over as far as I could to the parked-up curb and turned off the engine. Then I slid the Tarbell back under my coat while Rachel grabbed the bowling-ball bag, and we got out and started walking down the street, away from the cops.

We glanced back once, and I thought I saw the sleek silhouette of Solux's state car glide across the opening of the street ahead. We turned and started walking faster. The cars behind us began pressing their whiners, since there wasn't enough room to get by on the narrow street, but Rach and I pretended we had no idea who the assholes were who had deserted their car with so little regard for their fellow motorists.

But the whiners stopped when the new sound filled the streets. That terrifying shriek of something tearing the air, seeking a target, was unmistakable. The unseen missile was homing in on the device that Rachel had placed on the Imperator's car. In another few seconds we would hear the explosion, and the first real blow for freedom in the second revolution would be struck.

We started running. When the Imperator died, we wanted to be as far away as possible. The revolution would not be instantaneous. There would be arrests, repercussions, executions.

We had just gotten to the corner of 24th Street when we turned around for one more look. That's when we actually saw the missile, high over the buildings, coming from the north, moving faster than we could have imagined. But instead of whizzing to the east down Pennsylvania Avenue to home in on the Imperator, it came southwest, down the very street we had fled, like a huge dart thrown unerringly.

Right at the car we had deserted.

Unthinking, knowing nothing except what to destroy, the missile flew directly into the little car. The explosion that followed would have destroyed a platoon of tanks. The car vanished in a fireball, only the first casualty of the blast. Nearly a full city block away, the searing rush of heat staggered us so that we fell against a parked car. My Tarbell rattled on the pavement, and I grabbed it and put it back under my coat.

The explosion had destroyed every car within fifty yards of ground zero, and the walls of the buildings on either side of the street were toppling as though a giant fist had smashed them. People screamed everywhere. I saw one man on fire, running toward us until he fell. Then the only things moving were the flames. Dozens of people died, maybe more, depending on how many had been in the buildings. The carnage was so terrible that for a moment I forgot that the missile had been aimed directly at us. When I did remember, I didn't understand why.

I suppose I was standing stunned when I felt Rachel shaking my arm. "We've got to get out of here," she said. "Listen!"

Sirens were wailing all across the city. Soon cops, firemen, and healthers, all Hand employees, would be filling the streets. I walked up to a gawking driver who had slowed his car to look at the havoc up the street, opened his door, and yanked him out. He started to protest, but I shoved the

Tarbell in his face. He might have been as good a guy as ever walked the earth, but I wasn't in the mood to explain. We tore off west, figuring to weave around Georgetown before heading over to Kalorama Heights and the abandoned subway tunnel. *If* we were even going back to the embassy.

"Was it the Front?" I said to Rachel, my eyes on the streets ahead. "It was the Front's missile—did they want to kill us?"

Rachel's always calmer in a crisis than me. "It was their missile," she said, "but the last we saw of the homing device, it was inside a Pentagon garage, and the Pentagon belongs to the Hand lock, stock, and barrel."

"Goddamn them. Goddamn them *all*. Xenon said no bystanders would be hurt, and . . . did you see that man? Is that the price, Rach? Is that what freedom costs?"

She stuck to practicalities. "They must have found it. Then tracked down the stolen car, tagged us, put it on our car."

"But *why?* Why didn't they just arrest us?"

The radio, which had been playing mellow-40 hymns, gave us the answer.

"Attention! Attention all believers! Here is a bulletin from Washington Square in Washington, D.C. A cowardly attack has been made by the underground upon the person of our Imperator, Solene Solux. A missile was fired at the Imperator's car, missing it by inches. The errant missile instead hit a parked car, killing the innocent believers inside. The resulting explosion has killed many others and has also destroyed several apartment buildings. It is not known whether or not the families living in those buildings have met with tragedy. The Imperator had this to say about the attempt on her life."

Then the deep contralto of Solux's voice came over the air. "I am not concerned about myself. My primary concern is for those unfortunate believers who were killed or injured in this attempt on my person. I would have gladly given up my own life to save these innocents, but that was not God's will. I pray that God will take them to His bosom and they will find eternal rest.

"I also pray that the heretics who performed this vile and cowardly act, this so-called underground of atheists, agnostics, homosexuals, and other criminals, will be quickly apprehended and judged. And I call on all believers to help us in this quest, to capture these killers of innocents and—"

Rachel reached up and switched off the lies. "That's why they didn't arrest us, Gideon. Better anti-CFF propaganda. And in a way, it's deserved. My God, the size of that explosion. . . . ."

"Still," I said, "the Hand blew up all those people. . . . ."

"Just to discredit the Front, yes."

The sirens and the sound of the emergency vehicles died away behind us. The bowling-ball bag began to buzz again. Rachel unzipped it.

"Hey!" Beautiful said. "I been gettin' banged around in here like the charms on a hooker's ankle bracelet! What's with the explosions?"

"A missile," Rachel said. "It hit our car."

"Goddamn, that freakin' Marto ain't gonna stop until I'm a hood ornament on his limo."

"They weren't after you," I said.

"Hell they weren't—I got enemies *everywhere*. But we get me a good body, I'm gonna make the streets run red with their blood."

"Somebody already beat you to it," said Rachel angrily, zipping up the bag. The buzzing started again. "Shut *up!*" Rachel cried, "Or I'll stick my fingers in your eyes and mouth and use you as a bowling ball!"

We drove along toward the embassy entrance in silence.

CHAPTER 25

We had taken our small pocket flashes with us, so we easily found the loose cement block in the track bed where we had left our hand flamers. A few tongues of flame, and the cats and rats left us alone. At one point I saw a skell, his skin as pale and eyes as white as an albino. I shot at him and he vanished. Rachel asked me what it was, and I told her just a cat.

When we got to 98-C, Vivid and Literati met us at the entry hatch and relieved us of our weapons. Literati eyed the Tarbell with some respect. "A little heavier artillery, Eshanti?"

"Things are rough out there," I said.

"Yeah, I guess so. Guess somebody found out about the homer, huh? Now I wonder how they knew?"

Rachel looked at Literati like she wanted to kill him. "You suggesting that Gideon and I told them?"

Literati shrugged. "I'll let the senator deal with that possibility. Hand over the bag." She did. "What's in it?"

"A bomb," she said. "You're right—we're out to destroy the CFF, so we've brought a bomb in here that'll take the top off the whole embassy. Shake it up good before you open it. The triggering mechanism is in the zipper. As soon as you open it, bang. Go ahead. We're waiting."

My involuntary grin probably told him he was being bullshitted, but he still gritted his teeth when he grabbed the zipper and yanked it up.

"*Hey!*" Beautiful yelled. "Take it *easy!*"

Literati dropped the bag, much to Beautiful's dismay. "What the hell . . . ?"

"Holy *shit,* man! Whadda you think's in here, a bowling ball?"

"What *is* that?" Literati asked.

"Mr. Beautiful's head," I said.

"The demon?" Vivid said, her face pale.

"No, dumbass," the bag answered. "Mr. Beautiful the freakin' *cantaloupe!* Now get me outta here—it stinks worse than Mephisto's jockey shorts!"

"He's not a demon," Rachel said. "He's an android. *All* the demons are androids. And we found out a lot more. But we're not saying a word until you take us—and that—to see Senator Burr."

We were with Erin Burr in less than two minutes flat. The first thing she said was, "The plot failed."

"Yes," Rachel said. "The Hand must have found the device and planted it on our car. They were lucky we were near the motorcade at the time. But wherever the homer led the missile, it would have caused damage—terrible damage. If I'd known the missile was that destructive, I wouldn't have planted the device in the first place."

"Rachel—" the senator began.

"Was the Front ready to take out all those people along the motorcade route? If it had hit Solux's car, hundreds of others would have been dead! Are innocent lives the price of the freedom we're fighting for?"

"*Listen* to me!" Senator Burr said. "Our missile would have destroyed the car—and that's all. The size of the explosion indicates that the Hand used additional explosives. And they had to have been secured to your car."

"To our. . . . ."

"When the Hand put the homing device on your car, they added an explosive charge much larger than the payload of our missile. All the better to blame the Front for mindless violence. They killed their own worshippers to discredit us."

Rachel shook her head slowly. "I had no idea. . . . ."

"No. Neither did we."

"However they found out about the device, Senator," I said, "it wasn't from us. You have to believe that."

"I do. If you were traitors, this entire embassy would be overrun with Hand police by now. I know you're loyal to our cause."

"I wish some other people felt that way," Rachel said.

"You mean Derek Literati. He's a hard man to convince, but one of the finest agents we have. He's gotten . . . a shell around him since Marcus Vanders and Claudette Simeon disappeared. They were all good friends, and when they vanished something in him died. He knows you're not traitors. Because he's not dead or in jail. Or," she added, "in Hell."

"Hell," I echoed. "Hell is a little different than we realized."

"What do you mean?"

"We'll show you," Rachel said, opening the bag and folding back the sides so that the senator could see Beautiful's head.

She looked stunned. "What on earth . . . ?"

"Hey toots," said Beautiful. "So you're the Burr babe, huh? Not bad. I kinda like 'em older. I'm pretty old myself, y'know? A few thousand years, give or take."

"Meet Mr. Beautiful," I said. "Also known as the demon Pazuzu, but really just an android, like all his demon buddies."

"Yeah yeah yeah, but look, don't hold it against me. I got an idea of what you could hold against me, Senator, when I finally got something against which you could hold stuff, you get my drift."

"All too well," said the senator.

"Glad to hear it. I like a smart broad. With our combined brainpower and connections, hey, we could freakin' rule this town."

"What about Solene Solux?" Senator Burr said. "She's the one with the real power."

"Solux? That hermaphrodite freak? Don't insult my good taste, Senator sweetie. That sideshow exhibit has had a chip on its shoulder ever since it looked into the old drawers and couldn't figure out exactly what the hell it had in there. Who knows what's under those robes? Guy? Chick? It could have freakin' gills, for all we know!"

The senator smiled as she walked behind her desk and sat down. She was toying with Beautiful, trying to find out how much he knew. "But surely most people would be drawn to such a strong willed person?"

"Drawn? Yeah, and *quartered*. Hey, I been walking this earth invisibly long before Hell opened up, and I remember that misfit's humble beginnings. I heard all about Solux's dreams of glory, her eye on the presidency, them early clandestine meetings, propaganda bullshit, then the rallies . . . entire country starts gettin' in on it, lappin' it up like puppies. Then the talk show circuit, man, they start *cravin'* the freak. They start listenin', and then, man, they start *doin'*. Hey, I wasn't a demon, I'da been scared shitless. Nah, Solux never did a thing for me."

"Except created you," Rachel said.

Beautiful's eyebrows dipped into a V. "Excuse me, bitch. I been walkin' up and down this earth a million years before your ancestors were whackin' off in trees."

"Hardly. You were made when the rest of them were made, weren't you?" Rachel glared right back at him. "And that was probably anywhere from a few months to a year before Solux came to power."

"You're losing me, Rachel," said the senator.

"Yeah, and no wonder! She's babbling, Senator!"

"And we're losing you, Mr. Potato Head. For now." Rach pulled the sides of the bag up over the head and zipped it shut. She took it into the hall and left it with the guards, so we didn't have to hear it buzzing.

We told Senator Burr everything we had learned, about the demons being highly sophisticated androids, and about Hell being nothing but a virtual reality, so sophisticated and so advanced that we could scarcely conceive of it.

For a long time she just sat behind her desk, looking down. I knew how she felt. The knowledge had been so disorienting that it was as though we were suddenly living in another universe. Finally she looked up.

"I want Katerina in on this," she said, and pressed a button on her desk. In a few seconds, a businesslike and apparently humorless young woman walked into the office. The senator introduced her as Katerina Goertz and said, "Tell her."

We told her. "Solux's team of hackers and hardware is at least three generations ahead of anything you've ever seen. Hell isn't real, it's virtual. They're comgening the whole thing."

She didn't tell us we were full of crap. She didn't ask where we had found all this out. She just said, "How?"

I tried to tell as much as we had figured out. "The Hand might have been ruling like Luddites, but in reality they've been moving ahead full bore. They've developed cyberspace and decking technologies that are incredible. When they damn people, they don't physically send them anywhere. The victim's mind—and probably their nervous system—is linked to a network that generates an enormously complex virtual environment. Hell."

Then Rachel told her about the demons being government-created androids. Katerina still didn't say anything, but I could see the news affected her. She looked almost excited.

"So that's the secret to Solux's power," I concluded. "Phony demons and a phony Hell. The demons are somehow networked into the Hell system. We have one of their functioning heads and all the disks that ran his own program."

"That's the thing in the hall?" Katerina asked.

"Yes. Mr. Beautiful, he calls himself. We thought maybe the codes in his head might be of some use."

Katerina nodded. "They will be. We're constantly trying to break the ICE that protects the Hand's data banks in the Pentagon. If these codes can access any of the Hand's data, we'll be way ahead of where we are now."

"Possibly," said Senator Burr, "on the way to somehow crashing the Hell program?"

Katerina thought for a moment before she answered. "That's a big jump. It may be possible. In theory, at least, any data can be corrupted. But it's a matter of fully understanding their code . . . and it depends on the hardware. . . ." She seemed to be thinking out loud. "I'd need a lot of information, and I don't even know how much I'll get from this . . . head. If what's there is usable, I'll just have to start chipping away the ICE a layer at a time and see how far I can get."

"One other thing should help," Rachel told Katerina. "We have an informant inside the Pentagon who calls himself Deep Throat."

"You what?" Her expression melted almost to room temperature.

"He's a programmer who backs up data generated by the Hell program. He wants to help, but he's stuck inside for now."

"We've got to get him out," Katerina said. "His help would be . . . invaluable."

"Well," I said, "maybe if you break some of that ICE we can learn how to get him out of there. But cracking open Beautiful's head is the next step."

"Sounds lovely," Senator Burr said with a sweet smile. "But tell me, Gideon, Rachel, are you able to enter Hell at will?"

"It takes psychopomps," Rachel said. "Wireless decks. We left two of them with a friend of ours."

"Dante?"

I smiled. "You've been keeping track of us."

"As best we can, but you do get around. The reason I ask is that we have a great number of *missing* allies. Some are former government officials who resigned rather than serve under the Hand. Others are activists who the Hand deemed too subversive to remain free. All of them will be crucial to reestablishing an honest government when Solux is overthrown. Of course, the Imperator has apprehended as many of them as possible. When we learned they were consigned to Hell, we believed that restoring them to life was impossible. After all, damned is damned. But now there may be a way to rescue them."

"I get it," I said. "We could go to Hell and try and free them." The senator nodded. "One problem, though. Even if we free their minds from Hell, they'll still be prisoners wherever they're held."

"Do you really think they'd be well guarded?" Rachel asked. "After all, there's no reason to think they're going to try to physically escape."

"One more thing for me to try and learn under that Pentagon ICE," Katerina said.

Senator Burr nodded. "We have people in there. If the prisoners are there, and we could pinpoint their location . . ." She shrugged. "Anything is possible. But one particular person in Hell could really do us some good." She looked inquiringly at Katerina.

"Verdi."

"Yes," said the senator. "Jeremy Verdi. He's a wonder."

"Taught me nearly everything I know," Katerina said. "He was trained by his father."

"Verdi as in Verdi language?" Rachel asked.

"That was his grandfather," Burr said. "His father was killed in a . . . doctrinal dispute with the Hand. That was the last straw for Jeremy. Everything he loved had been outlawed. The Hand tried to recruit him as a technopriest, but he came to us instead. He wrote most of the ICE that protects our communication lines from Hand intrusion."

"If anyone on earth can crash Hell," Katerina said simply, "it's Jeremy."

I looked at Rachel and she looked back at me. We were both dog tired, but we knew what we had to do. "Okay," I told the senator. "Get somebody to get the decks from Dante..." I looked at Katerina. "And you see what you can find out under that Pentagon ICE. And since we haven't had any sleep in a long time, we'll make use of your bunks for a while."

"And then?" said Senator Burr with a smile.

"And then we'll go back to Hell. It's starting to feel like home."

CHAPTER 26

Before we retired for a few hours of sleep, we went with Katerina as she took Beautiful into a large room filled with antiquated computers. Large vidscreens covered one wall near the units, and at the opposite end were tables covered with a clutter of computer parts. It reminded me of Aldous Xenon's loft. I wondered if everyone in the underground were tinkerers and juryriggers.

Rachel handed Katerina the data disks and then unzipped the bag. I reached in, took out the head, and set it on the work table. Beautiful's gaze swept the table, taking in the parts and the tools. "What's all this?" he said.

I smiled at him. "This is where you make your contribution to the Citizens' Freedom Front."

"Contribution? Hell yeah, long as you get me a new body soon—maybe one of them citizens, huh? So whaddya want me to contribute? I can put a small army out on the street for you, march on the Pentagon and take that freak Solux by force."

"Actually," Rachel said, "we were hoping for something much smaller. Your brain?"

"My brain? Come on, honey, quit joking and find me a new bod. Something about six feet, well endowed, you know what I mean? What about old Eshanti here? 'Course I'd have to see him stripped first. Is he buffed?"

I shook my head in mixed disgust and pity. "Beautiful, you give new meaning to the phrase, 'mental midget.'"

"Hey, smartass, come on down here and whisper that in my ear—I'll chew your freakin' face off!"

His jaws opened and closed, snapping futilely in my direction. Katerina lifted him by one horn and turned him over, peering into the spaghetti-like tangle of his neck.

"*Whoa!* Hey, put me down! You hear me? Two more seconds of this and I'll have you in Hell getting your skin pulled up over the top of your head, bitch! Then I'll line it with drain cleaner and sew you back up in it again!"

"There should be a control panel somewhere here . . ." Katerina dug her wiry fingers into Beautiful's scalp.

"You monkeys! Solux is gonna whack every one of you! I get you losers in a Hell pit, I'll use your skulls for soccer balls! Every goal a header! I'm warnin' you!"

Finally Katerina found a catch in Beautiful's thatch of hair. "Yes, here we are. . . ."

"Hey, that's my access panel! Look, you wanna think twice about gettin' in there." With a click, the back of Beautiful's head swung open. "Okay, forget what I said about the drain cleaner. Forget the soccer balls. Just let me hang around—I'd make a terrific paperweight!"

"Quiet, stumpy," Katerina said, and flicked a switch. The light of life went out of Beautiful's eyes, and he said no more. His face went slack, empty of all emotion. He was inarguably what we had known him to be, a machine with no life other than what had been placed there by its makers.

Still, I couldn't help but feel a little sorry to see him become inoperative. For all his faults, he was a spunky son of a bitch. He would have kept squawking when all that was left was a voice chip and a speaker.

"So long, Mr. Beautiful," I said, although I didn't give the dead machine a pat on the horns. Katerina looked at me oddly, and I said, by way of explanation, "We went through a lot together."

"And I'm glad there won't be any more," Rachel added, to which I could only say amen.

The bunks in the sleeping room were just as unyielding as before, but by then we could have slept on cement. I didn't dream about going to Hell. I was too tired to dream.

When Charles, the multi-server robot, awoke me, I didn't jump out of my bunk. In fact, his half-metal, half-flesh face somehow felt reassuring, like a faithful old family retainer. "Mr. Essshhh-anti," he said, "it is now 1600 hours, and there is a meal and nuh-nuh-news awaiting you."

I woke Rachel, and we met in a small dining room with Senator Burr, Katerina, and Derek Literati, who, true to form, scowled when he saw us. Our place settings held plates full of good, simple food, including turkey, fresh strawberries, brown bread, and hot, black coffee.

"My God," Rachel said, "where did you get strawberries?"

"We have contacts with many farmers," the senator said. "You'd be surprised how people close to the land value their freedom. Go ahead and eat, while Katerina fills you in."

Katerina had been busy while we were sleeping. The codes she had derived from Beautiful's head, along with the data on his disks, had let her chip deeper into the Hand's ICE than ever before. "It's tricky going," she said, "but we've learned a lot."

"Unfortunately not enough," Literati said, looking down at the dark and filmy surface of his coffee.

"Derek is referring to the matter of the missing commandos," Senator Burr explained. "We've come across nothing specific concerning them yet."

"But I am getting," Katerina said, "very close to accessing some highly classified files. What I *have* been able to access, though, are tertiary-level Hell data files. They confirm your data and our theories. The Front operatives and sympathizers who were condemned to Hell are being held by the Hand all right. They're in secret rooms in the Pentagon itself. *And* they're jacked into the Hell virt."

"All together?" I asked.

"No. Different Hell pits and tortures for each. The Hand is nothing if not imaginative." Katerina's face soured. "They've got flames, of course. They've frozen one of our people in ice. Whatever the victim fears most, that's what the Hand uses, be it rats or drowning . . . or even dentists."

"Now that's fiendish," I said, trying lamely to inject a note of levity into her depressing tale.

"It is indeed," Katerina said. "The scenario is constant drilling into a nerve, with only enough surcease of pain to make the agony ever fresh." So much for levity, I thought.

"How," Rachel asked, "can a government supposedly based on God be so adept at causing pain?"

"You're just figuring that out?" said Literati. "Took you long enough. Or maybe you were so busy causing pain that you didn't realize people were *suffering* it."

"That's enough, Derek," the senator said sharply. "You can't hold Rachel and Gideon responsible for this. And even if you could, they're our allies now." She smiled at us. "And the guiltiest sinners often make the most impassioned converts."

But Derek wasn't finished. "So we should try to recruit the Imperator?"

Senator Burr didn't say a word. She just glared at Literati. I was glad she wasn't looking at me like that.

"Sorry," he mumbled, and looked back down at his coffee.

"At any rate," Katerina said, "the Hand's tortures rival those of Dante's *Inferno*. In fact, they probably got a few ideas from him."

"And speaking of a more contemporary Dante," the senator said, "we've picked up the psychopomps from his apartment. So the gates of Hell are effectively open."

"They've been that way," Literati said, "ever since Solux took office." Well, I thought, at least he wasn't knocking me.

"So I guess it's time to go dangle our toes in hellfire again," I said.

The senator nodded.

"So what do we do?" Rachel asked. "Just go from pit to pit trying to free all the people on your list? I mean, since it's all virtual, they can't really hurt us."

"Don't count on it," Katerina said. "You could be hurt, even killed. From what I've learned, the reality and intensity of this virt is . . . overwhelming. If your virtual body suffers intense trauma in Hell, it can affect your brain wave patterns—increase your heart rate past its ability to pump the blood, cause extreme hyperventilation, even brain swelling. You could become a vegetable, and in a worst case scenario, theoretically implode.

"But not all the news is bad," she went on. "The demons in each Hell pit are only programmed to injure those they've been assigned to torture. This lets Hand ops deck in and out. I don't know, maybe the high-ups get their kicks from watching. But you shouldn't be attacked unless you attack first."

"So there are self-defensive features built into the program," Rachel said.

"Right. You fight them, they'll fight you. Some of the demons are ineffective, like the one in Pazuzu's Hell pit."

"Chamo," I said. "The, what is it, iambic pennameter guy."

"Pent*am*eter," Rachel corrected.

"Other demons are very powerful," Katerina went on, ignoring my futile attempt at poetic fluency. "You attack them, they'll kill you, maybe for real. So, for most of them, cleverness has to be your weapon."

"So let me get this straight," I said. "We have to go from pit to pit, figuring out how to outsmart each demon and free each victim? Judas priest, it sounds like one of those old pre-actideck comgames. I played a pirated one years ago, hated it."

Katerina shook her head. "It's easier than that. There's only one you have to free. He gets out, he can help us to free all the others at once. By crashing the Hell program."

"Jeremy Verdi," Rachel said.

"Exactly. We know now where they're holding him in the Pentagon, and you were right, Rachel, there's not much of a guard. It would be easy, once Jeremy was freed of the machine, to escort him out. Our moles know about all the air shafts and bomb tunnels in there, and now they'll know about these secret rooms."

"But if your agents can get to the rooms," I said, "why can't they just yank off the helmets and take the people out?"

Katerina shook her head. "Their minds have to be freed first. Otherwise, the violent transition would destroy their nervous systems. They'd never be the same."

I looked at Rachel. "No wonder Portillo and Ferlinghetti looked so whacked out when we pulled their plugs."

"That's something we don't want to happen to Jeremy," said Katerina. "We need that brain fully functioning."

"Is that likely?" Rachel asked.

Katerina nodded. "Reports are that, unlike the mobsters, Krystal Getty is as normal as she ever was, so there's no reason to think that Jeremy's brain waves will be altered if he's freed as the Getty girl was—within the logic of the Hell program. We'll have a couple stationed nearby in the Pentagon to get him out. If you can free him from . . . *Gack*."

"Something in your throat?" I said.

I was rewarded for my bad joke with an actual Katerina Goertz smile, the first I'd seen. "Gack is the name of the demon tormenting Jeremy Verdi, as if you couldn't guess."

"What's the scenario?"

"Gack is on one end of a long board, and Jeremy's on the other. Jeremy's end is over an abyss—bottomless, naturally. Jeremy has been starved, and the demon eats constantly. Gack moves, and the plank and Jeremy go into the pit."

"You think the virtual fall would kill him?" I asked.

"I do. So you've got to get Jeremy off the board with Gack's weight still on it."

"This demon," Rachel said. "Is he one of those powerful ones?"

"According to the spatial grids, he looks like a whopper."

"So we've got to outsmart him." I shrugged. "So far none of them have been top notch in the thinking department. Maybe we'll luck out with Gack."

"Gack," Rachel repeated. "He doesn't sound very bright, does he? I guess we might as well go."

We got up and Katerina led the way to the computer room. On the table were the two psychopomps and the remnants of Beautiful's head, along with some other machines I didn't recognize.

"We're going to monitor the two of you closely when you're in Hell—heart rate, brain function, how your minds and bodies react when you're there."

"Guinea-pigged all over, huh?" I sat down and let Katerina place sensors on my neck and temples. She did the same to Rachel, then stood back with Senator Burr and Smiley Literati.

"You're set," she said. "When you put on the decks, just think *Gack*, and that's where you'll go.

"Gack," I said. "Sounds like a lovely place to visit."

We put them on, thought *Gack*, and went back to that never-never-cyberland called Hell.

CHAPTER 27

Gack was big all right. The fattest guy I ever knew was my friend Larry Bergstrom, an ARC data pusher whose idea of a light lunch was two plates of quesadillas and four burritos. Gack could have split up to form a barbershop quartet's worth of Larrys and still have had a manager left over. He was also a lot more repulsive and smelly than Larry, and vastly outnumbered my old colleague in the breast department as well, having seven of them. His skin was a bright pink, where it wasn't covered with dirt and stains.

Gack was, as Katerina had told us, sitting on the safe end of a long plank. At least I think he was sitting. Those stumpy things barely protruding from the rolls of fat looked sort of like legs.

On the other end, the one hanging over the cliff, was a skinny blond kid in a sweat-stained t-shirt and shorts. The boy's bare arms, legs, and face were scarred as if by burns. He was in a wooden cage, watching as the demon scarfed down chunks of what looked like a huge hero sandwich stuffed with shell pasta.

When we got closer, Rachel and I could see that the pieces of shell pasta were in fact squirming grubs. "Howdy howdy!" the demon said heartily, as though he recognized us. "Wanta join me? Boy, this samwich is great! The maggots just burst in your mouth like little flavor packets—want a bite?"

"Pass, thanks," I said. Rach swallowed hard, then cleared her throat.

"Suitcherself. Needs a little more tar on it, though. Hey, you know what'd go great with this? Baby food. You got any on ya?"

"Uh, baby food?"

"Yeah. Fingers in particklar. Toddler fingers got more meat on 'em, but them baby fingers is sweeter. Mmm-*MMM*!"

"Hey!" The Verdi boy was calling us, and we looked over. He stuck his hands through the bars, pleading. "Can you get me something to eat? Please! I'm starving in here. All that fat slug does is eat, and my stomach feels like somebody scraped it with a bone. Please, just one of the maggots that drops from his sandwich! I'll eat *anything!*"

"Take it easy, son," Rachel said. "We're here to help."

A gigantic belch, reeking of tar and rotten flesh, washed over us from Gack's filthy tunnel of a throat. "'Scuse *me*," he said, and the words were no less odorous. "Say, if you wanta help, maybe you could get me some more tar for this samwich—makes them maggots slippy-slide right down. As for you, kid, shaddup or I'll splash some more acid on ya! Oh," he said, turning back to us, "the tar's over there, in the barrel right next to the acid."

"Get your own damn—" I started, but Rachel grabbed my arm and squeezed it hard, so I shut up.

"Sure," she said, "we'll be glad to." She walked over to several barrels filled with various bubbling liquids, and I followed, knowing she must be up to something.

"Use that there bucket!" the demon yelled, and Rachel nodded and picked up a huge bucket that had seen better millennia. "Go talk to him," she said, so I strolled over to the obnoxious pile of blubber.

"Maggots fresh?" I asked, not knowing what else to say.

"You betcha. I'm purty particklar about what I put in my mouth."

"Yeah, you seem to be a demon of taste."

"Ain't that the truth," Gack said, and punctuated his certainty by breaking wind. If his belch was foul, this was twenty times worse. I suspect fish swam up there and died, and then the cats that smelled the fish were trapped as well, and perished too. "Whoopsie-doo," said Gack. "Please fergive my rudeness."

I waved a hand in the air, as much to dispel the noxious green fumes as to acknowledge his apology. Then Rach was at my side, holding out the bubbling bucket to the demon. "Here you are," she said. "Add some tang to that sandwich."

"Aw, thanks," said Gack jovially. He opened his sandwich so that we could see the thousands of gray, yellow, and white maggots, all of them wriggling, and poured the vile black stuff over the mess. Then he closed the sandwich and took a large bite. I figured Rachel had spiked the tar with acid, but had my doubts as to whether even the stuff that had so viciously scarred Jeremy Verdi's virtual skin would have much effect on this appalling omnivore.

I needn't have worried. After four or five massive bites, Gack stopped chewing and stood there, his mouth open, maggots slithering out of it and down his chin to drop unnoticed to the ground. He dropped his sandwich, and the freed Gack-food, those that hadn't been sizzled by the acid, crawled off into the sanctuary of the nearby rocks, leaving trails of tar behind them.

"I don't feel so good," Gack said, staring straight ahead. "My tummy hurts." Then his eyes grew wide, and he started scratching at the place where his stomach was hidden beneath rolls of fat. "Agggg . . ." he muttered, choking on a combination of maggots and tar, as the acid kept working its way out through his flesh. "Agggg . . . gggaaaakkkk. . . ."

Whatever was in that acid was whizzing right along now. Bubbles popped on his skin, letting yellow fat and pink blood ooze out. His vast corpulence had become a giant mountain range composed of volcanoes, all erupting at once. Not a pretty sight.

Then he started to melt. Flesh, fat, blood, the little muscle underneath—running together until old Gack was hardly distinguishable as anything other than a pile of pink and yellow muck. But from somewhere in the mess came one final, bubbling cry of protest . . . "gaaaaaaaaakkkk. . . ."

"We've been introduced, thanks," Rachel said.

"Good work."

"Thanks," she said. "Now let's get the kid out of that cage."

It was a good thing Gack had melted in place. The weight of the gelatinous puddle was still enough to keep the board from tipping Jeremy into the abyss. I added my weight to the landward end while Rach walked out and unlatched the door.

"Thanks!" he said. "Now some food. . . ."

"Land of milk and honey coming up, Jeremy," Rachel said, but before she was finished the boy had gone, vanished just the way Krystal Getty had. I hoped the Front moles were there to get him out of the Pentagon safely.

"Well," Rachel said when she rejoined me. "Back to earth ourselves?"

"I can't wait," I said, but before we could think ourselves back, something shimmered in the air in front of us. Red-orange flames appeared, forming themselves into letters that read: *GARAGE*.

"Deep Throat," Rachel said. She took my hand and we both thought about the garage, and in less than a second we were there. In front of us was the familiar figure of Deep Throat, fingers twitching nervously.

"I'm taking a great risk in coming here," he said in a trembling voice. "Solux has ordered an increase in security. Don't think they haven't noticed your presence in Hell—they have. Luckily for you, not until after you'd been there and gone. There's more live monitoring now of all the pits, so stay out of Hell completely if you can."

"We have absolutely no desire to come back," Rachel said.

"Maybe you'll be safe then. But I'm in danger. They're ferreting out the spies and moles in the Pentagon, and they know there's a leak in the programming team. They're very close to tracing this WELL to me. You—or the Front—have to get me out of the Pentagon as soon as possible. I mean, you don't know what they do to their own who turn on them . . . it's horrible."

"The Front *wants* you out," I said, "to help crash the Hell program. How can we find you? 'Deep Throat' won't be on any office door."

"My name is Thomas Meaculp," he said. "Employee Code EKF64793, KFOWUVSX. Tell them to hurry! I must go. Now."

As he winked out of sight, Rachel and I thought ourselves back to earth. As before, it was like coming out of a rank well into fresh country air.

We took off our helmets to see a smiling Senator Burr. "Well done," she said softly. "Our agents have successfully shuttled Jeremy Verdi out of the Pentagon. As we speak, he should be in the back of a van which will eventually bring him here to the embassy."

"That's great," Rachel said, pulling the sticky sensors off her skin. "But we've got someone else in the Pentagon to bust out." We told her about Deep Throat, gave Katerina his name and code, and she said she'd run a locate on him from the Hand files right away.

By the time we finished telling the senator exactly how we had freed Jeremy Verdi, Katerina had found everything she needed. "Thomas Meaculp has a small private office in area three, section fourteen, suite F.

That's a subterrane, but he comes above at meal times to mess room 84. We've got an agent in the kitchen who can access that mess when he does, bring him into the dry storage dock."

"So how do you get him out?" I asked.

"Hijack a foodstuffs delivery truck. One goes in to that dock at 2300 hours. Meaculp will be eating dinner then."

"At eleven o'clock at night?" Rachel asked.

"He works second shift," Katerina explained. "It should be easy to bring him out in the truck."

"But how will he know what to expect?"

"He won't. Our agent on the serving line will contact him."

I frowned. "What if Meaculp thinks it's a Hand set-up? He's paranoid as hell. He might not go along."

Senator Burr finally spoke. "He would if you were in the truck."

The first thing I thought of was, why do I have to get the shit detail every time? Why can't I just sit around the embassy like Literati? But the senator had a good point. And since Rach and I were the only ones who had seen Meaculp, I could also guarantee we had the right guy, and not a Hand agent with a tracking device up his ass.

"Okay," I said. "Into the belly of the beast again. Do I go alone?"

"Hell no, partner," said Literati. "I'll be right with you."

"You?"

"Think I trust you to go into the Pentagon by yourself? I want this Deep Throat guy too bad for that."

It went a lot smoother than either Literati or I thought it might. I only had to kill one man.

CHAPTER 28

Fortunately, the man I killed wasn't an innocent. The two poor chumps who were driving the delivery truck ("Lamb of God Meats—Abattoir Fresh") went belly-up at the first glimpse of Derek Literati's autopistol. We waylaid them on the cloverleaf at the George Mason Bridge and Washington Memorial Parkway, tied them up, and stuck them in the back of a Front van for release when our operation was over.

Getting into the Pentagon complex was easy. They checked the truck, of course, but they looked for explosives, big bombs that threatened to make a crater out of the whole building, not the two small plaz autopees we had under our tidy white coats. We were waved on, and drove around to the mess hall loading dock on the north side.

A woman was standing in the darkness just inside the door, her face in shadow. "Pretty warm night," she said.

"Might rain, though," said Literati. The passwords given and returned, we opened the back of the van, unloaded several crates of meat onto a pneumodolly, and steered it up the ramp, onto the dock and through the door.

The large room was refrigerated and dimly lit. Standing in the shadows against the opposite wall, Thomas Meaculp was shivering from the cold, and possibly from fear as well. I stepped far enough into the light to show him my face and smiled reassuringly. He smiled in return, and his shivering decreased. "Let's go," I said, and turned toward the outside door.

Just then, another door opened, and a man in an all-black spansuit came in, looked at us, and said, "Meaculp, what is this?" He had a .230 God's Justice holstered at his hip.

Meaculp looked from me to the man in black, his mouth goggling like a gaffed fish.

"I thought as much," the man said. "We've been watching you, believer—or should I say *un*believer?"

"Hand security?" I asked.

"Yes. And who are you?"

"We're butchers," I said.

"May the Lord strike me dead if *that's* the truth," said the man, pulling the .230 from its holster.

I was quicker, and shot him once in the middle of the chest, as if I had been trained for such work. The silenced autopee was scarcely louder than a belch. "So he did," I said as the man fell forward onto his face. "Like I said, we're butchers."

Meaculp stood there, unable to move. He may have seen tortures in Hell, but I doubt he had ever seen a man shot down before. I grabbed him by the arm and walked him to the door, while Literati dragged the dead man behind some crates. The woman followed me.

"I have to come with you," she said. "I can't stay here now, not after the shooting."

I nodded, and we went out to the truck. Meaculp and the woman hid in the back. We got out with no further problems, met the Front van at the Tidal Basin, returned the bound deliverymen to their truck, and drove back to the embassy.

In the dining area, Jeremy Verdi was sitting at a table with Rachel. She got up and hugged me, holding me so long it almost got embarrassing. "It's okay," I said. "I'm fine." I grinned at Jeremy. Three empty plates sat in front of him. "You're looking better than the last time I saw you, Jeremy. Not still hungry, I hope?"

"Feel great," he said, beaming. The scars from Hell had vanished. "Ate four cheeseburgers and a quart of high-caff cola. Thanks a lot for what you did down there—or *in* there. I knew it was a virt all along, but that didn't keep the pain from being real."

"How did you know?" I asked him.

"Some of the edges weren't sharp enough, little holes in the programming, occasional gaps in Gack's movements, stuff like that."

"You up to speed on the program?"

"Kat's given me the debrief, but I been thinkin' about it while I ate, and a lot of it's fusin' my circuits. I could use some e-journal pieces on intentionality engines and Chinese box logic structure—and some more sugar. But what would help most is your Deep Throat guy. We're gonna need reams of data if we're gonna devise a crash bug. You spring him?"

I nodded and pointed. "Meet Thomas Meaculp."

"Uh, Tom is fine," Meaculp said.

Jeremy leapt to his feet and shook the man's hand. "All *right!* The brain trust is complete. We'll get together with Kat soon as she—"

He was interrupted by the entrance of Senator Burr and Katerina Goertz, both of whom looked way too serious for the happy occasion. The senator put on a smile for Meaculp.

"Mr. Meaculp, it's a pleasure to meet you. If what these young people say is true, you may be the most important man in the country right now."

Meaculp blushed scarlet. It was quite a leap from faceless bureaucratic drone. "Oh, well, I . . . it's good to be here."

"We're sure you'll be of great help to our cause."

"Oh, I hope so, but you see, I'm really not all that good a programmer. I mean, I know the general architecture of the Hell program, and I have ideas about ways to crash the system, but actually programming something that complex. . . ."

"Don't you worry about that," said the senator. "I think you and Katerina and Jeremy should put your heads together now and see what you can come up with." She turned to Rachel and me, and the smile grew several degrees cooler. "Rachel and Gideon, I'd like to ask you to join me in my office please. Derek, I'd like you to come too."

Rach and I didn't miss the glance that she exchanged with Katerina, who also looked at us strangely. Now what? Did they have some false Hand-planted evidence that we were traitors to the Front? Was Literati coming along to pop us?

In her office, Senator Burr sat at her desk, with Rachel, Literati, and me across from her. She took out a sheet of paper and looked at it. "In the past few hours, Katerina has broken through more of the Hand's ICE to discover the fate of the commandos who disappeared six years ago."

I thought Literati was going to jump through the ceiling. "What? Where are they? Are they alive?"

Senator Burr held up a hand to calm him. "In a moment, Derek. I just want to tell you, all three of you, that what you're about to hear will be extremely . . . disorienting. Even more so than learning that Hell was virtual." She looked down at the paper. "This is a highly classified memorandum to Transgressions Leadership from the Hand of God Command Council. It concerns an operation that took place six years ago with the code name *Born Again*. I'll read it to you:

"'Several months ago, the CFF launched a godless terrorist strike at the heart of the Pentagon, with the intention of assassinating our beloved leader, the Imperator. Thanks be to God, the strike was unsuccessful.

"'The official story was that all the terrorists were killed in the fighting, but, due to the successful completion of the *Born Again* project, the truth is being revealed to the Transgressions Leadership.

"'The Lord delivered six of the CFF terrorists alive into our hands. These six were then given over to the Imperator's technopriests that they might fulfill the will of God by transforming these sinners into new people, instruments of the Hand of God, through experimental technology and procedures.

During a period of five months, Hand scientists rebuilt these captives, resculpting their skulls, altering their facial appearance and fingerprints, implanting new retinas.

"'But they did not stop at the physical. They installed dozens of memory overlays and Jung banks to create totally new personalities, new minds to replace the old. The six terrorists were transformed from enemies of the state and of God into pliant servants of the Hand.'"

Senator Burr stopped reading and looked up uncomfortably. "There's a list," she said, "of the commandos who were captured and the names of the new identities they were given."

By now Literati was a tightly coiled spring. "Marcus," he said. "And Claudette? Are they still alive?"

The senator nodded her head. "Yes. Let me read the list. All of the names will be familiar to you, Derek. . . ." She looked at us then, and I thought I saw pity as the strongest of the emotions sweeping her usually passive face. "And some will be to you." Then she read, "'Harold Balk became Adam Schonbrun. Leena Gordon became Deirdre O'Connor. Vic Tavaleo became James Hennelly. Mick Malone became Swivel O'Leary.'" She put the list down.

"That's only four!" Literati said. "What about Marcus?"

"Marcus is here," said the senator. "And Claudette."

"On the list?" Literati asked.

"On the list," she said. "*And* here." She looked back down at the paper. "'Marcus Vanders became Gideon Eshanti. And Claudette Simeon became Rachel Braque.'"

CHAPTER 29

There are no words to describe what hearing that news was like. It wasn't like hearing that your mother or father or best friend or wife has suddenly died, because, as unsettling as those things are, they're within the realm of possibility.

But to be told that you are not who you think you are, that you are someone entirely different, and that all the thoughts, emotions, features—in short, all the elements that make you *you*—are *lies* . . . that's something else again. That's something in a whole different galaxy.

And I guess that's why we couldn't believe it.

I laughed. Rachel was totally expressionless; I laughed again, trying to make her see the humor in it.

"You don't believe it," Senator Burr said, holding the paper in the air. Literati took it like a man in a dream.

"*No!*" I said. "It's crazy, absolutely nuts!"

"Why do you say that?"

"Because I *know* who I am! I mean, what if somebody told you that you weren't Senator Erin Burr? What would you think?"

"First, I'd think they were crazy. Then, if it came from a reliable source, I'd look at the evidence. And when Katerina brought me this memo, that's exactly what we did, Gideon." She leaned forward and looked at me intently. "We concentrated on you. We already had your data files, along with Rachel's. But when we tried to ascertain the truth of them, we failed every step of the way. Gideon Eshanti does not exist before six years ago. Earlier than that, there's only a phosphor trail laid by the Hand. Follow it back far enough, and it vanishes.

"There is no one who knew you at university, no one who knew you in high school. You're in the computer banks, but you're not in the yearbook."

"That's ridiculous," I said. I was getting angry now. "I have my high school yearbook, and one from college, and I'm there in both."

The senator opened a drawer of her desk and took out a book I recognized. It was my high school yearbook, the Ralph Reed Senior High *Banner* of 2081. "This copy belongs to Richard Humlin," she said. "One of our operatives brought it in just minutes before you returned from the Pentagon."

"Sure," I said, "Richie and I were both on the track team."

She passed the yearbook over to me. "Find your picture."

I opened the book. There were all the faces and all the names that I remembered—Noah Silva, Eric Brubaker, Dave

Rittenhouse, Nick Setthachayanon—but there was no one between Janice Emery and William Evans. I looked again, thinking that I was on the wrong page, that somehow my photo and data had gotten lost. I riffled the pages, hoping that I would magically jump back into place.

But it didn't happen. Gideon Eshanti was not in this copy of the *Banner*. Puzzled, I looked up at Senator Burr.

"They could prepare one doctored yearbook," she said, "and place it among your belongings. But they couldn't prepare three hundred more, burglarize the houses of all the graduates, and replace the spurious yearbooks with the real."

I could only shake my head and look at the place where I should have been.

"It makes sense," Rachel said in a voice so strange and flat that I thought someone else was in the room with us. "It explains our combat proficiency, why we were able to outfight the Hand agents that first night, why we know so much about weapons . . . why Dr. Clean told us we had already had facial reconstruction." She looked up at me. "Why we're both orphans, and have no siblings. You know as well as I do, Gideon, that we have no past."

"No!" It wasn't me protesting this time, but Derek Literati. He had leapt to his feet and was glaring down at me. "This is *impossible!* I know Marcus Vanders, I grew up with him, we were like brothers, and *you're not him!* I would *know, I would!*"

"I thought you looked familiar when I first saw you," I said quietly, afraid to add more evidence to convict myself of being someone else, but unable not to. "Maybe I knew you. Before."

"All right," Literati said through gritted teeth. "We'll settle this once and for all. "Stand up, *Eshanti*." He said it with violence, and I stood up facing him. We were only a foot or so apart.

Suddenly he barked, "*Five!*" and brought up his hands in a flurry of movement. His arms crossed and straightened, his elbows bent, he turned from side to side, now thrust a hip, now whipped out a hand, turned around, reached back, turned again, high-fived, all in a tenth of the time it takes me to tell it.

And I followed his every move, slapping his hands, bumping his arms and hip, as perfectly as though he were doing the lightning-fast series of movements in a mirror.

When we finished with our arms on each other's shoulders, his eyes were as wide and frightened as mine. I hadn't planned a thing, hadn't even thought about responding to his moves. I just did it, the way I must have done it hundreds of times when we were kids, to show the rest of the world that we were one, we were brothers, Derek and Marcus. Friends forever.

"My dear God," Literati breathed, looking deeply into my eyes. ". . . Marcus?"

I didn't know. I still couldn't believe it. I shook my head. "I . . . maybe. . . ."

He dropped his arms and stepped back as though he were scared of me. Part of me wanted to grab him and hold him. He was the only friend that I had before Rachel, and yet he was a stranger to me, as I was to him.

"You're Marcus all right," he said. "They might change the retinas, but they can't change the soul."

His face softened then, and he extended a hand to me. When I took it, he hugged me. In his embrace, I remembered him, and the memory made me know who I had to be, despite the thousands of other memories that told me I wasn't.

I sat down next to Rachel and took her hand. She looked lost. Derek knelt by her chair and took her other hand, and smiled at her. "Claudette," he said. "I'm glad you're back with us. Both of you."

"But how could they have done it?" she said dully. "Remake our faces, our bodies, our . . . minds?"

"Some rumors filtered through to us two, three years ago," said Derek, "about a Transgressions operation up in Annapolis. They had some elite infiltration squad there for some top-secret undercover op. But they weren't there to be trained. They were there to have something else done to them. The rumors said Transgressions had some new techs on facial remapping. Body surgimorphs, too. But what really got our attention was the story that this was supposed to be the ultimate undercover team, not just because they changed their appearance, but because they weren't going to be aware of their mission or even their true identities. The Hand was going to reprogram them. We never heard any more about it, though."

"But how?" Rachel said. "You can't turn thoughts into data!"

"The acti-deck did," I said. "Maybe the Hand has secretly perfected it."

Senator Burr looked at Rachel kindly. "Claudette, I know this must be terribly hard to—"

Rachel shook her head. "I can't . . . please, don't call me that. I know that . . . it must be who I am. But I can't change back, not that fast. Everything in me tells me that I'm Rachel Braque." She pressed her eyes shut, trying to make sense of it all. I knew how she felt. Exactly.

"I can't be Marcus either," I said. "I'm sorry, but . . . Gideon Eshanti is who I am. Maybe someday I'll learn to be Marcus again, but not yet. I don't have time to learn to be myself. Not while the people who did this to us are still controlling our lives. Let's keep doing what we've been doing. Let's tear down the Hand. Then there'll be time enough to be . . . Marcus and Claudette."

Senator Burr nodded brusquely. "A sensible decision. But there's another question that concerns me."

"Why?" Rachel said. "Why did the Hand change us? Why the different personalities? What else does the memo say?"

"Nothing. Just that Transgression Leadership should distribute to their subordinates the fictitious names under which the six would go into the world, to insure that they not be harassed or arrested in any way."

"They must have changed their minds a few days ago," I said. "What made them decide to kill us?"

Rachel abruptly looked up. "What about Brian Avery?" she said. "Seven were marked to be scrubbed that night, but Avery wasn't on the list."

"He was much younger than the others, too," I said. "He would have only been about twelve when the commando raid occurred. You know what I think?"

"What?" Rachel asked.

"I think Brian Avery was a red herring. I don't think he did a damn thing wrong in his life. I think the Hand scrubbed him just to screw us up, to try and tear apart the pattern so that we wouldn't put the pieces together in the right way."

"Sacrifice an innocent kid?" Rachel said. "Just to throw off anyone looking for links between the scrubs?"

"They've done far worse than that," Derek said.

"But we still don't know why the whole setup," I said. "Why the total personality reconstruction? Katerina wasn't able to find any more in the data banks?"

Senator Burr shook her head. "Not yet. There are related memos, but those are still under ICE that she has not yet cracked. I suspect, though, that with Jeremy here, they won't stay secret for long."

"New identities, new memories," Rachel mused aloud, "and then sent back into society. But where? They were all inserted on the fringes of Solux's kingdom of heaven on earth. They were all outlaws in some way. Except for us."

"And we *dealt* with outlaws," I added. "It's almost as if we all were placed into situations that might eventually bring us into contact with. . . ."

"The Citizens' Freedom Front," the senator finished for me. "Yes. I had thought of that. Even you two were placed into a branch of law enforcement in which you would deal with all aspects of illegal technologies, from which, were you so inclined, you might possibly be subverted into the underground. As they well knew, you already had a . . . predilection for it." She smiled. "But again, back to the *why*. We just don't have the answer."

"Maybe they tried to scrub us because what they had planned wasn't working," I said. "Maybe we didn't do what we were supposed to. Or maybe we were starting to become something the Hand didn't like."

"They may not have liked it," the senator said, "but I do. Your service has been invaluable to us. And I'm sure the Hand didn't intend that. But there's one other question. I have a possible answer, though I'd like your opinions. What did your commando team discover inside the Pentagon that made you abort your mission?"

"I think they . . . we must have learned about Hell," I said. "That it was virtual."

"I concur completely," Senator Burr said. "I wish we had learned that six years ago. The Hand might have been destroyed by now."

"It still will be," I said, and Rachel nodded in agreement.

CHAPTER 30

Jeremy, Katerina, and Tom Meaculp had been in the computer room for five hours straight when they finally stumbled into the dining room, their eyes bleary.

Rachel, Derek, and I were doing what we could to help the cause, monitoring Voice of God transmissions. Derek and I were on the two channels of state-run vids, and Rach was on the radio. There's nothing more boring than propaganda seen (we jumped to our feet expectantly when the three hackers came in).

"So," Derek said, "what's new?"

"A lot," Katerina answered. "Having these two around is like having half a dozen extra brains. I'm still chipping away at the Pentagon ICE, while Jeremy and Tom have been putting their heads together on the Hell program."

"It's altogether awesome," Jeremy said. "If what Tom's saying about Hell's on-the-fly texture generation systems is accurate, then they must be compressing data with string space fractals."

"You lost me there," I said.

"String space fractals," he repeated more slowly, as if anyone should grasp his meaning as long as they could hear the words. He was wrong. "They're only theory in the underground e-journals, but the Hand *has* to have them. Borrows a notion from physics. The compression program creates an ancillary, notional dimension in the memory manager and calls data from there when it needs it. Makes a system's memory potentially limitless."

"Sounds like that would rule out any memory overwriting bugs," said Katerina.

Tom Meaculp held up a finger shyly. "Keep in mind that the Hand's ICE systems are . . ." He struggled for the right words. ". . . prohibitively redundant and thorough. I doubt if anything we could make here with these machines would get very far in Hell. I'm not even certain the system *is* crashable."

"What about a virus," Katerina said thoughtfully, "that attaches itself to graphic libraries and overwrites images? The system might crash when it can't find an image it needs."

Tom Meaculp shook his head apologetically. "The crash would only be localized. That's essentially what happened when I first contacted Rachel and Gideon."

"Ah, we'll come up with it," said Jeremy, biting into the first of three cheeseburgers that Charles the multi-server had set in front of him. "We just need a blast of inspiration. And a case of Yoo Hoo Bold Formula."

"And," Tom said, "Massimo Eddie."

Jeremy lost his smile. "Yeah. That's what we need to talk to you ops types about."

"Massimo Eddie?" Rachel said. "The First Damned Man?"

"You got it." We sure did. Everybody knew about Massimo Eddie. The only person who was supposed to have seen all of Hell and returned to tell about it. But apparently what he saw had driven him mad, so that he could only relate his experience in bits and pieces. We had all heard some of the broadcasts in which the Hand had allowed him to tell about what he'd seen. The guy was as twisted as a cup of noodles. He was Solux's pet bogeyman, dragged out whenever the populace needed a good scare. Hell was real, all right. Just ask anybody who had ever heard Massimo's ravings.

"So what do we need that wacko for?" asked Katerina.

"You haven't come across anything on him beneath the ICE?" Katerina shook her head. "You will," Tom went on. "In fact, you'll have to if we want to locate him. It shouldn't be difficult if you're looking. Any high-ranking Hand official should have the location stored in his computer."

"You haven't gotten around to the why yet," Katerina said.

Jeremy swallowed another huge lump of cheeseburger. "Because he's got dope we need on Hell."

"How can he if it doesn't really exist?" Derek asked. "He's just another Hand con, right?"

"No," Tom said. "Massimo was head of the quality assurance technician team who tested the boundaries of the beta version of the Hell code."

"You mean like a guinea pig in a psychopomp?" I said.

"Exactly. Sections of the system were still buggy, and he suffered severe brain damage as a result."

"See, the way the pomps work," Jeremy said, "is they've got cutting-edge intentionality engines, ten times more complex than the old Acti-Decks. Basically they're for the guys who run the place, since they got to be able to get around fast. The pomps scan for the Hell areas you're aware of and offer them as an option. If you don't know about a place, you ain't gonna get there."

"That's right," Tom said. "But Massimo wound up in places . . . he didn't know about. Everywhere, really, and he wasn't prepared for it. It left him mad, prone to bizarre visions, and possessed by demons whose voices speak through him. But because he's the only person who has experienced the entire contours of the system, he's also the only one who might have the knowledge to bring it down. *If* he's sane enough to communicate it."

"But if the Hand knows he's got all this secret knowledge," I said, "why keep him alive?"

"One more fragment of the lie," Tom answered. "One more thing for people to believe in. And fear."

Katerina stood up and wiped her mouth with her napkin. "I'll have that location in ten minutes."

She was wrong. It took only five.

"He's at the old Lee Mansion across the river," she said, beaming. "They use it as a retreat for the Five Fingers, meetings, seminars . . . but Massimo Eddie is held in an upstairs room."

"Look," said Derek, "do you really need the guy himself? I mean, that's a major operation . . . or would talking to him be enough?"

"We just need data," Jeremy said. "It might even be in the form of a complex algorithm. If we got somebody in there to see him, who knew what to ask for and how to handle him. . . ."

"We've got connections with the cleaning service," Katerina said, "so we might be able to put one person in there. A woman."

All eyes, including my own, went to Rachel. "Do I need to volunteer?"

"Can you get her in?" Derek said. "Safely?" I liked . . . and distrusted . . . hearing my biggest concern spoken in his voice.

"Shouldn't be a problem," Katerina said. "I'll make the links now."

Derek stood up. "Jeremy, Tom, you brief Claud . . . uh, Rachel on what she has to get out of Massimo, while I clear this whole thing with the senator."

The cleaning service was scheduled to send in a woman the next day at ten o'clock. When the time came, Rachel kissed me goodbye and went off in a laundry van that would link with the cleaning service's truck. She had spent the previous hours learning, not about Massimo Eddie, but how to pose as a cleaning person. The proper security countermeasures had been taken, but nothing would protect her from using a drain opener to clean grout. Might as well wear a sign around her neck saying SPY.

It was my turn to wait now. I knew she had to spend the whole day inside the Lee Mansion, but I kept hoping she would show up sooner. Nonetheless, she didn't return until six o'clock, smuggled into the embassy beneath the rear seat of a British undersecretary's car. Everyone else gathered around her to see what she had learned—I was just glad she had come back at all.

Her white uniform was smeared with a dozen different colors of paint, but she was smiling. "I got something," she said, and took off one of her white leather, rubber-soled shoes and took out a piece of paper. It too was daubed with paints, but had some kind of formula on it. A lot of Greek letters, numbers, a couple of square root symbols, some brackets, and some other things I didn't even recognize.

"This guy writes like he's got the palsy," Jeremy said.

"It wasn't him," Rachel said. "That's my writing. Reason it looks so bad is I was trying to hold a mop and bucket while I was copying it."

"Well, it's a computer algorithm of some sort."

"Did he say what it was for?" asked Senator Burr.

"Matter of fact, he did. And I quote, 'Fight him, he's pro-grammed to win—the key, the key,' and then he smeared this on the walls with paint."

"It could be an algorithm to allow us to defeat the upper echelons of demons," Tom said.

"Whoa," I said. "Upper echelons? What's all this?"

"Look, we'll fill you in later," Jeremy said, turning back toward the computer room. "I really want to get right on this. Come on, Tom, Kat, let's board this and play with it."

"Vivid," said Burr as the three techs closed the door be-hind them, "let's get back to those infiltration plans. Fine job, Rachel. Take a good rest now. You deserve one."

Then Rachel and I were alone. "Doesn't anyone," she said forlornly, "want to hear about how I did it?"

I laughed. "I do, if for no other reason than you look so darn cute in that uniform."

She scowled at me, but then her face grew serious. "He really was mad, Gideon. Absolutely insane. I was never so scared in my life. He had . . . others inside him."

"How did you get in, Rach?"

She smiled. "You mean how did you get in, *Estrellita*. I went into the mansion looking scared. Not scared I was going to get caught, but scared of what might be in there. The guards were like most Hand guards—sadists. Nasty bastards. First thing they asked me after they checked my ID was why I looked so nervous. So I told them, in this really awful accent, that I had heard about a scary man in here, that my friend Carmen had told me.

"That was all I needed to say. They marked me as a fly whose wings they could pull off and assigned me first thing to go clean 'Big Ed's' room. I pretended to be even more frightened, and said that Carmen had told me all about 'Big Ed,' and please not to make me go in there. But they just laughed and led me upstairs to Massimo Eddie's room, unlocked it, and shoved me in, along with my equipment. They locked the door behind me and told me they'd come back in an hour."

She was quiet for a moment, then went on. "The room was like something out of a nightmare, Gideon. It was a fair-sized bedroom with a bed and a chair and a chest of drawers, but the rest was all paint, gallons of the stuff, as well as dozens of brushes, and all well used. The walls, ceiling, floors—everything was painted in every conceivable color. Maybe there were patterns, but I sure couldn't see any. It just looked as if someone had splashed it on without rhyme or reason.

"But when I saw Massimo Eddie, I realized I was wrong. He was in a smock so stained with paint that at first I took him for part of the wall. And he had these long blond dreadlocks and beard, so that you could hardly see his eyes. He held a brush in one hand and was looking at the wall as though he was trying to memorize it. Deep thought was involved in every touch of paint to wall, though I don't know what he intended.

"I called his name, but he didn't answer, so I scanned the room for cameras and mikes, but didn't spot any. Then I touched his shoulder, and he swung around and looked at me. And then we talked.

"I tried to make him understand why I was there. I told him that we were trying to end the thing that had destroyed his mind. And he spoke back to me in voices. Sometimes it was him, and sometimes it was other voices."

"He was . . . possessed?"

"Gideon, he was worse than possessed. Priests might be able to exorcise a real demon. But Eddie's demons are permanently integrated into his cortex, separate bits of comgen consciousness. They follow their own logic, and they're never going to go away."

"What was the painting for?"

"It focused his energies. Creating kept the voices quiet for as long as he could concentrate. But when I tried to get him to help us, they came out in force. It was as though he had a block programmed into his brain that kept him from revealing anything to me that could harm the Hell program."

"So what did you do?"

"I told him to fight it, and when he couldn't, when all the different voices kept screaming out of his throat, I told him to paint. And he did. He slapped the algorithm on the wall, moaning and grunting all the time, and I copied it just as he painted it. When ne was done, he collapsed, and I held his head in my lap for a long time, until he felt better. Then the guards came to let me out. As you can see, I had paint all over my uniform, and I guess they thought he attacked me or something, so they got a real laugh out of that.

"I spent the rest of the day cleaning their damn bathrooms and showers, with the algorithm stuck in my shoe."

"Why your shoe?"

"I figured it was the only place the guards might not put their hands."

I could feel my cheeks grow red. "And were you right?"

"They didn't bother me," she said, and kissed me lightly on the lips. I grabbed her for a longer one, and she showed no hesitation in cooperating.

"I was worried about you," I said when we came up for air.

"I know. And I was worried about you." She looked at me teasingly. "What would you ever do without me?"

"I don't know. But I know what I'd like to do with you."

"Gee, I don't know, I'm pretty tired. When a woman's been working hard all day. . . ."

"Oh, shut up," I said, and kissed her again. As it turned out, she wasn't *that* tired.

CHAPTER 31

First thing next morning, we had a meeting with the three techs—Derek, Vivid, and Senator Burr. I felt great, and Rachel looked well rested, but Tom had bags under his eyes, and Katerina looked wasted. Jeremy was as zippy as ever. It must have been the sugar.

"We learned a lot last night," he explained, nibbling on a Danish. "There was a helluva lot in Massimo Eddie's algorithm. Let me give you the background first. Hell's structure is divided into three large territories, each ruled by a major demon, Belial, Mephistopheles, and Beelzebub. Each one of these guys has his own sanctum in Hell, surrounded by the smaller Hell pits, like the ones that I was held in. But while anyone with a pomp can cruise the pits, you try and walk into the sanctums, you're gonna get fried."

"Why?" I asked.

"They're the personal domains of Solux's top three associates," Tom said. "The demons you've met up to now have been entirely computer generated. But the three major demons are idealized c-space reps of real people—the Engineer-General, who's also the primary designer of the Hell program, the Director of the Five Fingers, and the President of Churches United for the Imperator. And their sanctums are off limits to everyone except themselves . . . and Satan."

"Wait a minute," Rachel said. "You mean there's a c-space Satan in there too?"

Tom nodded. "Someone has to be lord in Hell. 'Better to reign in Hell than serve in Heaven.'" He pursed his lips. "Milton, I believe."

"Milton who?" Jeremy asked.

Tom sighed. "You need to get away from your computers and read more."

"So what's the drill?" I asked. "How do we bring these big boys down?"

"We don't have to bring down all of them," Jeremy said. "The grid goes from a demon to Satan, like one of those business charts. Satan's the top box, and the three demons are in a horizontal row beneath him, so you only have to go through one to get to the big guy."

"Why do we have to get to the big guy at all?" Rachel asked. Fair question, I thought. I was damn tired of messing with demons, robot or real.

"Because Satan himself is one of the last layers of ICE protecting the Hell-spawner program."

"Spawner program, Jeremy?" said Senator Burr.

"Yeah, the file server, the program that generates all the pits and lairs in Hell. Once Satan's ICE is wiped, we'll be able to launch a survey program into the code that generates an individual Hell pit. The bug will trace that code back to the spawner. That's the only way we can learn how to write the program to crash it. *Then* we have to figure out how to deliver it to the main computer room itself."

"Which is probably in the Pentagon," I said. "Guarded as heavily as Solux herself."

"We can access it," said the senator, "if we can find the location. Our people inside may be able to help. Mr. Meaculp, have you any ideas?"

"No, I've never been there. I couldn't even e-mail or modem the room. I had to download everything to disks and send them through a tube system to the address, *miraculum sepulcrum.*"

"God, I'm sick of Latin," Rachel muttered.

"One thing's for sure," Jeremy said. "We can't get any further until old Cybersatan's dead."

"And no doubt," Rachel said, "you want somebody for this job who already knows their way around Hell, and who won't be crashed out by the trip there, but will be ready to fight."

"You got it," Jeremy said. "The good part is that it's not going to be as bad as you think."

"Why not?"

"Because Massimo Eddie's algorithm told us, among other things, how to kick Satan's butt from here to Heaven."

"When this is all over," Rachel said with a thin smile, "I want a state named after me. So how do we beat Satan?"

"You beat Beelzebub first. His governing consciousness is that of Patrick Fallon, the President of Churches United for the Imperator. He'll be the easiest of the three to get through, since your Hell personas already have everything you need. Unfortunately, he's also the most repulsive."

"Repulsive?" said Rach. "Why?"

"Beelzebub was the Lord of the Flies," Tom answered. "And that's how he appears, as a giant insect made up of millions of flies and held together by the sodden dust of corpses."

"Lovely conceit," Senator Burr said softly.

"He's been programmed with the ability to reintegrate if he's blasted to pieces," said Jeremy. "So you need something to hold the pieces apart. But don't worry, you'll have it."

"And what about Satan?"

"Don't worry about him either," Jeremy said. "He doesn't know it, but thanks to Massimo, he's now programmed to lose. His only really effective weapon is his lying mouth, so don't let him throw you. Keep concentrating on blowing him away, and you will."

"Well," I said, "let's get started. It isn't every day you get to blow away Satan, even if he is just a bunch of data."

So we went into the computer room, plunked on our psychopomps again, monitored by Jeremy and Katerina, and away we went. I kept hoping that going back and forth to Hell so many times would make the damn thing easier, but it didn't. Although I kept telling myself that the pain wasn't real, my brain didn't believe me. But soon enough we were there, in Beelzebub's throne room, and I saw what Tom and Jeremy meant about repulsive.

The first thing that hit me was the buzzing. It sounded as though we were in the middle of a beehive. But these weren't bees. They were flies—big, fat, nasty, dark blue mothers. The grotto-like room was filled with them, and their presence in the air made it blue-black, like a dense, particulate fog. We didn't even open our mouths to talk, for fear the bloated insects would fly inside.

Things hung from the ceiling, and from twisted stalactites that extended in some places nearly to the floor. They had been people, but they were now only husks, sucked as dry as the president of Solux's United Churches sucked his parishioners of their money. It seemed fitting that his counterpart in Hell should be a bloodsucker.

Some of the forms were twitching, and I wondered if they were still alive. They were probably the damned, enemies of the state who Solux had ordered put to the mental torture of her cyberhell. Or possibly they were Patrick Fallon's personal enemies, and he came down here, dwelt in his cybernetic persona, and tortured them himself. Maybe he was even here now. But we didn't want to find him before we found something to fight him with.

It took us a long time. Jeremy must have miscalculated the visibility in the place. It was like walking through a thick fog you could feel. We had to keep shaking ourselves as the flies settled on us. I whacked one of them, but the black slime and dark red blood that smeared my hand discouraged me from smashing another.

I stumbled over the bazooka before I saw it. When I picked it up, its heft was rewarding. Rachel walked into something soon afterward, and I heard her hiss through her teeth. When she held it up, I saw that it was a bucket, the same one she had filled with tar and acid for Gack. Maybe our Hell personas had access to everything we had previously handled in Hell, like a learned memory or one of the quaint games of our great-grandparents, where your character gathered an inventory impossible to carry in real life.

It didn't matter, because we were hoping that these might be the only things we would need. I tucked the bazooka under my arm, put my hands over my mouth to try and keep the flies out of it, and shouted, *"Fallon!"*

And a voice answered. It was as thick and dense and buzzing as the atmosphere in the grotto, more like a hundred voices than one, and a blue light glowed through the constantly shifting curtain of flies, brightening with every word. "Who calls Fallon?" it said. "*Beelzebub* reigns here! Come! Stand before his throne!"

We walked toward the light. It seemed like it was hundreds of yards away, since going through the flies made inches feel like feet. At last we got close enough to see the creature that had spoken. It stood in a hollow in the face of a jagged cliff, thirty yards off the floor of the grotto, and what it looked like most was a fly.

It must have been nearly ten feet long from its bulging, multi-faceted eyes to the end of its swollen abdomen, and its wingspread would have made one of those extinct condors look like a canary. Those wings were trembling as though it was getting ready to fly, and I somehow knew it was going to come straight for two fresh-faced interlopers.

"Behold the majesty of Beelzebub!" it said. "Fall on your knees, mortals, and worship!"

"If we do," I said, figuring I could always spit out the flies that swarmed into my open mouth, "I'm afraid we'll crush a few dozen of your followers, flyboy."

That made the wings start in a-whirring. "You come to my sanctum, and then you mock me?"

"Sure," said Rachel, "but only until we're ready to swat you!"

That did it. Beelzebub came down on us like an old Spad biplane, spewing a greenish-blue ichor from somewhere under those eyes. A few drops hit my skin, and they felt like liquid fire. I threw up the bazooka and let it rip. The shell caught the big bug right in the head, smashing it to pieces and tearing into the body. Bug guts and blood went everywhere, and we both put our heads down to avoid getting the shower in our eyes.

When we looked again, the Lord of the Flies was in half a zillion pieces on the rock floor of the grotto. "The tar!" I yelled, getting a few of the demon's ex-worshippers stuck under my tongue.

But it was too late. The mass of fly glop drew together like somebody had turned on a vacuum cleaner, and in less than two seconds Beelzebub had reformed himself. Hell, he had even made himself bigger by the volume of however many additional flies and dried corpses had been within ten yards of him. He looked real mad.

"This time," I said to Rach, shouldering the bazooka again, "throw the tar *first*."

"Scum! I shall suck all the moisture from your withered corpses!" said the bake sale's nightmare, wings humming like mad as he slowly ascended.

"Withered corpses wouldn't *have* any moisture," I informed him as he rose. "*Now,* Rach!"

She flung the tar directly beneath where Beelzebub was hovering, and the cocky bastard didn't even get off a shot of sizzleskin before I sent another shell at him. I was closer now, so it ripped him even worse than the first one. He blew apart in much the same funky cloud as before, but this time he was doomed to stay apart. His countless pieces fell like heavy rain upon the tar beneath and stayed right where they had landed.

But that doesn't mean it wasn't trying. When I looked more closely, I could see that the tar was moving. Every piece of the demon had become a big blue fly, stuck tight in the tar, trying to join together with its mates. Eventually they stopped struggling and lay still, and, as they did, slowly the flies in the air started dropping too, until none were left, and we were standing in several inches of dead bugs.

"This," Rachel said, "is disgusting."

"At least we can breathe through our mouths again."

Instead of looking relieved at this news, Rachel's eyes widened at something over my shoulder. I turned around, half expecting to see that Beelzebub had reformed himself into a dead-fly-and-tar monster, but instead I saw an opening into the rock face of the cliff where the demon had perched. A red light streamed from it. "Was that there before?" Rachel said.

"Not that I noticed. Maybe we just opened it."

"The door to Satan's sanctum?"

"Could be. Let's see if the welcome mat has little pitchforks on it."

We walked toward the opening with a slow, shuffling gait, which squashed fewer dead flies than a bold tread. It was a noisy trek, with a lot of crackles and pops, and squashy liquid sounds, and I was glad my shoes were virtual.

The opening led to a tunnel lit by unseen hellfire. A good clue that the whole thing was virtual was that light sources here could come from the things they illuminated, pretty much ignoring some law of physics or another.

But we'd forgotten such niceties of natural law by the time we entered Satan's domain, the cyberspace at the end of the tunnel. The only good thing we found there was a laser rifle and a combat buddy, one of those lethal little piggyback pals, with which Rachel quickly armed herself. I still had the bazooka, and it was loaded for demon.

We knew right off the bat that this wasn't like the rest of Hell. There were no victims here, no instruments of torture, merely the most blighted landscape I had ever seen. Dead, skeletal trees poked up from the rocks, under a red sky with a smoking sun. It was a place for solitude, a place that Satan might come to be alone and think his dark thoughts.

I almost started to have some myself. Despite all my knowledge, there was a majesty and a dignity to this place, and Rachel felt it too. "So this is Satan's home," she said. "It makes me think of the Satan of *Paradise Lost*. A noble Satan, whose fall from grace was tragic."

"I know what you mean. Even though it's virtual, it's as though there's a . . . great power here. Almost a great . . . soul."

"My children. At last we meet."

The voice was soft and strong and so much at home in that place of regal despair that we turned slowly, not at all alarmed, to see Satan standing behind us.

He was the traditional devil, from his long, gaunt face to his cloven hooves and the spade of devil flesh at the end of his tail. His skin was as red as flame, and his eyes were slitted like a cat's. "Welcome to my kingdom," he said. "You have traveled far and come through much to get here."

He was as seductive as you would expect the devil to be. I knew I had to undercut his suave manner, make him angry so that he couldn't trick us. Or tempt us.

"Wherever *here* is," I said. "Inside a computer program. Not much of a Hell, is it?"

"No, you're wrong," he said silkily. "This is Hell. Hell, you see, is wherever I am. And Hell is wherever man's consciousness is."

"None of that matters," Rachel said, and I could hear her struggling not to be swayed or confused by his words. "We've come to destroy you, whatever you are."

"Destroy me? My poor children." His voice was rich with kindness, pity, even love. "If you destroy me, you destroy yourselves and you destroy what you think of as God. Don't you see? We are all one creature, one creation. Good and evil both dwell in you, as they do in me, for what is Satan but a fallen angel?"

"Spare me the metaphysics," Rachel said coldly. "You're no part of God, and you're no part of me. You're not even Satan! You're just a bunch of computer code, less than the lowliest bug on earth. At least a bug is alive."

"Oh, I'm alive, my dear."

"If you call it life. But you won't have it for long."

Satan shook his head. "So arrogant. So unwilling to listen to reason. Do you not see what I offer you when I extend my hand?" He began to pace back and forth, like an animal stalking its prey. "I offer you all the joys of the land of pain, I offer an erotic union of death and blood far more ecstatic than the puny human spasms you share in the dark, I offer you the full knowledge of the evil that lies deep in your hearts and minds."

"Thanks," I said, "but we'll pass."

"You shall *pass,* all right!" he wailed. "I shall eat your flesh, break your bones, and lap up the marrow! And then you shall *pass* out the Devil's arse and make your home in my chamberpot!"

I thought maybe at last we saw Satan's true self, and wondered what nut case had programmed him. "I'm ready to end this, Rach," I said.

"I've been waiting for you," she said.

Satan was raving now. Bloody spittle frothed at the corners of his mouth, and his eyes rolled. "Ha! Try what you can, my children! But when your bodies die, your souls shall fall into my care! For I am more than Satan! My power reaches beyond this plane into every crevasse of creation! I rule over every facet of existence—the sins you regret, the laws you break, the thoughts you think—I rule the United States of America! *God save the Imperator!*"

The monster's face changed then, seemed to lose its gauntness and mold itself, just for a second, into the insane countenance of . . .

"*Solux!*" I said.

"Yessss. . . ." And then the image of the face shifted. The round eyes narrowed again to slits, the flesh turned from a light brown back to blood red, and the jaw lengthened to a knife-like point. "Hell is *my* creation! All sin springs from me and is led back to me, just as all power in the earthly plane rests in my hands . . . in The Hand of *God!* I am Good! I am Evil! I am all! And I will destroy you!"

That seemed as good a cue for action as any. I threw up the bazooka, and Rach lifted her laser rifle. Her combat buddy was already rocking, blasting away with its twin barrels.

Satan, or maybe I should call him Solux, started blasting us with fire right out of his nose and mouth, like some demonic dragon, and I drew back. But the flames didn't hurt me, not at all, and I could only assume that Jeremy's algorithm was negating Satan's firepower.

With his main weapon gone, Satan/Solux's defeat was a given. We kept firing, driving him back, and he kept shooting streams of harmless fire at us. For a while, it seemed like a stalemate. He wasn't hurting us, but we couldn't do much to him except push him around.

But then, slowly, Satan began to slow down. His movements became less assured and more jerky, as though his battery was running down.

Then he stopped moving altogether and stared straight ahead. The pause was so abrupt that we stopped shooting, though the combat buddy continued his rattling fire. Satan ignored the bullets cutting into him, as his eyes widened and his mouth dropped open as though he saw something that horrified even him. I don't know what it was, but I'll hope to my dying day that I never see it.

Then he fell like a suit of clothes without a wearer. The life had gone out of him in an instant. Even the combat buddy's guns now silent, we walked slowly toward him, thinking he might be faking. But his eyes were dead, and his flesh was melting away into nothingness, revealing the viscera beneath, which also became insubstantial, until only the bones were visible. Finally, they too vanished, leaving us alone on the seemingly infinite plain of desolation.

CHAPTER 32

Back in the safety of the embassy, I repeated Tom Meaculp's quotation. "'Better to reign in Hell than serve in Heaven.' Maybe Solux became Satan because she knew she'd never have a berth up there."

"It wasn't enough to declare herself God's representative on earth," said Senator Burr. "She had to be the other side of the coin too."

"Don't talk about Solux in the past tense," Jeremy said. "She's still around. All you got rid of was her c-space representation. Not that that's any small beans, since it broke the last layer of ICE for our final run into Hell."

"It was . . . disappointing, though," Rachel said. "I expected more when Satan died. But he just fell down and faded away."

"That's c-space for you," Jeremy said. "It's not real-life magic, you know. The algorithm weakened the code that gave Satan life, and your firepower eventually wore away what illusion was left. The program deteriorated and. . . ." He snapped his fingers. "No more Satan. The next step is no more Hell, but we have to step lively."

"Your turn now, right, kid?" I said. "So send your bug after that Hell pit code, and then write the crash program." Jeremy didn't say a word. He didn't look like he wanted to. "So what's wrong? That's all you have to do, isn't it?"

"Well . . . it's not quite that easy."

"Things never are," said Rachel. "Spill it, Jeremy."

"Okay. If we were more familiar with the Hell code and had hardware even close to the Hand's cutting edge stuff, we might be able to program a bug that could find the spawner on its own. But we aren't and we don't, if you get my meaning. But human minds and computer code can interact."

"Sure," said Katerina. "The Acti-decks proved that."

"Psionic minds link up best with computer code. So if we can find a psionic who'll cooperate, we can use the psychopomp to scan and download data imprints of his psychic energies, and then embed them in our crash bug's code."

"We can have a psionic here in fifteen minutes," the senator said and nodded at Derek, who got up and left the room.

"The psionic," Jeremy went on, "will let us make a crash program that's not only nearly sentient, but will be able to sense and avoid ICE systems before it reaches them, which gives it a chance to get to its target."

"The Hell-spawner program," Rachel said.

"That's right. But because we don't know squat about the code structure, we gotta launch the survey bug, to let us know what we're up against. See, we can survey the code from here, but there's no way we can *crash* it from here."

"I don't get it," I said, feeling dumber by the minute. "Why not?"

The kid thought for a minute. "Look," he finally said. "Suppose you're a pizza maker, and you wanta make a great pizza for the Imperator. You could make a terrific pizza and send it to her, but she might not like the anchovies you put on it. So you find out what she likes first by linking with one of her flunkies—that's the survey bug. But once you find out and make the pizza you know she's gonna like, you can't send it to her via link, it's gotta be taken there physically so that Solux can jam it in her mouth, see?"

"Everything's food with you, isn't it?" I said. "So the survey bug's the link call and the crash bug's . . . the pizza?"

"You got it. The survey bug will make a map of the Hell computer code that the crash bug will follow once we've introduced it. But the problem with the survey bug is that it needs to be escorted by a human presence."

"Oh shit . . ." Rachel murmured. I think we both saw what was coming.

Senator Burr did too. "Why can't you just send this survey program in by itself?"

"Hardware limitations," Katerina said. "The psychopomps can't process data fast enough to keep up with the flow we'll be receiving." Derek came back into the room then, and nodded at the senator. I figured he'd gotten through to Link-a-Psionic, or whoever he had contacted.

"And even if it was fast enough," Tom said, "the psycho-pomp lacks the core memory to store the data, even for the few seconds it will take for us to download it. Only a human mind can hold that amount of data transmitted at that speed."

"And that," said Jeremy, "is why Rachel has to deck in and escort it."

"Whoa!" I shot from my seat. "What the hell do you mean *Rachel* has to do it! I don't like to let down the side, but the two us aren't permanent ambassadors to Hell. We wouldn't mind just dealing with some *human* bad guys for a while."

"Listen," Jeremy said, "you two have more experience with Hell c-space than anyone else we have."

"Damn it, Gideon's right," Derek said. "They've been to Hell often enough. Let *me* deck in."

The kid shook his head stubbornly. "No way. We can't take the chance on a Hell newbie with something this vital."

"Then I'll go," I said. "I've had as much Hell time as Rachel has."

"Yes," said Katerina, "but you're not as fit for the task. We've been analyzing the two of you as you deck to Hell. All our results show that Rachel's brain is much more efficient at processing visual stimuli. It has to be her."

All this time Rachel hadn't said a word. Now she spoke, so softly that we had to strain to hear her. "Maybe somebody ought to ask *me* what I think."

"Okay," I said. "Tell us."

"What's this going to be like, Jeremy," she said, "in comparison to what we've already been through?"

The kid didn't seem to want to tell her. He shook his head, shrugged, looked away. I wanted to grab him and shake him hard, but Tom Meaculp told her what she wanted to know, but didn't want to hear.

"Worse," he said. "Possibly far worse. This time you're pushing beyond the illusions, to the space beyond Hell. Up to now you've had a fighting chance, since the Hell program logic simulates and abides by an approximation of earth's natural laws. A demon is standing there with a sword, so you fight him. But now your consciousness will project into a completely abstract realm—the Hell source code itself. And we have no idea what that will be like. Instead of a demon, a few invisible lines of code may be your enemy. They'll be every bit as lethal as a demon, but you'll never see them coming. It could be so disorienting that you . . . lose your ability to function."

Rachel seemed more calm than I'd ever seen her. "So what you're saying is. . . ."

"That you stand a good chance of being deck butter," Jeremy said angrily. "That your brain could turn to cyber-slime, that if you survive, you might make vegetables look warm and witty, all right? God damn it, I'm *sorry,* Rachel, but this is the way it is, and it's the only way to do it, and if you don't go, the whole thing goes down the toilet!" When he finished, he had tears in his eyes, but I didn't know if they were because of what he was sending Rachel into, or because he was afraid his work might come to nothing if she said no.

She looked at him for a long time. Then she whispered, "Say please."

He looked back at her oddly, then licked his lips. "Please."

Then she smiled. "Now why didn't you do that in the first place?" She turned to Katerina. "I'd like to know one thing before we start. Kat, did you ever find out why the Hand changed Gideon and me, what their plan was?"

"No, Rachel. I'm sorry. The machines are cracking that ICE right now, downloading all the Hand files we can get, but that hasn't come up yet. We hope it will."

"Damn," Rachel said. "I really would have liked to know."

"You still will," I said. "Maybe it'll be here when you get back."

"Maybe," she said, and from her tone I knew that she was, if not scared, expecting an ordeal beyond those we had so far survived. I just wished I could share this one with her, for better or worse. "Can we do it right away?"

Jeremy nodded. "We're ready to go. You've never moved from place to place within Hell, but for the Hand pervs who're into that sort of thing, they've got a boat on a virtual River Styx. That's what you'll appear to be traveling on— until you break beyond the illusion, into abstract cyberspace. When you speak, we'll hear you."

"Is there any way," Rachel said, "that I could have a voice link . . . from Gideon?"

Jeremy thought for a moment. "Sure. I have one set up so that I can talk to you, but I can juryrig another in a few minutes."

While he was getting the second link ready, and Katerina was preparing the monitors, Rachel led me away from the others. "If I don't come back," she started to say softly.

I held up a hand. "Don't even think it. You'll be back all right."

"Just listen to me, Gideon. Don't try and make me feel as if this is a walk in the park. I just want you to know that I wouldn't have changed a thing If I die today, or tomorrow, or fifty years from now with our grandchildren around me, being with you during all we've been through in the past few days . . . well, it's been the best. I couldn't have had a better partner, or friend, or lover. I truly do love you, Gid."

"I love you, Rachel." It sounded so empty, so weak. Just a few words that could never tell her how I felt about her. I would have died for her. I wanted to live with her.

"If I come back," she said, "and my mind . . . and there's nothing left . . . see that I don't have to live that way. You know what I mean?"

I couldn't say anything because of the big lump in my throat, so I just nodded.

"I have your word?"

I nodded again. Then she kissed me, kissed the man who had promised to be her killer, if it came to that. We held each other for a long time, though not nearly long enough.

Then we heard Jeremy calling us softly and urgently, reluctant to interrupt us, but anxious too. God, weren't we all anxious to end this, to bring Solux down. "We're ready," he said. "The address is set to Spawner."

Rachel hugged me one more time, very hard, then walked to the lounge chair prepared for her and the psychopomp that would take her to a place worse than Hell.

She sat down, and Katerina outfitted her with monitors and fit the psychopomp over her head. Then Jeremy handed me my voice link mike, a plaz face mask that fit over my mouth and nose. I fit it in place with a strap, and sat down in the chair next to Rachel, taking her hand even though she wouldn't be able to feel it. Senator Burr and Derek stood nervously against the wall, trying to stay out of the way.

"When does she go?" I asked Jeremy, who was fitting his own voice link in place from his post at a computer screen. My voice sounded muffled.

"She's already on her way."

Suddenly, though Rachel's mouth didn't move, her voice burst from the speakers linked to the psychopomp. It was uncanny, as though I were hearing her ghost.

"I'm moving upstream—fast! It's . . . it's a tunnel, yellow and red walls, the water moving so fast, like I'm being sucked along. . . ."

"Focus on the Spawner, Rachel!" Jeremy said.

"Hang in there, Rach! You hear me?"

"Yes . . . yes, I hear you, Gideon. It's . . . so hot. . . ."

"Her heart rate's increasing," said Katerina, her eye on the small bank of monitors.

"There's a barrier ahead! It looks like . . . oh my God, I'm gonna crash right into it!"

"It's all right," said Jeremy. "That's the entrance. Just go with it."

"Heart rate's too high," Katerina said. "She could go into cardiac arrest!"

Jeremy thought for a moment. It was his call, and I felt certain he'd tell her to stay with it. But the kid surprised me. "Pull out, Rachel!" he said. "Pull out now!"

"No! I can hold it!"

"You stay in there, you'll die!"

"I can *hold* it," she said. Her hand in mine was hot and wet with sweat. I could feel her ratcheting pulse. ". . . I'm through! I'm through! Oh God, it's *madness* here. . . ."

"Commence data transmission," Jeremy said.

"Yes . . . yes. . . ."

Jeremy's screen was flooded with data, downloading into our banks so quickly that the constant torrent was indistinguishable as separate characters. "I'm getting it . . . okay, Rachel, it's coming through, yes, oh yes, keep it up, it's coming. . . ."

"I don't . . . I can't. . . ." Rachel's voice sounded weaker, and I gripped her hand tightly to try and let her know I was there and that she was here, her body safe with me.

But it wasn't safe. It was being controlled by her mind, and that mind—any mind—couldn't handle what was being thrown at it. I don't know what she saw or heard or felt. It was so powerful that she lost the ability to communicate it. But in spite of its power, she kept transmitting the data, until there was no consciousness left with which to transmit.

"That's it!" Jeremy cried as the last rows of data poured down the screen. "We've got it!"

"God *damn* it," Katerina said, "she's *flatlined*." She leapt to Rachel's side and yanked the psychopomp off her head. Rachel's nose dripped blood, and her eyes were open and unseeing. Katerina pulled her to the floor, and Derek was there in an instant with a respirator and a cardiojumper. All I could do was hold on to her hand and pray to a God that should have given up on this country a long time ago. I don't know whether he heard me or not, but if he did, he didn't help. After several minutes, Derek straightened up, tears in his eyes, and shook his head. I felt a hand on my shoulder, and when I looked up I saw the senator, her face strained. "I'm so sorry, Gideon. I'm so terribly sorry."

Katerina closed Rachel's eyes, and I looked down into her face for a long time. I just held her hand. I didn't kiss her. I didn't talk to her. I just looked at her and thought about how much I loved her. Then I put her hand over her breast and stood up and looked at Jeremy. "How long will it take," I said, "to make your crash bug now?"

"Four, five hours." He had his data, but he didn't sound overjoyed about it.

I turned toward the senator. "Can I have a car?" I said. "And the file on . . ." I looked down at my dead love. ". . . Claudette Simeon."

"Of course," she said. "If it's all right with you, we'll have Rachel's . . . *Claudette's* body stored until she can be interred with the respect that she deserves."

I nodded. "I'll be back. I'll help you the rest of the way. But there's someplace I have to go first. Something I have to see."

Derek got the file for me, and I found what I needed—the address of Claudette Simeon's parents in Alexandria. I was smuggled out of the embassy and, several blocks away, was given the code for a nondescript vehicle that sat waiting for me at the curb. It was dark by now, and I had no fear that I would be spotted.

The Simeon house was in the outskirts of Alexandria, in a cul-de-sac off a typical suburban street. It was an older neighborhood, and trees grew thick and tall around all the houses. I parked a good distance away and walked to the house, a split level well over a hundred years old. A few windows were lit, and I stood in the deep shadows of the trees, trying to imagine Rachel playing in the yard as a child, her teenage shadow drifting past the dimly lit windows. A young woman reading unsanctified books while sitting in the back yard swing.

I had come there to find Claudette Simeon, the Rachel I had known but forgotten. I wanted to taste the reality of her past, see the place where she had grown up and become the woman I would love. I wanted to pretend that, although the woman was dead, the girl still lived.

"Rachel," I whispered to the night. "Oh, Rach."

And then I felt her presence, as if she were standing close to me, though never to be seen again. And I heard a voice that in my grief and madness I thought was Rachel's.

But it wasn't calling my name. Instead it was saying:

"Vocabulum est serus. Ominus venire ab genitor."

The words, programmed into my subconscious long before, threw a switch in my brain. I reached out my hand, but instead of Rachel's warm fingers, I felt something hard and heavy placed against my palm, and I wrapped my fingers around it.

Around the grip. Around the trigger.

And I forgot Rachel Braque and Claudette Simeon. All I could remember was that I was supposed to kill Senator Erin Burr.

CHAPTER 33

By the time I got back to the embassy, the war had already begun inside me. I knew that I was going to kill Senator Burr, but I also knew I didn't want to. Still, I stuffed the small plaz pistol down inside the front of my pants. The sensors wouldn't detect it, and the Front wouldn't search me. I was a trusted member of the CFF now, a member whose strong and overwhelming intent was to kill my own leader

"Gideon," Derek said when he saw me, "Are you okay?"

"I'm fine. As good as can be expected."

"Nobody made you?"

"No. Didn't see a soul," which was the truth, although somebody sure as hell saw me. "How's Jeremy getting along?"

Derek smiled. "He's got it—the crash bug. In fact, we've got a meeting right now to talk over the final assault. Kat's been downloading Pentagon files galore. Got all sorts of formerly ICEd blueprints and plans. She's still pulling out stuff. But we're ready, brother." His face grew sad. "I just wish Rachel could be here for it. I'm so sorry about her."

"I'm sorry too. But it's war, Derek." I scarcely knew what I was saying. All I could think about was keeping him from seeing that there was anything wrong with me. I was acting, playing a role, while the real me was looking on with horror from inside, trying to get out. "We'd better get to that meeting," I said, patting him on the shoulder. Senator Burr would be there, waiting for me to kill her.

The meeting was to be held in the conference room rather than the computer center. I guess it was to spare my feelings, since Rachel had died there. It wouldn't have made any difference to me. The part of me that was in control could have shot down Rachel had I been programmed to.

Jeremy, Tom, and Vivid were there when Derek and I walked in, and they all gave me kindly, sympathetic smiles. I smiled back, wondering where Senator Burr was. Derek sat down, but I kept standing. It would be easier to draw my pistol that way.

There were two doors into the conference room. One was from the computer center, the other from the hall. Senator Burr came in from the hall just as Katerina entered from downloading the Pentagon files. Kat had a paper in one hand, and when she saw me and the senator, she gasped, and I knew that *she* knew.

I pulled out my pistol, the command driving me, and lifted it and aimed it at the center of Senator Erin Burr's chest. My finger began to tighten on the trigger. I could have pulled it before anyone responded, before the senator's dazed and unbelieving expression had turned to something else.

But I didn't. Agony tore through me as I told myself *NO*, I would not do this. The struggle took only milliseconds, but it seemed like hours. My own will was stronger than the other will inside me. Before I even realized it, the pistol was flying through the air. I turned to see who had knocked it from my hands, but no one was even close to me. It was only then that I knew that I had won, and thrown it away myself. The strength of my soul, unassailably mine, had defeated the will implanted in me from outside.

Derek was pointing his own pistol at my face, but he said nothing. No one spoke until finally Katerina softly said, "It's all right. He didn't do it. It's over."

The senator, no doubt surprised to find herself still alive, turned to Derek. "Derek, would you please search Gideon to make sure he is no longer armed?"

Derek picked up my pistol first, then patted me down. "What the hell were you doing?" he whispered harshly into my ear.

"He was trying to assassinate Senator Burr," Katerina said. "But he didn't. Though he should have—though that was the way it was planned—he didn't."

"Are you saying," asked the senator, "that Gideon is a Hand agent?"

"He was. At least he was programmed to be." Kat held up the paper she had brought into the room. "This just came in. It was in the most highly classified files. Top secret. But before I share it, Gideon, what happened to you tonight?"

"I went out to Rachel's home, where she grew up," I said.

"Someone must have followed me. They spoke to me, in Latin, the phrase I hear in my dreams. After that, the only thing I could think about was killing Senator Burr."

"But you didn't," said the senator.

"No. I didn't."

"Listen to this," Katerina said. "It's a portion of the Night of Re-entombment memo that was sent to Transgressions, ordering the scrub:

> "'The Hand programmed each of these remade people with voice-activated imperatives to kill top-ranking members of the Freedom Front. Obscure though related Latin phrases, which would certainly not be encountered by chance, are the triggers.
>
> "'Unfortunately, the imperative programming was buggy. Both Schonbrun's and Hennely's imperatives were activated, but neither target was terminated. God's vision of the prospect of losing control of these clandestine agents has guided the Imperator to order that all those agents be immediately terminated. Transgressions will also choose a sacrifice whose death will confuse any CFF functionaries illegally investigating the terminations.'"

"The boy," I said. "Brian Avery." I tried to get the rest of my thoughts in order. "We were the Hand's perfect agents. They planted us in strategic spots and waited. Except that they were sloppy, and the programming didn't work. So they tried to clean up their mistake and kill us. They got everybody but Rachel and me. And maybe the reason they didn't pull out all the stops to get us was that they thought if we contacted the Front, maybe they could get to Senator Burr through us. And they almost did."

"They saw you and followed you," said the senator, "and they gave you the imperative. If they did that, then they know we're here."

"They could come in here any minute then!" Tom said.

"No." Derek shook his head. "They'll wait to see if Gideon killed the senator. If not, *then* they might come in, despite the hostile act of invading British soil. So we've got to keep them in the dark. This place will be tied up tight, so we'll have to go out through the tunnel. But one thing first." He faced me. "Are you truly all right? Can we trust you?"

"If you couldn't, the senator would be dead," I said. "I still want to kill, but Solene Solux, nobody else. I'm ready to go through the real *Hell* if I have to, to help plant that crash bug."

He nodded curtly. "All right. Kat's found out that the Hell mainframe is located in a large secret chamber under the Pentagon. There are several underground accesses to the mainframe room, but they're too damn well guarded. However, the room is directly under the Pentagon chapel, which is one of the few areas open to the public."

"The Imperator very often worships there privately," said Tom, "and it's kept locked while she's in there. There are a number of crypts built into the floor of the chapel."

"Yeah," I said. "Where they plant good little Hand members."

"That's right," Derek said. "Their reward, beside eternal life in Solux's idea of Heaven, is entombment under the floor there. Well, the files show that one of the crypts, sup-posedly the late Minister of Faith James Robertson's, is a phony. It's probably Solux's entrance to the Hell mainframe."

"That's our way in?" I asked.

"Our only chance."

"The rest of the plan," said Senator Burr, "is contingent upon getting Jeremy into the Hell mainframe room."

"Jeremy?" I said. "No offense, but he's hardly built for combat."

"That's why you and I will be his escorts," Derek said with a smile. "We get him in, he does the rest."

"At which point," the senator continued, "you will signal me. The timing must be impeccable. The Voice of God must be in our hands by then."

"The Voice?"

She nodded. "It's not necessary to overthrow the govern-ment by force. The people will do that, but first they must see how they have been lied to over the years. If that hap-pens, not only the people in the streets but those in the government itself, even the Five Fingers, should rise up against Solux."

"But all of this," I said, "depends upon our crashing Hell."

"That's right, Gideon. So, while you put your heads to-gether over precisely how to accomplish that, the rest of us will continue to plan for the mobilization. But the longer we wait, the more time we give Solux to prepare. He must cer-tainly know by now of the defeat of his cyberspace Satan. For all we know, it could actually have been the Imperator himself decked in to his Hell. I would like to have you in the Pentagon by dawn, so that everyone preparing for work, and watching on vidscreens will see the truth. It could not be a better time for the fall of Solene Solux."

I looked at the stately old analog clock on the wall. It was just four hours until dawn. "What day is it?" I asked. I had lost track.

"Sunday," said Senator Burr.

CHAPTER 34

"So how do we get in?" I asked Derek. He, Jeremy, and I were sitting in a small meeting room. Derek and I were pounding down coffee, and Jeremy was swilling bottles of Jolt Plus. Enemies of the state indeed.

"We're going to drive right in, and we can have whatever we want in the car with us—bombs, guns, the works. Because they won't check."

I snorted. "Bullshit."

"Not at all. We're two Army of God colonels and one lieutenant. After they scan our codes, they won't dare search us. See, even big brass needs a little R 'n R. Our moles know when everybody goes in and out, and a car full of officers who answer our rough descriptions are due back at the Pentagon by dawn. Our people have already secured their car and are ready to grab them when they come outside."

"And you're telling me they don't have any grunts riding shotgun for them?"

"Not when they go to visit a homosexual brothel. You don't last long in the Army of God, something like that gets out."

I nodded, trying to keep the smile off my face. I didn't want to smile, now that Rachel was gone. But the thought of settling accounts made me as happy as I thought I could be. If we could get inside the Pentagon, I had the rest of it scoped. I explained the plan to Derek and Jeremy, and they thought it sounded good. There was just one stop we'd have to make when our official Pentagon vehicle arrived.

It pulled into Kaloroma Heights an hour later. By that time we'd been given uniforms that fit reasonably well. I didn't ask where they had gotten them, though I did wonder about the brownish-red stain on the collar of my jacket. We armed ourselves and then trudged through the tunnel, flamers and lights ablaze, until we reached the vehicle waiting for us at the other end. Front ops handed us our personal codes, as well as the code for the car, and we were off, with me behind the wheel.

I went into the Interface alone, leaving my jacket and tie in the car. The sight of a cross-colonel entering a speak would be enough in some places for the proprietor to hit a self-destruct and dive out the back.

"I didn't know if you'd be here or not," I said to Cynna Stone. She and the bartender were the only ones in the place.

"I'm almost always here, sweet Gideon. Where else do I have to go? What's the matter, get tired of your lady? Rachel, wasn't it?"

"It was." I looked her square in the eyes. "She's dead now."

The programmed sloe-eyed look left the hologram that was Cynna's face and was replaced by a frown. "The Hand?

"Fighting them. And I'm still fighting them. For her, and for me."

"Fight them for me too," she said bitterly.

"I will. With your help. You said you still had access to demolitions. I need a few things. Where do you keep your stash?"

"Upstairs. Small stuff only. The large pieces are in a garage in Rosslyn. What do you need?"

"A gas bomb, small but potent, capable of cleaning a large room."

"How high's the ceiling?"

"Probably no more than twenty."

"I'll give you max horizontal spread. Trigger?"

"Package bomb."

"Dead or out?"

"Out's fine. Longer the better."

"No problem. What else?"

"Four crevice charges."

"Compressed?"

"Better. I'm blowing stone. Maybe eighth-inch, four deep."

She nodded and went upstairs. Fifteen minutes later she was back, carrying a small cardboard box. "I nested them, safer that way. Wrapped the gasser. Here's a marker to write on it with. Any end opens, it goes. Out in thirty seconds, down for two hours. Time enough?"

"Definitely. Thanks, Cynna."

"It's okay. Listen, you ever want to . . . talk about Rachel, or old times, I'm here, you know? Nothing more . . . I mean,

I can't do anything more." She smiled at me. "Old times are all I have now. Literally."

"You were really something, Cynna. You still are."

She kissed me then, like a sister, on the cheek. It felt cool and light, a breath of wind just before winter, a ghost kiss. That made me think of Rachel, and she sensed my sadness. "Get it done, Gideon," she said. "Just get it done."

Back at the car, I tucked the box under the seat and we headed for the Pentagon. It was still dark when we pulled up to the checkpoint. We tried to look tired, which was no great challenge, while the guard scanned our codes. When he gave us a wave, we drove around to the western side, where we coded into an underground parking lot.

I felt like I'd been there before, and when I stopped the car I knew why. This was the garage Tom Meaculp had rendered, the place he had met us in his Deep Throat guise. Derek took the box from under the seat and opened it. The gas bomb was wrapped in brown paper to look like a sheaf of hards. I took the marker and wrote, "*Miraculum sepulcrum*—new code—enter immediately" on the packet. Then I handed it to Jeremy.

"Take this to any tube room. They're all over the place. Hand it to the attendant and then come to the chapel, in the northeast section."

"You've got your code card," Derek said. "Anybody asks you anything, just flash it, but they shouldn't. A tube room and the chapel aren't restricted locales."

We took a lift to the first level, and Derek and I headed for the chapel, while Jeremy nervously went to find a tube room where he could send the gas bomb to the Hell mainframe room. I carried the crevice charges in the small box, and every now and then pressed my arm against the pistol under my uniform jacket to assure myself it was still there.

The doors to the chapel were unlocked, and not a soul was inside. Derek stood lookout, waiting for Jeremy, while I searched for the false slab. The place was more like a modest cathedral than a chapel. The floors above had been removed so that a high, vaulted ceiling opened above the worshippers' heads. The style was old-fashioned, heavy gothic, not a touch of modernity except for the vidscreens on either side of the altar. When Solux spoke here, she wanted to be seen.

The chapel was dimly lit by unseen sources, and gas candles burned near the altar. A synchoir sang sacred music through hidden speakers, so softly that my footsteps seemed deafening as I trod slowly and carefully down the left side aisle, where the false crypt stone of James Robertson was supposed to be.

Walking over the carved stone slabs, I wondered what kind of honor it was to be trod upon in death by the denizens of the Pentagon. I didn't have much time to think about it, though, since Robertson's stone was the second I saw.

It read:

James Robertson
Deeply Mourned Servant of God
2012-2086

Beneath the legend was a carved hand, its fingers spread, a cross on the palm. I knelt and placed my own hand at the thin crack where the slab met the surrounding stone of the floor. I could feel a hint of cool air from beneath. Robertson's slab was a trap door.

I took the crevice charges out of the box, wedged them in between slab and floor, one on each side of the rectangular stone, and set the fuses on a twenty-second timer. When I had nearly finished, I heard Derek's voice.

"Someone's coming."

I froze, hoping that it was Jeremy joining us and not a platoon of Hand goons, but I needn't have worried. Jeremy's slim form, so out of place in a military uniform, slipped through the door. "I *did* it!" he said, and his voice echoed eerily in the huge chapel. Derek pulled the doors shut behind him and barred them as planned. If anyone found them locked, we wanted them to think the Imperator was having her early morning meditations. "I just went into a tube room," Jeremy bubbled on, "handed it to this woman, and said . . . no, I *ordered* her . . . to send it right away. And she said yes sir, and stuck it in a tube!" It was probably the first prank the kid had ever played that wasn't done over a net line.

"Time?" Derek asked, walking down the aisle toward me with Jeremy in his wake.

Jeremy looked at his chrono. "Three minutes twenty seconds ago."

"Got the charges set, Gideon?" I nodded. "Hit the timer."

I knelt by the slab, pushed the button, and trotted back to where Derek and Jeremy stood. My twenty count was a little fast. I had gotten to twenty-two when the slab blew, its pieces flying into the air and crashing down onto the wooden pews, splintering them. The loudest noise was that of the slab splitting and falling. The compressed explosives had done their work, if not silently, then softly. "Jeez. . . ." Jeremy whispered. Through the haze of smoke I could see an opening downward where the slab had been.

But then something unexpected happened. A slab that I hadn't set to explode suddenly flew into the air in one piece, as though launched by a spring beneath. Then another went up and crashed down, and another.

In three more seconds as many slabs flew into the air and shattered on the pews, and things began to rise from the exposed crypts. They looked like a gruesome combination of dead men and machines, meat and steel and silicon. The sight of them made my flesh creep.

One had a flesh face from the nose up, but the jaw and neck were metal. It had no mouth that I could see. Another had one hand of meat, but the other was grasping steel claws. The meat on all of them had rotted, and pieces sloughed off as they shambled toward us, revealing the yellow-gray bone beneath.

They had at least been given the dignity of interment wearing suits and ties, but those too had dried and withered, and the cloth tore and crumpled as they moved. But though the flesh of these dead Hand puppets had decayed, the metal and the computer brains had held up. They moved toward us, slow but sure, cutting us off from Solux's entrance to the mainframe room, her last blasphemous and twisted line of defense.

Derek, Jeremy, and I yanked our pistols from beneath our uniforms. They were powerful little autos, with thirty-shot mags, and were loaded with explorounds. I shot first, taking the closest of the creatures in the face. Dead flesh spattered wetly, and the bullet tore into the metal beneath, but the thing kept coming. Then Derek was shooting too, at the chest and head of another of the meats.

"Their *asses!*" Jeremy yelled. "Their operating systems are in their asses!"

It didn't take much maneuvering to get behind one of them, and I shot him in the left buttock. It was like a fist punching a hole through the rotten meat and smashing open the metal casing. I saw a few sparks, and then the thing fell like a brick. Damn it, the kid was right.

We kept dancing around with the dead bastards, trying to get behind them while they kept turning toward us. We fully living folks were faster, though Jeremy had a close call when he tripped in a pew and one of them threw himself on the kid, its metal jaws gnashing at his face. Fortunately its ugly butt was sticking in the air, giving Derek a great target. One round, and the thing was just so much dead flesh and steel.

We figured out pretty quickly that shots to the face disabled the creatures' video inputs, though their audio tracked us pretty well. Still, the blindness helped us to get behind them if we moved quietly. In another few minutes all of them were down.

"Just so much dead meat," I said, trying to ignore the twitching and the melting as we stepped over them.

"How'd you know their brains were in their butts?" Derek asked Jeremy as we headed for the crypt opening.

"Most logical defensive housing," Jeremy said. "Besides, there was a delay in the upper leg motion that made me think there was more in the pelvic region than just the mechs."

The opening led down a steeply inclined set of steps. The stairway was dimly lit. We gazed down, listening, but heard nothing. "This is it then," Derek said. "I'm punching in the code for the mobilization." He entered the code on the remote communicator linked with the Front HQ and slid the com back into his pocket. "Let's go. Sure hope they opened that gasser by now."

The stairs were long, cutting back on themselves several times. As we ran, I thought about Solux and the cyberzombies. The monster couldn't even let her own dead sleep in peace. She had to turn them into meat watchdogs for her private entrance to Hell. Probably thought she was performing a miracle, raising the dead. After all, she had already ascribed to herself most of the talents of the divine and the demonic.

The stairs ended outside a high, wide door. I took the brass handle and turned it downward. "Unlocked," I said, with a look at Derek.

"Why not? Who else would come down this way?"

I took a deep breath and pushed the door slowly open.

CHAPTER 35

From where we stood, which was obviously Solux's big entranceway into her warped kingdom, we could see the entire room. The only things moving were green wireframe designs on a huge vidscreen. Twenty workers and a dozen uniformed security types lay unconscious where they had fallen. A huge mainframe computer stood at the end of the room, and another long wall held nothing but smaller vidscreens showing different tortures in Hell.

For a moment I was caught up in them, overwhelmed by the horror. Then Derek patted me on the shoulder, and I turned around.

"Let's get to it. Where does it go, Jeremy?" Derek asked.

The kid pulled the silver disk out of his pocket and walked over to the mainframe, negotiating his way around the bodies on the floor. He looked at what I saw as a mind-boggling assortment of slots, drives, scans and keypads, then quickly pointed to an insignificant-looking dark slit. "Bingo," he said, and let the disk slide into it.

The program vanished into the bowels of the machine, and Jeremy punched a series of keys and sat back. "That's it?" I asked.

"That's it. Hell's hell."

"How long will it take?"

"Minutes."

"God," Derek said, "let's hope the Front stormed Voice HQ all right."

"We'll soon know," said Jeremy, going to the wall of vidscreens and flicking some switches. On several vidscreens, the familiar faces of the Voice of God announcers appeared, the ones who had been spewing government-fed lies for nearly two decades.

"Something's wrong," I said. "They're still on."

"Wait . . ." Derek watched the screens intently. Suddenly the screen went to white sight, the sound to white noise. "They're there," Derek said, and I heard the joy in his voice. "Now wait. . . ."

Then, on the screens that still depicted scenes in Hell, something began to happen. Streaks appeared, as though a painter had swept a brush across the screens. The backgrounds, the torture implements, the demons all shimmered. Only the victims remained untouched.

I was watching a pit in which demons were impaling people on stakes, with the tips protruding through the victim's chests, necks, and even mouths, when suddenly the stakes and demons *sizzled,* as though touched with an inner fire, and simply faded from view. The victims slipped to the ground, where they stood, amazed and unharmed, their bleeding stopped, their agony over. They looked about them as though they were reborn. We later learned that at that same moment every demon in the country fell over like a sawn-through tree, never to move again.

All the other screens showed similar events. People stood in blackness, as Rachel and I had stood when Asmodeus's pit had crashed, not knowing where they were or what had happened. And then all the screens went dark.

The white sight and white noise stopped on the Voice of God screens, and then we saw Senator Burr looking out at us. She said, "My name is Senator Erin Burr. This is a very special broadcast. Not of the Voice of God, but of the new Voice of Liberty. What you are about to see happened only moments ago."

And there it was, the things we had just seen on the Hell screens—the demons and Hell itself flashing, flickering, vanishing, leaving only the victims, revealing Hell for the lie that it was. Revealing it on every vidscreen in every home and office and public place across the country.

Senator Burr reappeared. "My fellow Americans, the true liberation of our country has begun. Solene Solux's rule ends today. You have just seen video input directly from the Hell data banks. You have just seen Hell crashing.

"That is correct—the Hell with which your former leader threatened you is a malefic, computer-generated illusion, rendered by the government with technology declared illegal by that same government, and used to create fear, a fear they used to perpetuate their unjust rule.

"Today, because of great acts of individual heroism, that rule ends. In the coming days we will need the help of all Americans as we move to form a provisional government that will restore rule of this country to the people. I call upon each one of you to help in every way you can. Those in the Army of God, in all branches of the Five Fingers, know that your dedication and devotion have been betrayed by a madman who wished to make himself both God and Satan, whose main goal was not goodness, but power. All of you, join with us. Throw down your arms, or take them up in defense of your country, and not the leaders who have lied to you all these years.

"I will formally address the country in a few days. Until then, I say with renewed energy and spirit, *God bless America*."

I turned to Derek, and just as I saw tears in his eyes, I felt them in mine. We had come so far, lost so much, but now we had a chance to reclaim our country.

Jeremy looked up from where he sat, grinned, and said, "So now what?"

"A force is set to try and take the Pentagon," Derek said. "I'm hoping it won't be necessary, but we'd better get to a position where we can join them."

"Can you give me a few more minutes?" Jeremy asked. "The bug's crashed Hell all right, but I want to disable this entire system to make sure no backup override goes into effect."

"Fine," Derek said. "Rip the sonovabitch out by its roots."

Jeremy took only three minutes to hammer the stake into the machine's heart. When he was finished, we headed toward the stairway to the chapel.

Before we could get there, the door at the opposite end burst open, and in poured several dozen Army of God soldiers, all armed to the teeth. A major holding a .1040 Hammer growled, "Who are you?"

There was no point in fighting. They'd take us down before we even had our guns out. And help was on the way. If we let them capture us we might be able to fight again, maybe even today. "We're the ones you're looking for," I said. "We crashed the Hell program."

A look I couldn't read spread over his face, and I tensed, ready to draw my pistol if he threatened to open fire, making my life as expensive to them as possible. But instead he grinned and let the muzzle of his weapon drop toward the floor. "Shit, man, we're not looking for you—we're looking for Solux."

"Solux?"

He looked around in disgust. "We never knew about this place. They told us classified records was down here. Very limited access. But once we saw what was happening on the corridor vidscreens, we knew what had to be here. This is it then? This is what Hell was?"

"Inside that mainframe," I said. "That's all the Hell there was. And the demons were only androids."

"And it's gone now?"

"Destroyed," Jeremy said. "With sure and certain hope of no resurrection."

"But Solux isn't here?" the major said.

"We didn't see her."

"General Russell ordered her arrest soon as the broadcast was over. A squad went to her quarters, and we were sent down here."

"Wait a minute," Derek said. "You mean everybody's turned against her?"

The major took us aside and spoke softly. "We in the Army of God have had to carry out a lot of orders that made us sick. You'd be surprised how many of us are in sympathy with the Citizens' Freedom Front. And you'd be even more surprised to know how many of us are Front agents." He glanced down at his bars. "And at how high up some of them are."

Then he shook our hands. "Welcome back to America," he said, and we were glad to be here.

CHAPTER 36

The changeover went surprisingly smoothly. There were pockets of resistance, still are for that matter, who continue to think that Solene Solux was sent by God, and that the CFF, or anyone who cooperates with them, are enemies of God and should be damned. To them, Hell still exists. What the whole country saw on its vidscreens was a hoax presented by the CFF. The android demons that were taken apart were also Front props. The real demons, you see, went back to Hell, appalled at the depravity of a country that would overthrow the very Mouthpiece of God.

Oh yes, to these people Hell is very real, and it always will be. More's the pity for them. They'll raise their children to believe it, keep the lie alive, set the stage for another Solene Solux to manipulate their hates and fears somewhere down the line. Hopefully I won't live to see it.

We looked for Solux everywhere during those hectic first weeks of liberation. Rumors had her followers smuggling her to Mexico or Canada. Some of them said that she had ascended to Heaven and would remain there until the country had purged itself of its sinful ways, and only then return in triumph with angels as her escort. A few violent fanatics were quickly captured, some, unfortunately, after they had already done some damage. But as long as they don't start shooting, they can sing the praises of Solux all they like. After all, it's a free country.

I became pretty well known as a result of the overthrow of the Hand of God. It got so I couldn't even go out on the street without reporters and photographers dogging my steps, wanting to know something that I hadn't already told them. I hadn't even been able to visit Rachel's grave at Arlington since the funeral three months before.

So Senator Burr made arrangements to get me into the cemetery after closing time. One early fall evening at dusk Derek and I drove out there. Her grave was on a slight rise, hidden by the Simeon crypt, which held an ancestor of Rachel's who had ridden with Lafayette during the first American revolution. Her marker was small and simple, and read:

Rachel Braque
2066-2095
She gave her life for freedom.

I had thought about having the name of Claudette Simeon put on the stone, but it was Rachel Braque who had fought and died.

Derek walked out of sight over the rise to keep watch and ensure that I would be alone at the grave. I didn't know what to say at first, so I just stood there for a long time as the sun sank lower behind the trees. Finally I started to talk, not knowing if she could hear me. But I needed to say the words.

I told her what she had meant to me, and how much I missed her, and that I loved her and would always love her. And I told her that I knew she was in Heaven, because we'd had enough of Hell. Then I started to cry. I hadn't been able to up to that point, but now I did, huge, heavy sobs that shook my body. I was glad no one was there to see.

Then I heard Rachel's voice. "*Gideon. . . .*" The door to the Simeon crypt creaked slowly open, and my heart thudded in my chest as I watched through a blur of tears, afraid to rub them away, to move at all.

Solene Solux stepped through the door, a pistol in her hand, and I remembered the other time I had heard Rachel's voice in the night, the words in Latin, the other lie that had nearly made me kill.

"Oh, what a pity," said Solux in a mocking voice of silk and steel. "Did he lose his love in my Hell? Well, you'll lose more than that, you miserable sinner! You'll pay with your life now."

She looked wasted, not at all like the powerful Imperator of a few months before. Her clothing was worn and dirty, her dark hair unkempt, her finely chiseled features now puffy. Her formerly glowing brown skin had dulled to a flat gray, and she smelled rank. But her spirit, or possibly her madness, burned brightly. She held her head erect, and her six and a half foot frame upright, and glared at me from yellow-white eyes.

"Did you think I could be defeated so easily? Me, who conquered a country with words? Who made my own Hell to punish the wicked? Who am both Satan and God in one?" He grinned and shook his head. "Oh no. My followers are in the millions. They believe in me, in my *immortality,* and they will help me to regain power. But before I am resurrected to supremacy, I must rain down judgment on my greatest enemy—the survivor of the pair of fornicating traitors who destroyed my greatest creation! Then, with you dead, my disciples will rise up and sweep the bitch Burr from power!"

"I have waited *weeks* in this tomb! I knew you would come eventually to mourn your dead sow! And now you are here alone, and I come from the grave, rising from among the dead, to smite you as a warning to all who would betray me! You die, and I rise again. King of Kings and Lord of Lords, to rule *forever!*"

Her grip tightened on the pistol, and I knew I was a dead man. My eyes closed involuntarily and I heard the shot, but felt no pain. When I looked, a blotch of blood had appeared on Solux's shoulder, and the pistol had fallen to the ground.

"Reach for it and you're dead!" shouted Derek, running down the rise. By the time he reached us, I had already scooped up Solux's pistol and was pointing it at her. She was laughing, laughing so hard that tears were coming from her eyes.

"Take me!" she said. "The Lord's blood is now shed. The Lord shall now be taken before the populace to be judged, and when I speak, my words will bring all the sinners back to my flock. Though bound in the deepest prisons, I shall live, and the true believers shall free me and restore me to godhood, though it take many years! Still, I shall reign! So take me before the people!"

"You're *right*," Derek said in an icy voice. "That might happen. But it won't. You'll never deceive this country again. Because I'm ending it now."

Before I could stop him, he pointed the pistol right between her eyes. But in spite of her wound, Solux had the swiftness of the mad. She whipped up a hand and dashed Derek's pistol from his hand, then turned to run.

I jerked up the pistol I held, but I didn't have to decide whether or not to shoot her in the back. She ran two steps, then stumbled and fell, her forehead striking the sharp granite edge of Rachel's grave marker with a sickening crack.

Solene Solux did not move. I knelt down, turned her body over, and knew. "She's dead," I said.

A red mark showed on her forehead but no blood ran from it, and I thought of the mark of Cain. I looked at the smooth surface of grassy sod over the place Rachel lay.

"What did she trip on?" Derek asked softly.

I shook my head. "There's nothing there." Then, slowly, I stood up and looked down at Solux's body.

She was a martyr now, nothing more. The long nightmare was over. Its dreamer was dead. Her eyes were wide open, staring. The madness had drained out of them, and all that remained was the fear of what she now saw.

"Maybe she'll learn what it's really like," I said.

"What?" Derek asked, although he knew.

"Hell," I said, still looking down at Solux but seeing far deeper than the grave, far below.

Down in that place where the fire is not quenched.